In White Ink

Elske Rahill

HEAD
ZEUS

An Apollo Book

First published in the UK in 2017 by Head of Zeus Ltd
This Apollo paperback published in 2018 by Head of Zeus Ltd

9 7 5 3 1 2 4 6 8

A catalogue record for this book is available from the British Library.

ISBN (PB): 9781786691064
ISBN (E): 9781786691033

Typeset by Adrian McLaughlin

MIX
Paper from
responsible sources
FSC
www.fsc.org   FSC® C020471

Printed and bound in Great Britain
CPI Group (UK) Ltd, Croydon CR0

Head of Zeus Ltd
First Floor East
5–8 Hardwick Street
London EC1R 4RG
WWW.HEADOFZEUS.COM

Contents

Toby   1

In White Ink   29

A Wife   81

Bride   103

Terraforming   129

Right to Reply   155

Dolls   199

Manners   217

Cords   231

Playing House   247

Tasteless   263

Acknowledgements   295

One way or another, these stories are for my children.

... *a woman is never far from 'mother' (I mean outside her role functions: the 'mother' as a nonname and source of goods). There is always within her at least a little of that good mother's milk. She writes in white ink.*

'THE LAUGH OF THE MEDUSA', HÉLÈNE CIXOUS

Toby

THE HARDWARE SHOP is dusty and cluttered, with a muddy, masculine smell that at once revolts and reassures her. There is a teenage boy at the till and a white-haired man sitting on a stepladder. The man goes downstairs to look for the bug bombs. He returns waving a tiny rectangular box above his head.

'Here you are, love,' he says. 'The last one.'

Valerie follows him to the till, looking as she goes at the rows of nails and brackets and screws, each presented in a trough with letters and numbers written on a label above them – codes she cannot read. She tries to keep her gaze away from the rumpled, pink face of the man: too much colour against the blanched hair and all around his eyes creases cramming like the unready petals of a peeled poppy bud.

'Unusual this time of year,' he says, handing the box to the boy. 'You must keep the house very warm, love, is it?'

'Oh,' says Valerie. 'Yes, I suppose perhaps.'

The man leans over the boy's shoulder, pointing at the till. 'There.' He says it softly, like a pleasant secret. 'Press Open, then Pets, and then you can put in the price . . . It's on the back. Turn it over – there, y'see?'

His voice is louder for Valerie, his accent clipped clean of nuance: 'Do you have a dog, do you? Or a cat?'

'A dog, yes. My husband's dog.'

'That's what it is. Has it a flea collar? There's flea tablets you can give them too, you know? Might be the best thing.'

The man points as he speaks. His fingers have an inflated look, spongy and pale – the nakedness of roots grown blind beneath a garden slab. Valerie wonders how that can be, given that he is in the business of hammers and nails and soil.

While the boy confuses the till, Valerie moves to a small pet section in the corner and chooses a flea collar for Toby, some flea tablets, and some dog treats to hide the tablets in. When she brings them back to the till, the boy is still struggling. The drawer jangles open and the man slides it closed again. 'Don't mind that,' he tells the boy. 'Start again. Just take your time.' He explains to Valerie how to use the bug bomb, warning her that there are rotten chemicals in it.

'Leave the house for the day,' he says. 'That's what I'd do, no two ways about it. D'you've any kids, do you?'

'One. A baby.'

'Keep him out of the house for the day.'

'A girl. Yes, she goes to crèche, so . . .'

She tries to imagine 82 cubic metres because the man says that's how far the poison spreads. She asks him is there anything else he has, because her house is quite large and one bomb won't be enough for the upstairs and the downstairs. He sends the boy to get a spray for the furniture.

'You're sure it's fleas?' he says, pulling a reel of paper from the top of the till – a translucent strip with rows of ghostly purple zeros printed on it. He tears the paper off and throws it in a basket by his feet.

'Yes,' says Valerie.

'You've seen them?'

'Yes.'

'You can't kill them by squashing – you know that? You have to roll them.'

'Oh yes. I know.'

A few days after they began, Valerie looked it up on her husband's computer. Rolling, not squashing, said the Internet, and vacuuming. Vacuuming everything over and over. She has vacuumed twice this morning – that's what had Joanna late for crèche – and right now Dolores will be arriving to do the weekly clean. Valerie left a note instructing her to vacuum everywhere, and to bleach all the floors.

The man ducks beneath the counter.

'Unusual this time of year,' he calls. 'Unusual for Ireland actually, to tell you the truth, love.'

He reappears flushed and pleased, wire-cutters in his hand.

'I wasn't going to order in any more of them bombs, we sell so few. It's more in the heat you'd tend to get fleas. The continent. Rotten stuff in them things. Should be banned.'

The teenager returns with the spray, his face set in eager determination as he approaches the till. He smiles for approval as he gives Valerie her change, still smiles as he puts it all in a blue plastic bag with *Carrier Bag* printed across it in faint black letters, nods like a man as she takes it.

Valerie stows it immediately in her spacious cream leather handbag. She doesn't want to arrive at the hairdresser swinging that flimsy carrier bag like something haggled from a street seller, bright bug spray glinting through the cheap plastic.

At Saphron Hair Design Valerie catches herself in the mirror, being helped into the black robe like an invalid, and she can see at a glance that her new gold-sheen lipstick ages her and that her eyes are overdone. She sits on the swivel chair and looks down to avoid the mirrors all around her; the shock of her profile, the dregs of shadow settling beneath her eye sockets. She will ask for her roots to be done today. Then she will feel better.

A man puts his hands on her shoulders and speaks to her reflection. He says his name is Justin and he will cut her hair today because her usual stylist, Lauren, is out sick. His smile, she knows, is meant to reassure, but he can't conceal the sneer on his lips when she tells him she likes it the same every time. His gaze flitters over her pearl-stud earrings, her kitten heels. 'Sure. If you find a way that works for you... why change?' He has a quiff like a tidal wave, a gold hoop spearing the flesh of his brow.

'Well yes exactly,' says Valerie.

Fashions come and go, but every woman has an ideal hair length for her face shape; when she finds it, she should stick to it. It was Valerie's confirmation day when her mother explained that. They had a girl in to do her hair, and Valerie sat at her mother's vanity table, in her new blue suit with the shoulder pads and the sailor collar. She requested an up-style, but her mother shook her head.

'Know your own face, my girl. Every woman has an ideal hair length, but it's only a clever woman who knows what it is.'

Side by side in the mirror, they looked together at all the secrets of Valerie's face. Valerie might make the most of herself, her mother explained, by letting her hair fall just to her chin, giving her a bit of a jawline and sweeping inwards, to soften her look. When she was finished speaking, her mother stood behind her, wrapped her hands firmly around Valerie's shoulders as though to strengthen her, and sighed into the mirror.

While her hair is cut, Valerie leafs through a magazine from beginning to end, then starts at the beginning again. Her fringe is still clamped up in a big green clip when the hairdresser abruptly stops cutting. Valerie's breath snags, and, keeping her head down, she glances up carefully at the mirror. The hairdresser is frowning a little, pecking slowly at her scalp with long, clean fingers. She swallows quietly, forces her eyes back to the magazine – a 'sneaky snap' taken from far away, that shows the naked face of a celebrity on a hotel balcony. Valerie always uses a lice treatment before a hair appointment, and a leave-in repellent – she has nothing to worry about. But there is a twinge behind her ear, a twitching impulse to scratch. She forces breath out slowly through her teeth. She can feel the drag of her own cheeks, the foolish heaviness of her mouth, lipstick cloying.

'What colour did you say you usually go for?'

'Oh,' says Valerie, 'Caramel o6 is the one Lauren uses.'

Red rings have been drawn around the flaws in the star's face. *Guess who has crow's feet?* says the title.

On the walk to Grafton Street, Valerie keeps her eyes on the pavement ahead. She can feel how her new haircut sleeks over the contours of her skull and curls girlishly at the nape, making the shape of her head painfully conspicuous. She will need to sort herself out before shopping. She tugs a lock in around her chin. It's supposed to draw a nice curve around her face, but the man has made her hair a little too short, exposing the rough cut of her jaw. Already, she is dreading collecting Joanna from crèche. The minders will notice she has had her hair done. They will try to compliment her or, worse, they will say nothing but giggle together when she is gone. They will think the hair is too youthful for her face.

The cosmetics department is Valerie's favourite part of the store, and she always does a little browsing before picking up her monthly skincare supplies. Today she is distracted, though, flitting from counter to counter but collecting no samples, making no enquiries, taking nothing in. To take advantage of the free gift offer, she buys two bottles of her usual cleansing milk instead of one. The girl at the counter

7

is beautifully made up in this season's mango-yellow eye-shadow and coral-pink lipstick. They are the kind of colours Valerie might buy and never wear. You need delicate features and a porcelain complexion for colours like that.

'It's a great offer,' says the salesgirl.

'Yes.'

Martin often teases Valerie about her lust for bargains. He tells their friends about it – 'Vie knows all about shopping! Shopping is Vie's speciality! Nothing a woman loves more than to spend her husband's money. Am I right, lads?' and the husbands laugh, and she smiles, and the wives roll their eyes in sympathy, 'Oh don't mind him, Val. My Brian is just the same . . .'

Valerie's mother used to say that your skin is the one thing you are stuck with, the one thing you must look after. These days she has to make a particular effort to keep her skin decent. Since the baby it has grown temperamental and prone to blotches.

After the birth her cheeks were covered with fine red lines and pricks of blood that twinkled like mocking stars. They were burst vessels, the nurse said, from the pressure of pushing. They would clear up in no time. The swollen lips were nothing to worry about either; they were a result of her biting down for the final push, determined not to scream, not to make a spectacle of herself.

'Is that the baby?' she'd said when the head showed. 'Yes,' said the midwife, 'touch it.' But she hadn't. 'Are you sure that's the baby?' – because the head, faceless and purplish, looked like it could have been her own insides – a kidney or a prolapse. When they pulled the rest of it out, it hadn't cried as she'd expected. 'Is it over?' she said. 'Can I sleep now?'

The nurse pried something from its mouth with polythene hands, and Valerie heard a faint mewl. They handed it to her wrapped in a green towel and told her it was a perfect baby girl. It cried then, but only a little, with no enthusiasm. In its open mouth a wound-pink tongue curled like a fern. Its fingers stretched wire-tense and gossamer-fine, casting dark shadows on the lap of her polka-dotted hospital gown.

The salesgirl slides the gift into a tasteful beige bag beside the cleansers and ties everything up with a neat black bow.

'I've popped in a nice sample of our hand cream,' she says.

'Oh that's lovely,' says Valerie. 'Thank you. I might give it to my mother. She's in a home now, you know, but she still likes to look after herself, never without her hand cream and lipstick . . .'

'Oh,' the girl nods, 'that's a nice idea. I'll give you another one then, for yourself.'

The girl doesn't understand what Valerie is telling her; her mother – Mummy – who has always been the smell of soap, and ironing water, and Red Door perfume, who has always known how things should be done, is old now, and in a home, and sits all day by the window, and makes an ugly sucking with her mouth. She can no longer oversee a room of dinner guests, making matches and soothing out old resentments with her quiet, dignified gait and soot-heavy lids.

It's when Valerie reaches into her handbag that it happens – the barely perceptible landing weight and in an instant the tiny prick, building already towards an itch. She feels for her wallet and grips it hard, squeezes her lips against the compulsion to scratch the back of her wrist. She would give way to madness if she responded to every sensation that moved over her skin, and she must not encourage her imagination, which is learning to taunt her with little stings and tickles. Even her eyes have started to play tricks – a speck of dust that hops; a cleft of wood that hatches larvae fine as the hairs on her child's back.

Valerie looks up at the girl, who is patiently smiling. She smiles back, lifting out her hand, tilting her wrist very slightly to catch the shape of it. Yes. It's there all right, angling on the hill of her knuckle, the fleck of its body poised for escape. She opens her purse. She will not make a spectacle of herself.

'Take your time,' the nice girl says. But Valerie can feel the red patches under her eyes, the perspiration on her palms.

*

The interior of her car is chemical-clean and air-conditioned. It is dim in the car park, but Valerie flicks on the roof lamp, a thatchy rectangle of yellow. She moves bits of herself into its glow. There is nothing on her ankles, nothing at her cleavage. She runs a palm around the back of her neck and down the lobes of her ears. There it is – from nowhere she feels it land. She raises her arm to the light, watches it pivot in the crook of her elbow, the humped back peaking puce with her blood. She brings her fingers down on the porridge-soft fold of skin, and presses firm. It bites again but she can feel it, a tiny grain beneath her touch. Ha! She has it.

It's not the catching that's the problem; it's what to do afterwards. She rolls hard, pushing a finger back and forth until she is confident there is no risk of escape. Then she traps it expertly between thumb and forefinger and rolls it some more before leaning close to inspect it. It's surely dead now, or crippled at least, legs like crushed lint; jagged, crooked filaments.

In the rear-view mirror, she examines the papery creases under her eyes, the thin film of skin restraining a liquid swell beneath. She will need to fix herself before collecting Joanna.

*

She parks in a loading bay, rushes in and out as though in a great hurry. 'Come on, darling,' she says to Joanna, loudly so that the girls – the pretty foreign classroom assistant and a trendy young mum with a baby on her back – understand she is not being rude. 'Mummy is in a bit of a hurry today.' She shakes Joanna into her coat, hooks on her bag. Joanna is a quiet, obedient child. She slips her hand into her mother's, but Valerie can't bear it – the coolness and certainty of the touch, the fine bones closing together like a bird's wing. The itches are starting up again, convulsions of them running over her wrists and under her arms. She pulls her hand away, clutches the back of Joanna's coat as she guides her across the road. It's a beautiful coat – well cut, made from pure lambswool. Valerie was delighted to have found it in the January sales.

The flexibility of these thin arms always surprises her when she loops them into the straps of the child seat. She smooths the plaits either side of Joanna's face, straightens her shoulders, light and round as ping-pong balls, and pushes her bottom into the cup of the seat before pinning the little chest with a final click. 'There now,' she says. She hands Joanna a box of raisins and switches on the DVD. The entertainment system is in the back of the headrest on the passenger seat. It makes journeys far more pleasant for everyone. They are educational cartoons, and it reassures her

to hear Joanna shouting back at the characters, 'Square!...
Triangle!... Green!... Smaller!'

Valerie knows she is not what people call a 'natural
mother'. She is not 'made for it', the way some women are,
with slings and breast pumps and all that. But she does her
best. With what she has, she does her best.

Today Joanna is particularly quiet in the car. She is not
replying to her DVD. As Valerie brakes at the lights, it dawns
on her with irritating obviousness that the child could be
choking on the raisins, and she twists her head around to
check. But the raisins are forgotten. Joanna is occupied by
the handbag. In all the flurry of fixing herself, Valerie left
it in a mess on the back seat. Nothing has been put away
in the designated pouches. It's all lying on top: the gold-
smeared tissue, blush-stained powder sheets, the tube of
Barely Lipstick. The bag from the hardware shop is billowing
messily through the zip-trimmed gash.

'What did you buy, Mummy?'

It still surprises Valerie to hear Joanna speak. It began
suddenly, when she was eighteen months old. There was
no evident process to it, no first word. She hadn't even said
Mama. Then after her first week at crèche, Joanna began
to talk. A little lisp at first, but she spoke in slow, correct

sentences, and she was polite – always please and thank you and pardon. Now, at two and a half, she speaks like an adult. On hearing the child request her teddy last night – 'Mummy, please may I have Lucy Bunny? Thank you very much, Mummy' – Martin gave a satisfied, nasal chuckle.

'Glad we're getting our money's worth! The price of that place...'

But this sudden articulacy, these precocious manners, only make Valerie feel separate from the child, wary of her, and sorry for her willingness to learn the rules.

Valerie tilts the rear-view mirror to look at Joanna more comfortably. Her daughter straightens herself into her default position: ankles crossed, shoulders back. She is small for her age with a straight, flat fringe and sweeping lashes; an eerily dainty creature. Valerie allows her gaze to travel up her daughter's body – the waxy nubs of knees, the boxy pinafore, the too-fine hands resting one on top of the other on her lap, her whole presence dispassionately tidy and compact. She is an unusual sort of child certainly, not boisterous or messy like other toddlers. If you didn't like her, thinks Valerie, you might call her prissy.

'They're for Toby,' says Valerie. 'Treats for Toby.'

'Oh.' The child nods, but after a pause she says, 'Please did you get me a treat please, Mummy?'

'No darling. Not today.'

This morning, Valerie parked beside a lovely Mini – brand new, bright yellow, glossy and neat as a boiled sweet against the landscape of silver Land Rovers and smog-grey vans. She drove up beside it on purpose, aligning her car in one steady swoop. There was a box of lavender tissues on the dashboard, and, hanging from the mirror, a small teddy bear in a ballerina costume. The type of young woman who might drive about in that car would be efficient and fit, independent and busy. She would have hair sleeked back into a satiny ponytail. It would be nice to buy a car like that for Joanna someday.

'What treats for Toby, Mummy?'

'Treats, Joanna. Just treats, darling.'

'For good Toby.'

The child loves Toby, a dense package of heat and breath, flat, wiry fur, and foxy snout. Sometimes she sits beside him on the floor, curves her arm over his stiff back and tilts her head towards him. 'Toby,' she sighs, patting him lightly with parted fingers. 'Good Toby.' His back is a dirty white with grey flecks and one big splotch of rust, but when Joanna talks about him she says she has an 'orange dog called Toby'. His tail has been docked but a good three inches of it remain, so he sits all day wagging the sad little stump – too short for a tail and too long for the neat nubbin that tradition demands – waiting for Martin, his beloved master, to come home and pat him on the head. Martin will be at after-work drinks tonight, so Toby will sit and sit until it's dark, banging that blunt stub on the tiled porch floor.

'Why do they dock the tails?' Valerie asked her husband once, 'and why are they still born with tails, after all the breeding? Why do the tails remain?' The reason mustn't have been very satisfying, because Valerie can't remember it now.

She never liked the dog. She should have said it when Martin first came home with the puppy – she should have made him get rid of it, but it was after her third miscarriage, and she was still cautious then, grateful and glad to be a wife, determined to rise to the role. Making a marriage work, her mother had told her, was largely about learning to like things that might at first seem tiresome. 'And the secret,' she said, 'to a really happy marriage is to make him believe he is in control.' When her mother said that she winked in that elegant, warming way she could. 'But of course, darling, it's you who is in control.'

Valerie buys Martin's shirts for him, and his socks and his underpants even; she sends him out every day to work and then she buys the things she wants – that new coffee table; the wooden mini kitchen for Joanna. Joanna; she even named the child. Why, then, does it feel not at all like her mother's victorious, conspiratorial wink?

She was right, though; Valerie has learned to like being a homemaker. There is a delicious guilt, now, in leafing through interior design catalogues, fantasizing about all the different ways she might redecorate the dining room. But Toby is nearly five, and she still doesn't like him. As time goes on, he only smells worse; his lopsided gallop grows only more irksome. It's a secret she hardly admits to herself: that she hates to be greeted by Toby, hates the pleasure Toby takes in Martin's return or her daughter's head-tilt, the way Toby laps up the meaningless words of praise, 'Good Toby.'

In the evening while she waits for Martin, Valerie often allows herself a gin and tonic, and as she drinks, she listens to the steady tap of Toby's half-tail on the tiles, faster and harder as the moment approaches, the sharp yelps of excitement when the car swings into view, the scuffle and bump as he leaps at the porch door because he can't contain his excitement, and then his panting joy – pure dumb doggy joy – when Martin pats him on the head.

As an afterthought Valerie tilts her chin up and says, 'I'll get you a treat tomorrow, Joanna,' but the child is asleep, her head flopped to the side, the soft peaked mouth drooling onto the seatbelt. Valerie almost doesn't notice it – she is about to turn back but then she looks again and there it is – the familiar fleck perched insolently on the curve of her daughter's cheek, and Valerie's breath hooks high in her chest.

HROOOOO – it's the four-by-four behind her, a man at the wheel wearing an ill-fitting suit jacket. He honks again, longer this time: HRNMOOOOO. The lights are green and she must go. Oh and God, what is she like? There are tears now; her eyes are watering, liquid seeping out like the ooze and split of an overripe fruit because her daughter, Valerie's own and only child, is asleep with fleas hopping over her skin. She is a ridiculous woman and everyone knows it; a mush of a face pasted over with make-up, hobbling the streets with the hair of a pretty child and fleas in her expensive handbag; weeping at the wheel, holding up traffic. That hairdresser today – the way he ran his eyes over her; he knew she was a joke. And that stupid teenager, handing her the plastic bag, smiling and smiling at her like a hungry pup and laughing behind the smile. She can feel the creatures under her clothes, burying into her, creeping around in her nostrils. She will poison them, but will it even work? The bug bombs, the spray, the vacuuming. Or are fleas forever part of her now?

One of the women on the Internet said that she still had fleas after a thirty-year battle. 'Will I ever feel clean again?' she blogged.

*

Toby is already frantic at the porch door – he always knows when Joanna is coming home. Valerie opens the back door of the car very slowly and crouches, her stub heels sinking into the plush gravel. If she presses down on the flea, she will wake Joanna. She will have to pluck it off. She needs to be careful and deft. She brings her thumb and forefinger together on either side, but her nails are too long, the acrylic lacquer too thick. The flea drops immediately onto her daughter's hand. Valerie lowers her head to assess the angle but – Ha! She feels the skin pleating around her lips as she huffs a quiet laugh, the tightness springs from her chest – it's just a fleck of cut hair! She licks her finger, touches the speck, and lifts it gently away.

Valerie leaves her handbag in the back seat for now and brings in only the plastic bag with the things from the hardware shop. Toby knows better than to jump up on her nice skirt. While she moves to the kitchen, he orbits her like a satellite, leaping into the air, trembling with all the tempered aggression he has been bred for.

The kitchen is immaculate but for a mug in the sink with a ring of tea dried into the base. Dolores always does that – leaves the house spotless except for some tell-tale sign of her passing-through. Valerie has spoken to her about it several times.

With relish she removes her purchases from the hardware-shop bag and lays them out in a straight row. What pleases her is the variety of sizes and shapes – the tall can of spray, the tiny bug bomb, the pillow-shaped bag of dog treats.

Toby begins to nose at the bag and Valerie pulls it out of reach. Then she notices a few of the bone shapes at the bottom. The packet of treats must have split. Toby's paws skitter on the floor as he resists the urge to jump. 'Sit!' says Valerie. The dog lowers his hind quarters, quivering in a half-squat.

Valerie slips her shoes off. The underfloor heating makes the soles of her feet tingle as she lowers the bag to Toby's height. Toby hurls his weight into the suffocating plastic, nosing blindly around the bottom of the bag in a frenzy of snuffing and licking. He inhales nostrilfuls of the stuff, misses the treats and tries again, his tongue dark through the plastic, claws skating coolly on the hardwood floor.

Valerie's mother – Mummy – must have her handbag by her at all times now. For hours sometimes, her fingers scurry and scrape at the lining, searching. She is getting worse. That's what Valerie thought last time she visited – she is drawing further into that terrible mindscape of pretty napkins and perfume bottles, staring out at Valerie through shrinking, pinkening eyes.

The bag could smother Toby. Stupid creature. The

sharpness of his claws makes her think of the hairdresser again, the metal in his flaccid brow, how it must have hurt and how the man wore his mutilation like victory. Valerie tries to pull it off him but he pushes in, all snorts and huffs, so that she has to put her palm on his spine and push down. 'Sit, Toby.' Toby can't resist the order. His bony haunches collapse, the little peaks of his pelvic bones hiccupping with desire for his bag of doggie treats. He raises his rear again, and lowers, hovering, awaiting permission to move. Valerie puts a hand on the rough, oily sack of his neck. Inside the loose skin there is something craggy and solid – his voice box; his throat. As she peels the bag down off his nose, she notices, flapping at the edge of her vision, his docked tail – that mutilated knob of gristle, wagging and wagging and wagging for approval.

'Why are you wagging, Toby? Stupid creature, why are you wagging?'

Poor dumb Toby; pleased with his treats. Toby, waiting for Martin's pat, waiting for some orders to obey. Poor mutt. He thinks he's pleased with his draughty porch, his Sunday walks, his treats and that amputated appendage.

'What a life, Toby. What a joke.'

Valerie draws the bag tight around the dog's head, stretching the plastic thin over the shape of his muzzle and his long skull. Watching the suck of the plastic catch and tug on his loose eyelids, she thinks of the day her ears were pierced. It was her mother who brought her. The jeweller used a red pen to make a dot on each lobe. The quick stamp of pain and the victory of no tears.

Face low with his now, Valerie can smell the oily sleek of Toby's coat, the hot, healthy sweat, the sandy traces of excrement on his scraggle-bearded belly. She is on top of him now, her skirt hitched up and her legs pressing on Toby's stringy muscles, the slosh of his stomach, the graceful chains of bones. Valerie retches loudly, for she can feel the greasy heat of him shifting on her groin. He bucks, but she has him, her knee jabbing into his neck, so he lowers his head silently. With both knees on Toby's sharp shoulder blades, Valerie reaches for the handle of the built-in rubbish bin, pulls it outwards, and grabs the new sack that the cleaner has put in it – a heavy black one. She pushes one knee down on Toby's head; his eye. Toby whimpers, that is all. Weakly, hopelessly, he shows her his teeth. Poor Toby. Stupid docile creature. With his head twisted on the ground, she opens the sack over his wincing face, scrunching it closed at his throat. Toby begins to growl now. He scrambles for some kind of leverage on the glossy floor. His hind legs kick and scratch. He jerks, and the force of it draws streaks of pain through her. She clasps and pulls until the bag is over the whole rat-like bulk of him. Because of the closing fan of her daughter's cool, small hand in hers, the bones like quills and the flesh like fruit – because of Joanna she knows she can't let go now, for she can see how the fleas would infest the delicate curls of her ears, how his filth would ruin her winter coat. In one snap he could remove the dimple-knuckled hands that like to pat his stinking hide, sever clean the soft bones and supple nails. Valerie heaves the bag up and is proud of her strength as she gets some swing on it and smacks it down, lifts it again as he whimpers and sags, and she heaves and smacks heaves and smacks and there are distant crackles like dry leaves being trodden down, then a fainter, daintier snap, but she will not stop until the bag is heavy and still and her shoulders ache and she knows it is done.

Slowly, painfully, she straightens her back and opens her jaw to the ceiling. The smell must have been here for some time – maybe even before the black bag, because the shit is on her arms in foamy globs and smeared with curious greasiness over her thighs, and she realizes that must be why she retched. She hears her own voice, soft and adult and reassuring. 'There,' it says. 'Now. There.'

In the shower, Valerie makes the water as hot as she can bear. She uses soap, an exfoliator, then shower gel with a loofah.

She must visit her mother tomorrow. She would rather not. Last time she went, things were worse. Her mother's hand scuttled like a sea crab across the floor of her empty handbag. 'My powder,' she said, 'someone has taken my powder.' She had that look Valerie had caught on her once before. It was when Valerie was a child – maybe eight or nine – at a dinner party. Her father's work colleagues were there, and their wives, and some other important friends of her parents, and everything was going well. There was a fire crackling in the good room, and Valerie knew it was a success by the way the men nodded genially at each other, and the women admired each other's dresses. It must have been the start of the evening, because Valerie had been asked to offer around the snacks and then to play the piano and everyone had clapped, but afterwards she found herself standing useless in the room of beautiful dresses and mahogany furniture, all the strangers looking at her back and her front, and smiling, and she had gone in search of her mother. She found her in the kitchen, arranging canapés on the oval silver platter that Valerie had always longed to touch. Her mother cut a beautiful shape – her head was bent, her neck arcing in that way that made Valerie think, always, of waterfalls. Suddenly she was a singular thing, where before she had been all of it – the food and the fire and the floor polish and the rhythm of the house. Valerie approached her quietly, needing to be near her, but finding no excuse for leaving the party. Her mother didn't notice her, and when she raised her head, about to lift the plate, she was wearing a private face. Her lips had dropped to a lax pout, grave tightness at their edges and – the part that sent a ripple of terror through Valerie – her hooded eyes were round and bewildered beneath a twisting brow. When she saw Valerie watching she pulled her face into place – the dusky eye-sockets, the muscular cheeks. She pushed the tray into Valerie's hand and told her to take it around the guests. All evening, Valerie felt the roundness of her mother's eyes, the ugliness of her mouth.

That was the look her mother's face had the last time Valerie saw it. Valerie made only a short visit, for she had Joanna with her. When she turned to leave, though, the old woman clutched Joanna weakly by the shoulders.

'Vilie,' she said, 'my little Vilie Vie.' It was a pet name she had used for Valerie when she was a child, but her voice was hateful and flat. 'My silly little Vilie. You think I made the whole world, don't you?'

The child stood very tense, her cheeks wrinkling, perhaps about to cry. Her grandmother shook a finger close to her face.

'No, no, little Vilie. Don't come to me with your tears, darling. I only tried to help you live in it, my darling. It was the other girls and boys made it, you silly goose you, and you thought it was me made it all.'

Valerie will not bring Joanna there again.

She hurries into her clothes – her jogging gear seems the only thing at this late stage in the evening.

Downstairs is fine except for the smell of bleach. The cleaner might be responsible for that, for all Martin knows. First she closes the French doors that look onto the night; the flat lawn and the discreet line of wheelie bins pushed against the wall. As she bolts the top latch she hears a gentle rustle beneath the silence outside, but she will not look at the big black bin. Her mind is playing tricks; she knows that. She hurries all the same, and is glad to twist the key and pull the heavy curtains shut.

Because of the shower, her body is hot to the night air that has gushed in noisily through all the open windows. She imagines steam lifting off the back of her neck as she moves from room to room, closing the big double doors of the breakfast lounge and the small window of the under-the-stairs lavatory. She imagines how her body must look to the fleas huddled in the chill upholstery – streaks of red and yellow, a whirl of nourishing blood moving in the dead atmosphere.

In the car, Joanna is still dribbling soundly onto the harness. She hasn't had her dinner; there's a risk she'll wake hungry in the night, but Valerie will take the chance. Joanna begins to stir against her mother's shoulder, but Valerie rubs her back and shushes her, 'There now, there . . .' Valerie puts her on the toilet upstairs and runs the tap to make her pee so that there are no accidents in the night. Then she lifts her into bed. She can sleep in her pinafore just this once. The cleaner has changed the sheets and Valerie wonders if Joanna is old enough to appreciate the pleasure of crisp cotton against her cheek. She pulls the duvet to her daughter's chin and pries open the plaits, spreading the child's bright hair over the pink Egyptian-cotton pillow case.

Joanna's hair is the same colour as Valerie's once was. On the hairdresser's colour chart it is called Caramel 06.

Down in the kitchen Valerie puts a new black sack in the bin. The bin is clean, but something about it makes her think of maggots – the white chubbiness of them; the way they can materialize from any kind of filth; the way they are almost certainly there, at the bottom of the outside-bin, writhing blindly against the plastic; and the way they work diligently on things that are dead, curling out of eye-sockets and nostrils . . . She puts Dolores's mug in the dishwasher and slices a wedge out of a lime, ignoring the drips of juice on the granite. She puts three ice cubes into a glass, squeezes the lime over the ice, and drops the wedge in on top. Now the gin, and now the spit of fresh tonic from a chilled can. Valerie has a silver stirrer that she uses to swirl the drink. She sits at the kitchen table. Now she can turn her attention to today's shopping. She has brought it all in from the car, and she removes the cleanser and the free gift from the bag and sets them out before her. She will enjoy this as she sips the drink; she will enjoy unwrapping the generous sheets of crepe, swivelling the top of the cleanser until it pops up, ready to pump, and discovering the treats in the free gift bag. Her ankle twitches, and forgetting herself for a moment Valerie scratches along the bone. It is a comfort to know she has the bug bomb. She will wait until Monday to light it – Monday after Martin has left for work and before she takes Joanna to crèche.

She's left the porch light on, and it is glowing now, an orange cube against the dark outside.

In White Ink

ALREADY I AM losing the shapes for you. You are not face or hands or voice, but only sensation – breast-brim and skin-yearn and the cell-crave of our division. The ink I have used to set you down – the marks that make the letters, that make the words to make a story stick – I think it is the kind that will not smear, but swim cleanly from the page like a shoal of sated minnows.

There is a sign recommending that passengers with sea-sickness stay on deck and look out at the horizon, but closed eyes and closed-up limbs seem the only way to wait the nausea out. I keep low, crouched down with the cradling of the boat, knees drawn in, face tucked down, hands clinging barnacle-still to myself. In the little dark this makes, I try for your smile your foot your ear, but there are only the words that pull away, and then even the lines where they were perched begin to scramble. Already, the ages and stages you are made from bunch and cross, so that when I look for your age I cannot find a number. But there you are, I see you now, the lines all ajumble – here, sleeping in your buggy with buttery thighs and feet like handkerchief knots; here a map of Ireland in a sonograph of my insides; and here – but no that is not you yet – the mossy chin, the widening shoulders, the snarl – not yet, no. It is your parting smell that will lead me to you – the sweet, moist liveness of your skin – Oh now I have you – there you are opening your eyes at first light.

You wake too early – a ravenous mouth; a need; a wild, snorting, pulling thing, ferociously rooting for survival. Sleepily we lump you from his hands to my arms to milk, and there you mew and smack and, frantic for it, you miss and miss and catch and miss and latch. The lock and pull of you sends a rush through the other breast and three white arcs cross the bedroom – elegant, confident shapes, and shocking for their reach – leaving a sprinkling of tiny blots on the mirror of our wardrobe and we laugh and sigh and stay it with a cloth and promise each other we'll change the sheets after breakfast.

Ready to smile, you keep the nipple within suckle-clamp,

two palms suckered to the swell-and-wobble globe that is now your touchstone. Your mouth is a stretch of red-sharp gum, a serrated streak of tooth cutting through, and your smile curves open like all sorts of understanding. Waste of cream on your lips, you look me in the eye for the first time this morning and say something – you laugh, suckle some more. A satisfied little puke and I promise your daddy again about the sheets.

Seven a.m. is your happiest and most demanding hour. Daddy makes a play of changing your nappy, pretending surprise and horror, as though he has not known these smells each day since you came, and you chuckle because his face is twisting and opening and making great noises and maybe you feel big, like your shit is a powerful thing. Maybe you feel like a monster and a lord.

Back in bed we babble and laugh because we see why everything is so funny for you, and you rub Daddy's beard until you get bored and I read to you – a story about a prince and a tower and a golden-haired woman whose tears can heal, but you are not concerned with that, only with my voice now, the way it moves up and down, faster and slower and is still the same voice; the way that contrasts make shapes; the way the pages can rise and turn and new ones appear beneath. Then I eat your toes and, holding your fat balls of hands, I walk you up and down my tummy where you used

31

to grow, folded into yourself in a wordless complicity only us, and play airplanes and congratulate you loudly when you move the beads up the abacus and I tell myself to cherish it now; your baby scent.

Because I know these are the things for forgetting.

We play Mozart and lay you back in your crib under the mobile with a clumsy elephant and a bright zebra that pivots, twirls, and creakily slides, and you sleep while we make love quietly under the covers, laughing a little because just for now in the fractured rise of light, before the words begin and the witnesses come, before my mind gathers these colours into the white of day, we know the heart is made of flesh.

Now you can speak, and I don't know what sounds to make for you. Mothers are supposed to sing to their children, but I have a terrible voice. They should tell stories too. That is something I think I can do. But what can I say?

I could tell you about this time last year, when you were a bump – still so miraculously neat that I could conceal you with a princess-line or a baggy jumper. If I lay on my back the whole shape of you raised under my skin; we saw your head already; blades of your bottom; thick of your thighs.

This time last year your father blindfolded me and walked me onto the Luas – I could hear the bell and the doors shushing closed, and I could feel the tracks beneath us as the tram rolled on. The scarf he had tied around my head kept slipping down over my nose. It scratched my eyes and made my cheeks twitch. It smelled of him. I kissed him just under his ear, breathed his skin, and he kissed my mouth. He said it was a surprise but I knew where we were going.

When we got to Smithfield I gave up on the blindfold, which disappointed him, and we walked from the station to the square, where they were selling Christmas trees and wreaths. It was very cold. The tips of our fingers were numb and our breath made clouds. His nose was red – the whole bulk of it from the nostrils up the hump, inflated and glowing with cold. Without meaning to, I knew how easy it would be not to love him. A moment is all it would take; a moment to trip myself up and let fall a thing that could never be gathered up again; spilled milk. He wrapped his scarf snug around my throat, tucking in the ends.

We picked a nice, symmetrical tree that smelled of Christmas, the kind of Christmas that happy families had, the kind – please believe me – the kind we wanted to make for you. We asked the man to lop the bottom off the tree, to make it small enough to fit in our flat, and spent ten euros on a tree-stand. Your daddy hadn't budgeted for the stand at all, but we agreed that this was an investment – we would use it for years to come. I remember that because I wondered if we believed it.

On the tram a sign said: 'Happy Christmas! Please do not bring trees onto the tram. To do so is a crime. Offenders will be prosecuted.' There was a picture of a Christmas tree under the print; white gaps in a green triangle. We had no money for the fare on account of the tree-stand. When the conductor came around your father stood me in front of the Christmas tree. The branches stuck out either side of me and the needles poked my back. I laughed and so did he. The man looked at us and raised his eyebrows. 'Come on, man, you can't throw us off. We're pregnant,' said your father, and my skin pickled.

You haven't tasted pickles yet – they are not like the foods you eat now, which are tepid and mildly sweet. Pickles are cold, sharp-tasting foods preserved in clear and bitter liquid. I cannot know what you will think of pickled onions or pickled gherkins or pickled eggs, but when you taste them, you will know the kind of thing that happened all over my skin when he said, 'We're pregnant.'

The conductor turned away. It was a look like disgust, only kinder. Young love, he thought. I could see it in the way he shook his head, knowingly. Young love. He didn't know anything.

I rubbed my tummy, making circles on your back with my hands, my skin taut against your growth. Your father bent over, catching his breath between his guffaws. We laughed into each other's necks. I laughed against his chest, he laughed into my hair.

You stretched your shape and kicked and I wondered what the bony judder of my ribcage meant to you, shuddering over your capsule like strange weather, but I hoped I was keeping the cold on my surface, outside you.

I could tell you that when you were born the morning sun lit the white walls of the delivery room as though it was summer, and there wasn't as much blood as people would like you to think. Your head was crumpled like a passion fruit as it came out. Then you opened into a baby, drinking the light with your new skin, your gasp. Your fingers splayed and curled, exploring the air like tentacles.

You smiled the moment you emerged, and you opened your eyes, though people don't believe that. A thousand expressions moved across your face – O of wonder, scrunch of disgust, all the full curves of joy – a flicker-book of everything you would feel between now and the close of your life. People don't believe that either.

For the birth, they wanted to numb me up. They said it again and again, in a tone warning and urgent, as though something would happen soon that would be too much. The pain was fine, though, more fine than anyone would like you to think, and not really what people usually mean by pain. When I told them you were coming they insisted your birth was hours away and told me not to push. 'Trust me,' said the midwife with a smile, 'you'd know all about it if it was coming.' But you and I knew. We laboured in secret towards our separation, me nodding obediently at the professional grimaces. 'Don't push yet,' said the midwife, and 'Close your mouth.' She said I would scare the other women with my sounds – not the tearing cries she wanted but noises darker and dirtier than a scream. Your father rubbed my back and said, 'Shhhh. Listen to the doctor, baby.'

The sight of your head shocked them.

'Oh,' said the midwife, turning to the trainee, 'no warning that time.'

To me she said, 'Alright, you can push now. Come on, push now, push.'

She called your father 'Dad', and told him to put a vest on the heater. She was trying to distract him, I thought, for he was eager to put the mask of laughing gas over my face and the more I said no, the more his eagerness grew. The vest was striped white and blue with poppers between the legs, and I knew that it measured from my belly button to just under my breasts.

You had hardly left my inside when your daddy cut the cord, and you and I were two. I didn't recognize your face.

They asked your name but I couldn't do that, not yet. I could only call you 'baby'. 'Hello baby.'

They taught me how to swaddle you, but you hated to be swaddled. You hated to be folded up again, tucked in and stuffed over yourself and made to fit. You liked to stretch your arms, your legs and toes and scrawny neck. Silently you moved like that in your glass box, extending into the world with tiny extremities and glad, glad of it all.

For three days I could not sleep but only look at you. The joy that came was an engulfing kind; a terrifying, snatching kind full of claws and wool and feathers, and the shapeless terror of silence, and I knew already it was not the right kind for a thing like you, that needed to stretch and open.

For three days I tempered it, tempered it down into the practical chores I could make from it: nappies and feeding and biting your nails blunt so you could not nick your cheeks and scalp; the appallingly delicate skin you came in.

When you were three days old, a respectable shade of milk replaced the garish colostrum, and I had soothed it down enough for words. I told you something true then. I whispered it close to your skin that smelled like coconuts. 'I love you,' I said, but thought, I have no idea though, baby. I have no idea who you are. He named you then, but I still have no idea. Your life is a journey out of me, a one-way street.

*

When you were four months old and I was sitting my exams, I didn't go back to sleep one night after your 4 a.m. feed. I couldn't rest. You snored a baby snore in your crib at my back. Your daddy slept beside me. I tried to tuck myself into the hot curl of his body and his breath but his presence played a cool fever on my bones. I got up and went into the other room of our flat.

The window was silver from the steam of the drying laundry, and the street lamps glittering through. It was cold outside, but when I opened the window, the air hung still. I remember that because it sent a surge of fear and giddiness through me, the way the night refused to move into the warm, as though some law had been suspended here in the unpatrolled hours. There was just the sound of night traffic. Trucks, mostly, lumbering through, rumbling the tarmac, casting their gaze over our walls, our floor, our table, our buggy. Sitting on the couch I tried to study, some Greek myth about punishing gods, hubris, jealous women – but by the time I reached a full stop I had forgotten the beginning of the sentence. I didn't understand anything.

I took the scissors out from the drawer under the hob, and the Pritt-stick from under the television, and I gathered all our photographs around me.

By the time you woke for your seven o'clock feed, I had made you a book. The book told our story. It began when your father and I met. It chronicled our holidays together, the drunken karaoke, the kisses in the kitchenette while we waited for the coffee to splurt up through the funnel of that aluminium espresso pot your daddy had back then. That was before we heard that aluminium leaks into the brain, making you confused as you grow old, making you forget the references you are made from: your car keys; your phone number; names.

I found the notebook this morning. The photographs have been hurriedly glued. In all the pictures, we are smiling. There is a narrative scrawled beside them in baby language. I have written you a story that is simple and not a lie. I say how in love we were, how happy, and the photos seem to prove it. I do not tell you that the morning-after pill was too expensive, and 'risk of pregnancy' a thing inconceivable. Anyway, that might have been a different time. I am no good on dates. I do not say that you were planned, but nor do I tell you what my eyes might have meant, shut into the pillow in the moment of your conception. I do not explain the tedium of slumber-rape, the horror of daily sniping, the way these things wear and wear until the fabric is too thin to handle.

I write that your daddy was happy when I said 'We are going to have a little baby.' That is not exactly how I put it, but I think it is what he heard. I tell you we both laughed and were happy. I tell you that he kissed my tummy. I do not tell you what happened then, lips to skin, faces, eyelids, shoulders, looking at each other in the twilight under bed-sheets. I do not mention the glaze that sometimes crept into my eyes, or how I resolved that with forgetting I would make it good. It would be to betray you, to tell the words he used, his hand wrapped from behind around my neck, and pushing, pushing: 'Mine now. You are mine now.'

There are pictures of Halloween, when we tied an orange silk scarf around the bump, and your daddy drew triangle eyes, triangle nostrils, and a smile of triangle-teeth to make you a pumpkin. 'Bump-kin', we called you all night. We went out and had dinner with many people I did not know. The girl opposite me was dressed as Catwoman. She had a sultry sweep of eyeliner across each heavy lid, and a way I could not read, of gliding her eyes over you, and when asked if she would one day like children she looked your father in the face and said, 'I am just back from an abortion. I flew back this morning.'

She left halfway through the main course, and the host smacked his forehead. 'How stupid,' he said, 'to have seated her opposite you pair after what she's been through. Silly Jules – I just didn't think. . .' I don't tell you that part, or the desire that happened as we looked at each other, me in my witch costume and she dressed as Catwoman, weak smiles wavering across the black tablecloth and 'ghoulish goulash'. Perhaps I seemed smug, moving my hand over and over you like a crystal ball; as if I thought I knew something she did not. That was not what I meant by it, though. Not at all. I don't tell you because I know it is easy to misunderstand, and I know I have a terrible voice.

In any case, she slipped off without a scene and all night he introduced my belly with a joke accent, 'This is Bumpkin, and this be ma witch . . .'

I was dressed in black; the top had enough room for you at the front, and the back was bare except for a web of black ribbons laced over my skin. He had lifted a long silver wig from the pound shop, which made me look glamorous and gothic. In the photograph we are beautiful and extravagant, grinning with our dark, painted mouths. My eyes are frilled with fake lashes of purple and silver. There is an envelope stuck to the page opposite, with the orange scarf tucked into it.

The next page is a picture of the two of us with the Christmas tree. We are standing on either side of it, holding the bark, chins raised, goofy smiles, green sprigs flecking our arms. My face is pale from vomiting – it didn't stop after three months like they said. My nose and eyes are pink. 'They waited and waited and waited,' says my handwriting, 'for their baby to come out and meet them.' This must have been close to the birth because you are a tight mound under that big sweater of your daddy's.

There is a photo of me an hour after you were born, my mouth touching your furred head, the hospital sheets pulled up over my breasts. There is one of you under the Christmas tree, asleep on a big toy sheep. You arrived on Christmas Eve and the tree was still up when we brought you home. The needles were a little dry, but still green, and I think they still smelled like Christmas. I have written: 'At last Mammy and Daddy could take their baby home. They had never ever been happier than when the three of them went to bed that night.'

That is true. I want you to know that. Neither of us had ever been happier.

In sleep I am dark and hairy all over. The hair I have is wiry, humid, kinked and disparate like the crunching scraggleweed found at the root of a penis. My mouth is slimy, hot, fanged and chomping, and with my many arms I can reach far on either side. My many arms – or are they legs? – are for reaching and for moving. One by one, the arm-legs move slowly on a tightrope of spun silk. My many eyes show a disco-ball vision of our little room – the damp-mottled ceiling and the lino floor and the curtain-hooks. I cannot see you at first, only flashes of our room: the hinge of the door; the cracked twirl of wicker on our laundry basket, but then there you are, right in front of me, twirling like a suckling on a spit, but you are smiling in a serene daze, smiling with love at my many eyes and my many legs and the fangs in my hot and dirty mouth, and I am turning you before me, swaddling you around and around in reams of white muslin, leaving only your lovely face exposed. What will happen next? What will happen to your lovely face?

There are many parts to the story, but it would not be right to share my dreams with you. That would be to tug at the fraying cord between us. That would not be fair. Like I said, it's a one-way street.

I could tell you that when you were a bump, and we walked through crowds, your daddy stretched out his arm in front of me so that no one could bang into you.

In one of your books there is a picture of a man throwing his coat over the puddle, and his lady is smiling sweetly with cheeks that are apple-red and apple-round, gathering her skirts over her foot and tilting her ankle like a pony, so I think it would make sense to you, if I could say how his gesture made me blush. 'Bloody ignorant,' he said to the crowds. 'Bloody ignorant! Foreigners taking up the street. Excuse me

– my girlfriend's pregnant!' I could say how wonderful it was to be protected like that, because you will not know what I mean if I tell you how my face burned and my eyes stung, how I tried to like it.

I think I could blame him, though. I think if I tried, I could make a good case, but there are so many parts to the whole that telling it is always wrong.

After the birth he said 'All over,' and 'That's my girl,' and 'My son. My son.' I wanted some other words. I was exhausted and in shock, my body shuddering back to the shape of me; nothing he said could have been right. It was his voice that felt like a fist, thrusting in at the space between me and you – 'All over,' he said, 'it's all over now.'

In the pub your daddy's friend smiles; 'Your fella said something so beautiful just now.'

'Oh? What did he say?'

I watch her pretty lips part and touch.

'He said watching you feed the baby makes him wish he had breasts.'

I try to giggle but a cackle comes out. 'Oh. Boob-envy,' I say. The words sound bitter. I buy us both another drink.

★

For your first Halloween we make a little pixie of you. You have a felt bonnet that ties with a ribbon under your chin. It has a purple, peaked tip and pointed green ears. I dress you in a soft green babygrow and purple booties with curling toes and bells on the ends. Your daddy wants to put green face-paint on you and take a photo but I say no – not your face. I don't want anything on your cheeks, soaking through to the magnificent complexity of blood and flesh that your skin protects. He says, 'What makes you think you know better than me, what's okay for him and what's not? It says hypoallergenic. He's my son too . . .'

When you are all-dressed-up, you feed rhythmically. Your eyes roll back, lids close and flutter and shut. 'There,' I say, 'there now my little pixie, my pixie baby.' Your daddy leans over you and, mimicking my tone, he says, 'There now, your mother is a bossy bitch, isn't she, little pixie? Yes she is. But soon you will be a big boy and we will do what we want. Soon you will be my big man,' and I frown, and he laughs and kisses my cheek and I smile.

You fall asleep on the breast and I use a finger to release the vacuum between your lips and my skin, pry you carefully out of the pocket of heat between us, and lay you in your crib. Your daddy is watching something on TV and I am still in my nightdress with the nursing straps and the milk stains, so I take a shower.

When I come out of the bathroom, you are not in your crib and your daddy is gone. Your buggy is here and you are not. You are not in your rocker or your playpen and your daddy is gone. I phone him on his mobile and he answers. 'Look out the window,' he says. He is across the road, on the street outside the chipper, looking up at me where I am standing by the window in my towel. There is water trickling from my hair down my neck, and a pool is forming at my feet, but he is too far away to see that so it doesn't matter. On the road between us, the cars swash him in and out of view. 'You don't trust me,' he says, 'I can hear it. What do you think I have done?'

My voice is wobbling and rising to a terrible shriek; 'Where is the baby?'

'Guess.'

'Where is the baby? Tell me now. Tell me now.'

'Use your mother-instinct,' he says. 'What do you think I have done?'

'Where is he?'

'Say please,' he says. 'Don't be so rude.'

'Where is the baby please.'

'Try again.'

'Please tell me where the baby is.'

'He's safe. If you trusted me you wouldn't be such a psycho about it.'

Then there is a tinkling – your bootie bells, and then your

cry and I know where you are. In the boiler closet, strapped into your car seat with the straps that are growing too tight – there you are, disgruntled from a nap you didn't mean to take, a creased little goblin mewling in the dark. When I lift you out something shifts across your face; for a moment this is a changeling child and in a dizzy pause I listen like an animal for your cry – out in the corridor, perhaps, or down on the street. I bend to smell you. There is green paint daubed like camouflage on your cheeks.

That night I take your book from where I keep it in the drawer beneath the oven. I use a hole-punch to make a pair of eyelets on a blank page. Then I thread the purple ribbon through one hole, and hang a little bell on it. I put the ribbon out through the other hole, and knot the ends at the other side. The book does not close properly now, but I don't mind.

I can't find the thing to say. Looking through your book I can't trace it to the moment when tedium turned to torment. I can't explain why it became less possible day by day: baking him meatloaf, sitting on his knee, dragging running jokes to death, flinching when he spoke to his mates, his voice changing into someone else's, his laugh a spray of bullets – huh huh, huh huh, huh – giving you suck, giving him head, cleaning the toilet.

They called in a lot, the mates. One afternoon they sat on the couch. They were just back from a trip to Thailand.

'They like us Irish lads,' said one, ''cause we're nice to them – the English guys abuse them an' all. Terrible.'

You were nestled in the crook of your daddy's elbow, sleeping. 'Do they, yeah?' he said. 'Fuck's sake. Terrible.'

Then they told him about one girl in particular, and it must have been a funny story because he laughed that laugh, and you woke up. I wanted to take you out for a walk but he wanted to keep you and show you to his friends. You cried and clawed my T-shirt but I had to leave you. Please understand. My milk would have tasted like metal, like boiled blood.

The sequence of the book is all wrong; I can see that now. After the bell there is another page with your passport photo stapled to the corner. You look startled and are wearing a tiny Hawaiian shirt. That was the spring. Halloween came after. The passport was for our holiday in Spain.

You were only three months old then, four months at most. Getting the photo right was tricky, because no hands are allowed in shot and you could not sit yet.

His aunt said we could use her timeshare house and we left the day the exams finished. I remember warm evenings, you burbling in your buggy, eating out of doors, children running in and out of houses in the dusk, parched fields, white houses.

At night you slept on a double bed, couch cushions penning you in, and we sat by the pool with candles lit and talked and drank wine and dangled our feet in the water.

While he was putting you down one evening I stood by the water in a new white dress. We had bought a bottle of bubbles that day to entertain you. I blew some up into the air; big, slow, wobbly ones at first, then streams of little ones that petered into dots. I could not stop then; I blew more and more, dreading the bottle ending. I watched the bubbles turn slowly like glass planets, and they caught the light of our candles, vibrating with invisible colour, bouncing on the surface of the pool, trembling before they popped. I knew it was beautiful. I knew how happy I could have felt.

Your daddy came out of the house. He had been watching me. He had the camera in his hand. 'You look so beautiful,' he said. 'In that white dress. I tried to take a photo, but the memory was full.' My chest hurt like a tightening screw and all I knew burst into ribbons of solitary sounds.

He wants you for your first Christmas. He puts his foot in the door and says he will keep it there until I talk to him and when I push him he grabs my wrist and asks if I am trying to make him hit me. 'You'd love that,' he says, 'wouldn't you? I'd never hear the end of it.' I am not doing myself any favours, he says, or the baby either. If I co-operate with him, then he will co-operate with me and my neurotic demands, he says, he will feed you whatever hippy shit I want and put you down for the regimented nap, and he will not call unexpectedly at night to take you. I remember the mediator saying that co-operation is key. I am not sure I know how to co-operate. I think what she really meant, was bargain.

His big sister phones me to ask, and then his father and they both take the same line: They were expecting you for Christmas. Why should they pay for what I have done? Why should their Christmas be ruined? They didn't have me down for a sexist. Your grandma has bought you a stocking saying 'Baby's First Christmas' and everything.

So it was me who said yes. But you see it doesn't matter that it is Christmas – you don't yet know the difference. This time is the worst, though, because this time it is three whole days and nights he takes you for. He collects you on the morning of Christmas Eve, an hour earlier than planned. A pallor falls over your face when the buzzer sounds. We listen for the heave of the lift, and I open the door for him before he knocks. You cry a lot and squirm when he pulls you off me. He stations you behind his head, hanging a hand at each of his shoulders, to bunch one of your wrists and one of your ankles tight in each of his knotty fists. I think he is hurting you. Your eyes widen at me but what can I say that will not make it worse? I give him a cooler bag with bottles of breast milk, and tubs of cubed avocado and chickpeas and butternut squash. 'Butternut posh,' he says. He struggles to take it and to restrain you at the same time. You scream so loudly that I think he might give you back, but he just juts his lower jaw, as if to make it bigger, delving ridges along his collar bone. He holds you firm and you do your worst – mah maaaah mahmahhhhh.

The mediator said to ignore such performances. She said that even very young children can be manipulative. I should try to be rational, she said, and remember that two parents are better than one. You will thank me for it in the future, she said. But I can hear you wailing all the way down in the lift and out on the street and long after and I lie in bed for some time, looking at the wall instead of your cot and trying to remember what the mediator said; trying to be rational.

I will stay here until you are back. My parents think I am with 'the father's side' for Christmas. My mother makes sure to say it, whenever she is seen with us, 'She is with the father, of course.' They don't know what I have gone and done now.

In the evening I text to ask if you have calmed down, if you have some colour back. He doesn't answer so I wait an hour and phone and he doesn't answer so I call his sister's house, where he is staying, but it is a wrong number, so I call her mobile and call and call and text and call and no one answers.

That night I have to pump your milk with a squawking machine, and I think I feel blank but maybe not because I make a sound too like squawking; a terrible sound like braying and squawking at once; nothing as pretty as a weep.

To steady myself I look through the book I bought with thick, matt pages that I will read to you when you are back with me. It is an edition of 'The Night before Christmas' – the kind of book with illustrations that tell lots of stories, not just the one in the poem. Hidden tiny on one page is a family of mice hanging mini stockings by their arch in the skirting board. On another, a reindeer munches illicitly on a mince pie meant for Santa. They are the kind of scenes a child might look at over and over, discovering new details every time. Every year, I think, you will find new things. Every year. Because I still think that maybe I can read this book for you every Christmastime, even if it is a few days before or after; that such things have wiggle-room.

They do not answer, they do not call, and then on Stephen's Day your daddy sends a message:

> He wants you to leave us alone. Your harassment is making me angry. I cannot be a good father when I am angry. What are you trying to make me do?

I read the Christmas book and look for all the secret tales. Every six hours I pump a bottle of milk and put it in the freezer. Then I drink a glass of water, to keep hydrated.

The next day he brings you back. You are wax-faced, blue-lipped, and your eyes are so big. You do not cry, but your big eyes grow bigger and you open your palms to me and before I can stop it my voice has betrayed us. 'My baby,' I say. 'Oh my baby.'

He swings you out of reach. You do not cry, even weakly. You say mah mah mah very quietly and you put out your arms as he holds you away. 'He doesn't want you,' he says, 'you know that, don't you? Just your tits,' and oh, your eyes – oh no your eyes, big, round, pink-rimmed – sorry oh sorry it was me who said yes, it was me who bargained you away, and so I say, 'Sorry, yes I know. Sorry sorry sorry please let me feed him now please I am sorry,' and he lets me take you. His lip curls as I take out my breast and he says in a babying voice he thinks is mine, 'Your mummy is a bitch, isn't she? Yes. You don't know that yet, do you?' Then he moves his eyes up my neck to my face, and with a flat voice he says, 'Someday he will hear about this and he will know what you are.' This sets a bitter thing coursing through my veins. How is it you don't taste it?

While he is there you stay limpet-locked into me, feeding, but when he is gone your hands dangle, and then your head.

You splutter and vomit something lumpy and lurid blue, and your eyes roll blind and your neck won't hold—

The ambulance men make me go back in to put on my shoes. They make me give you to them and put on my shoes and coat and I say, 'But look but look but look at his lips please look at him—' and one of them puts his hand on my elbow and walks me back to the lift. 'It will only take a minute,' he says, 'to put on your shoes. Come on now and get a coat. We have him. We will get him in the ambulance and you get your shoes now, love.'

On the way to the hospital I phone him to ask what you have eaten. He threw out the bottles of breast milk, he said. He could not touch it because of what I am. A stinking bitch is what I am with stinky little paps – a tit-Nazi, he says. 'My mates call you the tit-Nazi.' I didn't want him to let off steam this Christmas with the lads, he says, he can see it now – I didn't want him meeting girls and so I let him have you so that his big sister would make him stay in and listen to you cry. I ask again what you have eaten and he says you had formula and baby biscuits, like his sister's baby. It doesn't do his sister's baby any harm. He is hanging up now, he says. He is having a pint and I am to stop looking for attention.

'He had formula and baby biscuits,' I tell the ambulance man, and he writes it down. 'What brand of formula? Do you have the box?' I shake my head. 'When was the last dirty nappy?' I can't speak; just a terrible breath rushing in too deep and fast, wringing my voice to a gasp. He offers me a sedative and I shake my head.

You are curling soundlessly into your pain, and it takes two of us to hold you out straight so they can do the scan. A nurse holds your feet and I press your shoulders flat, your eyes grow wide in focus and roll back, and you don't make a whimper. I whisper all kinds of things about Holy God. I ask them to give you something for the pain and they say they can't, not yet. I chant good boy good boy, with my face at your cheek. The radiographer rings someone and says a word I haven't heard before but will always know now – intussusception – and a doctor arrives very quickly, and then they say the word again and they tell me it is urgent. A nurse explains it to me slowly, like I am foreign or very stupid, and I am grateful for that because words are starting to slide for me and I am struggling to understand. She says your guts have folded into themselves and they are just getting the operating room ready and they will do their best but I should stay here and let her take you. There isn't time to put you under for it and it is not a nice procedure but it is usually a success. I will not want to see, she says, and my distress will make it worse for you. I can wait here in the corridor. Now your father is here and I don't know how he found us. His back is straight and his eyes brilliant with rage and he wants to go and watch them through the glass while they do it and they say okay but the nurse says, 'Please wait here, Mum. No good can come from watching.' I sit on the floor beside an arch containing a statue of the Virgin. She is cream-coloured and her robes are freshly painted blue. The nurse brings me a plastic cup of very cold water before she is paged away. Oh Virgin Mother, I will do anything. I will do anything. I will do anything—

When it is over, they say you have to stay in hospital. You are in a cot with high bars and cannot eat but only take glucose from a drip at first, and then blackberry-flavoured glucose-water from squat glass bottles with disposable teats. They have inflated your guts to straighten them out and it was very painful for you but it is over now. 'It's over now, my pixie,' I say, 'we're alright now. It's over.' I wonder can I blame him, but the nurse says no, there is no known cause for the thing that happened. It sometimes occurs, especially in boys under two, and no one knows why. They will keep you in for three days in case it happens again.

There is a chair beside the cot and the nurse says I can stay with you. She will get a blanket and she might be able to get me a mattress for tomorrow night. Your father says, 'Why should she be the one to stay? I want to stay.'

And the nurse says, 'Go home. He needs his mother. Go home please, sir. Have some sense.'

He says, 'There is no law that says she gets to stay . . . This is sexism. I am calling a lawyer.'

And she says, 'Have some sense and some respect.' She is a lovely hulk of starched pink, taupe French plait, great red-scrubbed hands clasped before her. She stands beside me until he leaves and then she moves us to another ward.

We stay for three days. There are lights on all the time, fizzing in strips along the corridor, boxes holding quiet little creatures with tubes in their noses and lumps of hard plastic bandaged to their hands, their machines yipping. I cannot tease out the promises I made while they were hurting you, delivering you back to me from the pain and the blue lips. All I can say is thank you to the nurses. Every time I see one, 'Thank you, thank you.' The nurses scurry back and forth, swishing curtains, speaking to babies in a tired, panicked hush. The other babies slide in and out of my periphery; a bony one in a sling, its face crooked, smeared as though someone has tried to erase it. The nurse coos and kisses its head. 'Contact is good for him,' she says, 'they heal quicker with contact,' and I tell her thank you thank you, because the other babies are all possibilities of you.

You want to feed but I peel your fingers off my buttons. 'No, no. Be a big boy now. Have some water.'

There is a playroom with coloured beads on lines of meandering wire, and plastic trucks, and thin Ladybird

Classics with careful watercolour pictures, their card covers held on wonkily by loose hoops of thread. The one you want is *Rumpelstiltskin*; a story of a little man who gets a maiden released from a dungeon cell by spinning gold from straw. 'Not that story,' I say.

You nod. 'Jes, Mama. Jes.' The price for the gold is to be the maiden's first child. It is a promise she soon forgets, beaming at the newborn in her arms. The mother's mouth opens in horror when the little man comes through the bedroom window to claim the child. You like the picture of the baby. 'Bebe,' you say, 'bebe.'

It all comes right in the end, because the mother ventures into the wood on a dark night and learns the name of the little man. Her face can be seen peeking through the branches, and on her smile the yellow glow of the little man's fire. There he is in the clearing, a terrifying creature no bigger than a toddler. He prances around the fire, back bent, crooked fingers, leering mouth. 'Rumpelstiltskin is my name.' Once she speaks his name she is free from her promise. She gets her baby back, and it looks just the same as it did on page three.

Even so, I do not like reading you that book. I hide it on a high windowsill in the playroom, so that you do not keep pushing it at my hands, opening the cover. ''Gain Mama, 'gain.'

For three days I cannot sleep but only look at you and listen for your breath when you doze, and when you wake from the sugar and the beeping and the insectile buzz of the lights, I give you each of my forefingers to hold in your fists and I walk you up and down the corridors and lift you to look at the big fish tank. I say, 'Look! Fish. Pretty.'

And you say, 'yook. Ish. IpwEee.' My breasts swell hot and sore at first, but I will not poison you again with all my braying rage. By the third day, your milk is gone.

'Just be decent,' is what they said at the legal aid office.

I looked through the rails in Oxfam but there was nothing suitable there. I looked in the discount rail in Penney's too, but the blazers were all too big and in any case I don't know if a blazer is what they meant.

Your daddy has borrowed a suit, I think, because it is too broad on the shoulders and too long on the arms and he keeps shrugging himself and shifting, as though by doing so he might make himself big enough to fit it. He clears his throat a lot, bobbing the mealy bulge of his Adam's apple, and he won't stop looking at me while we stand in the lobby. There are plastic orange chairs fixed in rows along the walls, but I can't bring myself to sit. If I turn my back he will see my bum and the back of my knees, so I stand with my profile to him – the most anonymous angle I can find. I can feel his eyes on my cheek. He cannot do anything with his looking, he cannot change anything with looking. I try to remember that but still I cannot turn my back. His friend is with him – the one who thought he said something so beautiful. She is trying not to look at me. His sister is there too, and his father. They both nod frantically at me with straight lips, and mutter something. All of them are dressed up for a day out, dressed decently, but I hadn't the sense or the wherewithal to borrow something.

The legal aid person told me she would meet me at nine thirty in the lobby. She turns up ten minutes late but it feels like a long time because of your daddy looking and looking and clearing his throat. She is a pear-shaped woman in a tight woollen trouser suit. She has a small, avian head and very fine, close-cut hair dyed canary yellow. She looks at my knees, and winces, and I know that I am all wrong. I am wearing a pale blue dress pilled from too much washing and a little stretched around the neckline from a year of your tugging. It is too short and shows my too-skinny arms, but I thought the blue dress was better than the red one.

'Hi,' she says, and shakes my hand briskly. She has a gravelly, smoker's voice. 'Okay,' she says. 'How are you? Are you alright? You'll be fine, just stay calm.' She ushers me into a stairwell, and sits on a step. 'Sit down,' she says. 'Now, it's not brilliant news because Friel is on today – he's known as The Bull. He drinks and he's not a big fan of young mothers, but he's usually fair. Gruff, but he doesn't make outrageous orders. Just don't be crying or speaking out of turn. He doesn't like hysterics. Make sure to show respect – that's the main thing. Brush your hair before we go in. Brush it now while I'm speaking to you and put it up – here, I have a bobbin – my daughter's. Right, so the father is taking you for custody and access, is it? Don't mind the custody, we'll contest that. We should put in for maintenance. I see you haven't done that. Did no one tell you to do that? Not to worry. You just relax now. But you're giving him guardianship I assume? There's no point refusing, he'll get it anyway. If his name is on the birth cert he'll get it. This child has the father's name – yes?'

She opens a briefcase on her lap and there is nothing in it but the court summons, and an A4 pad, and a biro. She puts the case on the floor, pulls a foot onto her thigh, and rests the pad on her bent leg – 'Okay, so tell me quickly – what's the story?'

I begin with Christmas, and she says, 'No, go back. Go back.' I go back to your birth and she says, 'No, go back to the beginning. Where did you meet the father?' I go back to Freshers' week. I didn't like him, to be honest, but he was persistent. I had forgotten that. I am telling her about missing one of my exams – waiting for him outside the door of the exam hall with you pulling at my earrings, waiting and waiting because he said he would look after you while I sat the exam, but his phone was off, and he did not show. I am telling her the way he sneered when he came in that night, when a voice comes over the intercom. I can't understand what it is saying. My solicitor holds up a finger to silence me – 'Hang on,' she says, 'wait there. It's the callover. I'll be back. Wait there.'

I am alone in the stairwell and I am afraid he will come in so I stay standing with my back against the wall. After a few minutes my solicitor comes back all a-fluster, tilting forward on the axis of her hips and tucking the briefcase under her arm. 'Quick quick,' she says, 'we're up.'

Your daddy is representing himself. This means he can interrogate me on the stand: he will put questions to me and I will have to answer him. Even though he put in the order, he asks to go first, and my solicitor concedes. Because he is representing himself, the judge must hear him out.

Until I threw him out, he says, he was your primary carer. I was in college. I was enrolled full time, and the college records to prove it. He says I gave you to him until he started seeing someone else and now I won't let him take you. Before he began to see someone, I didn't even want to have you for Christmas, he says, I made him take you for Christmas. He has a letter here to prove it, with twenty signatures at the end – people who saw him at Christmas, with his son.

'She looks all innocent,' says your daddy, 'but your honour I can assure you the girl before you is—' Judge Friel waves his hands to stop the pelt of rehearsed words. He assures your daddy that he is well aware that this country is crawling with black widows. Well aware, he says – it's because of the constitution. He tells your daddy to save his breath, he is no eejit, he says, and he wasn't born yesterday. He has seen enough in these rooms to know that they come in all shapes and sizes. He shouts then, tells me to stop making faces for him to see out of the corner of his eye and stop the crying; that it won't do me any good.

Your daddy has a box of letters with him – letters I wrote to him apologising for being difficult, saying that I love him. 'She admits to being irrational,' he says, 'on three occasions.' 'In one,' he says, 'in one of the letters she even admits to being depressed.' He says I am unwell. He hopes I can get the help I need, he says, holding a shoe box towards the judge.

'I'm not looking at these,' says the judge. But he has heard.

'And she wanted an abortion,' your daddy says, 'she didn't want him. She wanted to kill him.'

When it is my turn on the stand your daddy says, 'I put it to you that you are irrational,' and 'I put it to you that our son wants us to be together.'

I open my mouth to speak but I have a terrible voice, stuttering and strangled and unsure because I am afraid I might shriek. My solicitor makes eyes that I can't read. The judge tells her to please deal with her client.

'She is very nervous, your honour.'

'I can see that. If she is old enough to be a mother then she is old enough to speak up. She will have to speak up if she expects me to listen to her. I am losing patience, I'll tell you that now, counsel. As I'm sure you can appreciate, I have a lot of cases to get through before lunch.'

I once felt like a warm and powerful thing, because I am your mother, but now I know I am weak, my account all patchy and nuanced, my story a box of handwritten concessions and unspoken protests, and things I can't recognize; things misshapen, discoloured, forgotten. I am not sure enough to find the words. I have not made lists of dates and I have no signatures.

That night I get a text message:

Are you happy now that you have cut our son in two?
Someday he will know it is you who did this.

An hour later he sends another:

Someday he will see what you are.

Easter Sunday the springlight wakes you, and you smile and watch your hands above your face, catching hot geometries of sun as it slices through the gaps that frame and cleave our bedroom curtain.

I suppose to you our flat is a whole world, but to me it is a box. Sometimes it is such a small box and I need to get out. I can't wait, so I change your nappy quickly, and dress you, and for breakfast I give you a flapjack in the buggy, instead of porridge. 'Special treat my Pixie-Poddle,' I say, 'today is Easter.' I put on a dress I haven't worn since before you – pale yellow for spring. It brushes softly against my hips. I am pretty again.

'Pwatty,' you say. I don't feel guilty about the flapjacks. I have put dried apricots in them, for the iron, and desiccated coconut instead of sugar. And in any case, I have to leave.

Once you are finished eating you writhe out of your buggy and we walk very slowly in the shadowy streets between tall buildings and out to the broad roads, the dormant water fountain, the light and sky of College Green. Grafton Street is almost empty; just some morning-after couples and the melancholy twang of a busker wrapping himself in his own low, clear sounds; stopping and starting; closing his eyes to locate the note where it is staggering somewhere in his voice, his fingers lax and effortlessly strumming, strumming regardless while you stand and watch him; your feet turned outwards and your belly pushing full sail before you. You tilt your head, your hands perched at your chest.

I am bewildered by the busker; I can't understand how he can go on strumming, how he does not stop to marvel at you as you stand like that – how he is not struck by the miraculous detail with which you are made – the shocking blue of your eyes, your dimples – one in each cheek and one by your chin – and the funny way you clasp one finger now with all of your other hand – how he pretends not to notice it at all; refuses to be flattered by your rapture. I call, 'Poddle on now, Baby, come on,' and you start towards me and then stop. You turn and wave bye-bye to the busker by showing him your palm and opening and closing your fist.

Then you waddle up and demand to be carried, 'Cawy Mama, cawy.'

It is slow, carrying you with one hand, and steering the buggy with the other, but there are no crowds to obstruct us as we make our way to the park.

For the ducks we have brought a batch of flapjacks that didn't work out – too tough and dry for you – and you squeal and grin and stomp, press your sticky splayed fingers hard together, giddy with delight to see the mother duck dip and dive for the crumby lumps, her mustard-coloured babies twirling abstractedly about her, sniping occasionally at the water's surface. We stay for a long time, even after the ducks have lost interest and I allow you to squat unnervingly close to the water and murk it with hard, dry oatflakes.

Afterwards we do a circuit of the park. You strap your car into the buggy, tucking him in cluckily. You push him slowly, the buggy tilted on its hind wheels, his two front tyres peering over the blanket, his headlights facing the sky. You put a finger up to your lips because your car has fallen asleep.

I let you throw ten one-cent coins into the fountain, and coax you back into your buggy with a carton of grape juice and your car, who wants a cuddle.

As we leave the park a man in a very crisp suit jacket, very tight, clean pants, spits at us. It lands on the back of my neck and when I turn to look at him, I see tight lips shrinking up off his teeth like they are melting from the sight of us. 'Is that your kid?' the man says, and for a moment I am going to answer. 'Little slut, what age are you? A bastard isn't it?' he says. 'It's the likes of you that's the problem. Fucking scrounger whores!' As I walk away he shouts after us, 'Dressed like a slut it's no wonder you get knocked up at fifteen! Laundries were the right idea! At least you'd be of some use there!'

It doesn't matter. I have wet-wipes under the buggy and I use one to clean his phlegm from my neck.

You fall asleep on the way home and are still asleep when we take the slow, smelly lift up to our flat. Hidden around our flat – on our bookshelf, in your box of blocks, under the mugs and behind the spider plant – are twenty tiny chocolate eggs wrapped in brightly coloured foil. When you wake we will hunt for them together. We can have ten each.

I unlock the door, push it with my back, heaving the buggy in after me. While you sleep I try to read but can't sit still. I walk around the small space with bleach-spray and a cloth and check on all the glinting little eggs. I cannot look at you. I cannot bear the lovely rhythm of your sleep, the smooth and shallow lift and sigh and the bigger, rutted inhalation then, followed by the long, easy current of your breath: your wet, slack lips; your eyelashes casting dark wings on the curves of your cheeks. I can't look because I know it is still here – the debt – lurking in the too-clean light and the dustless corners, waiting.

Every weekend I file documents in a warehouse. I file them alphabetically. I earn just the right amount – low enough to keep the single mother's allowance; high enough to buy you the leather first shoes instead of the polyester ones. The warehouse is high-ceilinged and unheated and there are two other temps there, boys my age, filing in different parts of the building. The stuff on the floor is like brushed card and worn felt and it burns if I move around on my knees between the boxes. One of the boys fancies me, I think, even though I have you and I have said so. But I suppose he cannot understand what that means; how silly things like sex are now, how beside-the-point, and cinema dates, and banter, and how it is a relief not to feel hands on my throat at night and tendrils winding around my tongue.

We file all day and with each hour that passes, I calculate what I have earned and what I will use it for: the gas bill; that jigsaw; free-range eggs. The boy gazes at me a lot over his filing cabinet. He is bored, but also he has notions. He has rust-coloured hair and sweet, rust-coloured eyes and when he looks I am aware of the way my face moves as I file; I am afraid that my thoughts move over my face, and I wish he would not look. From his eyes I think he sees a girl who is fragile, closed and fidgety, but that's not how I feel at all. I feel dangerous, tentacled, with blurring edges.

I carry the book in my rucksack. I know I have to burn or drown it but that is hard. Even if the story is all askew, there are bits of you in there all the same, and bits of me.

His access ends at six o'clock every Sunday evening. I wait outside his door and at exactly six he opens it and pushes you through in a buggy with huge tyres like an SUV. He watches me unstrap you and lift you into the hammockish buggy I have brought. Then he hands me an envelope with this week's maintenance. On the back he has written:

> €30.00 as decreed by the powers that be. To be spent on my
> son not on nail polish or coffee with friends.

You are always blank-faced at the handover; eyes staring steadily at your knees. I kiss you as I strap you in. I won't expect you to speak until the morning. The mediator said it's normal – some children even get pains in their tummies and cramps in their legs and so on but it's all psychosomatic, she said; parents should not be manipulated by such performances. 'Kids are very adaptable, they grow out of it.' She wagged a finger at me. 'I only wish the mothers would do the same.'

You are wearing the clothes I dressed you in on Friday morning – everything down to your socks. Last week he sent me a text message explaining why this is. It is because the first thing he does when I hand you over is strip you down and put 'Daddy clothes' on you instead; the last thing he does is put the 'Stinky mummy clothes' back on you. He says they smell like council flat.

We take the bus home. Your buggy folds against my knee like an umbrella, and you sit quietly beside me, holding one finger with the fist of your other hand. I look out the window, knitting. I am trying to give you space, like the mediator said. It's a hat for you for the winter. I can knit without looking because this bit is all the same – just round and round and round for four inches.

You pull yourself up, standing on the seat with one arm hugging the headrest, wobbling with the bus. You put the other hand on my chin and pull my face around to look at you.

'Smile to me Mama,' you say. 'I am your little boy, smile to me.'

You use both hands now to mould my face into a smile, pushing up the corners of my mouth. 'Like that,' you say. 'Keep like that.'

My college tutor calls me in to discuss the exam results. You are asleep in the buggy and I park you in the hall and leave his office door ajar in case you wake or someone tries to steal you.

He has a long, tea-coloured face with such kind lines on it that I feel ashamed for failing him after all he did for me during the morning sickness months. He even gave me ginger nuts from his wife.

Yes, he says, they are disappointing results – maybe it was too soon to come back? I explain about missing two papers. I could repeat but I don't think the grant will cover it; I would have to pay and I don't know if it is possible. He has spoken to his wife about me, he says; his wife thinks the college has failed me.

'Oh no,' I say. I mean it, and oh, it is good to hear my own voice again, honest and reassuring. 'The college has been very nice; very patient. I don't know what else they could have done. You have been so supportive, really.'

'Well look, let's appeal,' he says. 'Go to the college counsellor, say you were depressed or overwhelmed – whatever – you might have to exaggerate. Get me a psych report and I'll make them waive repeat fees. Sorry, I think it's the only way. Then take a year to figure things out; do try to come back. My wife is very adamant.'

Your second Halloween falls on a Wednesday and your daddy wants you for the day. I say okay, the day but not the night. I arrive to collect you at 5 p.m. and it is already dark outside. He opens the door, wiping his hands on a tea towel. He steps back. 'You will have to come in if you want him.'

There is music playing; a man with a guitar and a lovesick voice. There is a big bowl of marshmallow skulls on the coffee table, and another of bright jellies shaped like witch's hats. A sheet of beads closes his kitchen from his living room, but they are tangled into a clump, so I can see through to the worktop where there is a single beer bottle with a wedge of lime stuffed into the neck, and a pumpkin with spilled guts.

'I'm just carving the pumpkin,' he says. 'Would you like a drink?'

I shake my head and scan for you. Your daddy nods at one of two closed doors. 'You will have to go and get him, if you want him.'

You are at the other side of the door. It must be your daddy's bedroom, because the other room has a plaque on it saying 'Bathroom'. There are other children in there with you. I can hear their voices, 'Pow pow . . . Hoiyyyy–ya!' but I can't pick yours out.

The bedroom is warm. It smells of his sex, and of sleep and cologne and damp. The headboard is all curling black bars, and there is a leather belt fastened casually to it. The belt makes my throat taste of acid.

You are standing on the bed dressed in a Spider-Man costume. The costume has padding for muscles – a strap-on six-pack running up your torso, and big foam biceps. You are holding a balloon sword, standing with your feet splayed. There is a big lozenge of black painted across each eye and your cheeks are red with a fading mesh of webs over them.

Your cousins are there. One of them is hurling himself into a wall, falling, getting up and hurling himself at the wall again; 'Hoiy-ya!' he says, 'Hoiy-ya!'

The smaller one is running in a circle saying, 'Nee-naw, nee-naw, nee-naw.'

You look at me, and then you turn your back, revealing a flimsy polyester sag, the heartbreaking flatness of your tiny bottom.

I say, 'Hello my Pixie,' and I cannot stop the smile, for any moment now I will hold you. Your cousins continue to run and crash and maybe you don't hear me.

Your daddy is standing too close behind me. At my neck I can feel the cold beer on his breath.

'He wants to stay with me for Halloween,' he says. 'He told me. Why don't you come back for him tomorrow?' He has a second beer in his hand. 'Have a drink with me,' he says, 'before you go.'

I take the beer, but I don't drink.

'Do you want lime?'

I shake my head and I open my mouth again to say your name but no sound comes – my mouth tastes of soil, as though my tongue is stuffed back with clay and sand and even breathing is impossible.

'He had his dinner.'

I close my mouth and nod. I am not sure what expression my face makes but it causes him to roll his eyes.

'Yes,' he says, 'a *proper* dinner... he had peas and carrots and potato.' Then, as if he has just remembered, 'Oh, by the way, you can expect a summons in the post. I'm appealing the order. I'm going for custody. I'm not sure you're fit, to be honest. You can't really look after him, can you? Temping part-time and living in that shithole? I'm asking for a psychiatrist's report on you. I'll be subpoenaing the college counsellors. It's time I stood up for myself. I won't be paying you any more either, for the privilege of seeing my son. I have a new solicitor. She thinks it'll be easy enough to sort out.'

You are standing on the bed now, looking at me with all that facepaint blackening your eye sockets. Your daddy nods at the cousins, 'How're you girls?' and the bigger one lunges at him like a little rhino, his shoulder bouldering forward.

'I'm not a girl I'm not a girl I'm not a girl . . .'

Your daddy laughs, bending to protect his groin from the child's fists. 'Alright pal, okay.'

'*You're* a girl.' The boy pummels his knees. 'You're a girl!'

You look at me, the sword hanging down at your side. I try to smile and I take a breath. I am going to say, 'You want to stay with Daddy, Poddle?' I am going to say it gently; no pressure. But your face is so dirty with that paint, your eyes so pale in the alien crescents that I don't know what shape my face makes, and my voice – there is too much bubbling for too long in my chest, too much that is ugly and hateful, blood simmered to a thick and pungent metal, and when it comes my voice is a scratching sound, about to break into a fury shriek and so I swallow some beer and you keep looking at me.

Beside me, your daddy is looking too and smiling.

'He's two and a half,' he says.

I nod.

'It's time you let go.' His smile is tight and curling. He makes a little laugh sound – 'Huh. Weird, isn't it? Not even three years ago, I watched you give birth.'

I shrug and sip the beer. I think he has rehearsed this. I think that because of the stiff, unnatural little smile, the Hollywood twang in his voice, and the pretend laugh, like a cough – *huh*.

'Do you know you shat yourself?'

I shake my head. 'I think I would remember, if that had happened.'

His mouth lifts now into a big gleeful grin. 'Nah,' he says, 'Women forget. Once it's all over, they forget. It's proven. Science.'

Then there is a hissing sound; something cold and light on my face. I look up and it's you, stern-faced stretching your little hand towards me in the Spider-Man hex – the two middle fingers folded down, pinkie and forefinger pointing. Fastened to your arm in a web-patterned wrist strap is a silver can. Streams of white silly-string come shooting from the can, but they slow as they approach, landing silently on my hair and tumbling into little squiggles on the carpet.

'Mammy has boobies,' you say. 'Mammy has boobies.'

Your daddy laughs. 'Ahhhhhh!' he says. 'Web fluid! No Spider-man, noooo!'

To me he says, 'Lighten up, sourpuss. Is it a wonder he wants to stay with me?'

The arms are spinning you around and around. They are awkward, stiff, ungraceful arms, spindly and blank and efficient instruments. I cannot stop them but now I need to because – how did I never see it before? They are not wrapping you, but winding you back, peeling off the days and hours and moments that you are made from, undoing you down to where you started, and I know then. I remember then, the hinge of your conception, the pragmatic surrender-route that made you, the dull and shameful choice to hurry a thing to its conclusion, rather than resist the knuckle and thrust and neck-clamp of him. I still know it though I have tried to slide out of it, avoid the reckoning, spin a yarn and knit a tale.

Now my arms are still but nothing can stop the spindle, nothing but waking, and there is no name that will chase away the debt. It's you, my darling. I see it now; the bargained chip, the straw of gold, the thing set going, the milk once spilled.

★

Now you are almost three and you have his words in your mouth and his name sewn into the collar of your coat. It is a one-way street; I never thought otherwise. Friday is when his weekend access starts. We meet in the park. I hold your hand as we cross the road, but when we get inside the park gates I let you run on alone.

Your daddy gets down on a knee and opens his arms, the way of returning fathers in family movies. You play your part – great baby grin between the dimpling cheeks – perhaps you have watched these movies together.

You stop and turn to wave, opening and closing your palm at me, before tottering on into his arms. You have a little knapsack on your back. Usually it contains only your favourite car, maybe some medicine, if you are ill, and your animal-shaped vitamins. This time I have put your vaccination book in too, and your passport.

Your life is a journey out of me.

I am sorry, please believe me my darling, I am sorry that I have added no explanation for you to read. I could not make the marks on the page for you. I could not set the letters out. I tried. All night I tried but I could not manage even to put your name down. There is nothing I can say, no language I can speak but screech and claw.

He has you now. A concept sprung cleanly from his voice; a man-born son. I have left no mark on you but a neat scar hidden in the dimple of your navel.

Up on deck there are dogs growing restless in their cages; barking and whimpering and howling in the sharp sea spray. A sign says to sit upright and look at the horizon, but by now it is too dark to see that fine discrepancy between water and sky, and up here the smell of diesel and the hound-cries make it worse. I prefer, anyway, to hunker down into the dark and sickly swell, down there in the belly-heave beneath the sea-line.

Through the heavy doors and into a toilet cubicle I lurch to kneel and vomit over and over. The toilets are clean, bleach-white, filled with a saccharine peach-scent smog that clings to the tongue with the burn and the bitter hurl from the dirty inside. I rest here, face to the porcelain seat; bleach and peach and pale vomit and bright bile.

I was never sick like this until you began, and so I almost like it – the endless stir and wrench, the acid weakness and, with every wave of nausea, some awe at the force of it, the crippling pull and retch. It is a keepsake from my time of making you.

I know I have slept because as I wake I am fantasizing about rocking home to death, drowning in a plunge of sea. It is only the cold that frightens me; the way it would trickle under the clothes and then spread through the tissue to the hot and blood-dark places as my heart slowed to a stop. Apart from the cold I think I might like it; the slosh and crash of water, the great to and fro, the pulse of the ocean fighting this ship like a parasite. I wonder what it was like for you; what you heard and what you knew as you stemmed out to flesh in the liquid crannies of me and if it sounded something as comforting and frightening and as mighty as this.

Now I will add the last of that story here. When I can stand and walk, I will bring this to the deck and toss it away into the sea; the bell that heralded your first change, your bracelet from the hospital, your sand-dull curl tied with a ribbon, and all my threadbare yarns.

In the ferry giftshop I bought another book for you. It is blank with a hard cover, powder blue to match your sex and lines for keeping my letters straight.

I will begin at the beginning and I will be clear this time. I will put your story in; dates and weights, perhaps, and your first word. Your first word. What was it? Will I put the *ma ma ma* of hunger? Was that a word? Or *look*? Or *mine*?

A Wife

After 'A Mother' (Dubliners), by James Joyce

GER, CHAIRPERSON OF the Gaelscoil na Cnoic Naofa Parents' Committee, had been bustling about the clós and corridors for almost a month now, her head swivelling about doorways and her expansive round haunches stuck out behind her like an ostrich's plumage. She held a clipboard and made vague enquiries and vague requests, pulling the laminated photograph out of her bum-bag and telling anyone who would listen about the Brides Again evening.

But at the end of the day, it was Kathleen who arranged things.

'If you're going to do it,' Kathleen's mother used to say, 'do it right,' and, to elaborate, 'If you want something done right, do it yourself.' These, Kathleen thought, were the best pieces of advice her mother had ever given. She tried to teach her daughters the same thing, to drill it into them, so that they would come to expect it of themselves, so that they would be ashamed to be late or to only half do their homework.

When she was twenty-nine, Kathleen had married urgently out of practical good sense. She had spent her secondary school years at a convent boarding school. (She would have sent her own girls there too, only it was closing down next year.) Despite being a prefect, sporty, slim in her youth, despite having the resources and the taste to dress well and behave properly, and despite going to the races with the more popular crowd at school, Kathleen had never made any lasting friends there, and when the Leaving Cert was over and all the girls dispersed, she found herself alone. Some of the girls went to UCD, but Kathleen had taken an events management course at a private college. She was a good-looking girl back then, with champagne-blonde streaks through her copper hair and a high ponytail. She worked out twice a week at the gym and went for a swim every other day. The worst her enemies might say of her was that she could look a little insipid, if she didn't highlight her hair regularly and colour her face in with make-up. But the few boys enrolled on the course were scrawny and unambitious, and she graduated at the age of twenty-two with only a handful of disappointing cinema dates behind her.

Still, she did not lose heart. Even if she could be pale sometimes, and her lips not very full, she was quite presentable. She knew how to dress and how to walk, she was never caught without well-manicured nails – things like that mattered in her line of work. Straight after college she found herself a good position at Party Pro, managing the corporate gigs. She was good at the job, and was given ever greater responsibilities. She liked the big events. She enjoyed wearing the name card around her neck, using the walkie-talkies, and co-ordinating people. She enjoyed her own fierce efficiency, and liked to say 'imperative'. 'It is imperative that everyone be in their places for seven...' she would say, and 'It is imperative that we have a team we can rely on!' She began to make an effort with the men she met at work, but none of them was very impressive. Many tried to start something with her, but never with the sort of passion or adoration she had hoped for from a lover.

She began to worry that there was not, as she had been led to believe, someone for everyone. She soothed her bouts of panic by walking for a long time on the treadmill in the gym, her ponytail swishing reassuringly to the beat, and sometimes by eating large amounts of Turkish Delight in bed while watching TV. The intense romance she had once imagined looked less and less likely, as the fat began to gather at her hips and under her chin.

But, as her mother would say, Kathleen always had great get-up-and-go. When she heard that three of the girls from school were getting married that year – and had not invited her – Kathleen took great joy in surprising them all by sending out generous wedding invitations. She would marry Graham, an accountant at her father's firm.

He was much older than her. Until recently, her mother had explained, he had been dedicated to a woman who suddenly married someone else. He had no children. She had hoped to marry a solicitor – that had been her mother's secret ambition for her – but she knew she had to be practical, and, according to the nice suit he was wearing, and her father's familiar attitude with him, he was good at what he did. She liked his clean, oval nails and the gentle way he passed the salad bowl that first evening when he came to her parents' house for dinner. By the time the leg of lamb came out she had made up her mind. She smiled at him softly over the pavlova roulade, and said that she never drank anyway, so she could drive him home. A year later he took her to dinner one Friday evening and asked the waiter for his best champagne, before proposing calmly.

After eighteen months of planning, the wedding day went off without a hitch.

She had never quite given up her romantic notions, though. Sometimes, if she was very early collecting the girls from school, she would read novels about true and forbidden love in the car before going to wait in the clós. They were about affairs between rich ladies and workmen, or romances set in Victorian times. Sometimes she read racier ones too. And sometimes, but not often, when the girls were at school and the au pair was out, she climbed into bed with a small wooden box of real Turkish Delight – translucent, sugar-dusted little cubes of emerald green and red, which she popped into her mouth whole – and watched a DVD with Colin Firth in it. But she made sure to be a good wife. She always had his coffee on when he woke, she prepared a wonderful meal every evening, and she continued to have her hair done and look after her skin. She understood that the little things mattered. When Graham had a work do, Kathleen was always the most attractive and well-dressed wife in the room, and she knew Graham appreciated it by the way he introduced her as 'my lovely wife – yes, I know, she's a little out of my league!' She could engage in conversation with his female colleagues too. 'I was a career woman myself,' she would laugh, '. . . in a previous life!'

Kathleen once found a brown envelope on a shelf in Graham's office, in amongst his books. It contained cards and letters and odd little keepsakes; a paper hat from a Christmas cracker, train tickets, a piece of ribbon. There were photos in there too, of the woman he had loved, whom he never spoke about. It comforted her to see that even back then the woman was far looser around the middle than Kathleen was now, and it looked as though she had bad skin. Nonetheless, there was one photo where Graham was smiling at the woman in a way Kathleen had never seen him smile.

She had made the right decision, though, marrying Graham. Her first impression had been spot on – he was a decent man through and through. It took them seven years to conceive. They had all the tests but still the doctor couldn't tell them why it didn't happen. Kathleen kept it to herself. She knew people would suspect – she suspected it herself – that it was her coldness that was to blame. She hadn't the warmth, perhaps, the passion to make anything grow in her. Graham kept it all very quiet just as she asked. She knew that some men shied away from all the investigations, but not Graham. He attended all the tests and meetings and funded every treatment without question. He was a good husband and a good father. And he had his head screwed on. He researched the property market and didn't take big risks – they hadn't been hit as badly as some by the recession – and he looked after his daughters, saved for them, planned ahead. When Cliona was born, it was he who had suggested the au pair to help Kathleen with the housework, and she had to admit she enjoyed how the other women envied her when she mentioned their holidays in Portugal and the South of France. Not package holidays either. 'My Graham,' she would say, worrying sometimes, even as she spoke, that the girls would find the familiarity of her tone incongruous with the grim-faced man they had met, who, even after twelve years, still nodded at Kathleen politely, and looked through her like a stranger when she told him things about her day, 'my Graham insists on doing it right. A villa in the South of France, he says, or nothing at all. And I have to confess... it is just *gorgeous!*'

Kathleen had said to Graham before, though, that they would encounter problems if they sent the girls to a non-fee-paying school, but he wouldn't listen. He was all about saving their trusts for college and sending them to the coláistí. The Irish second levels got the best leaving results, he said, and there was no point even putting the girls' names down, unless they sent them to one of the feeder Gaelscoils. No point at all.

And for a while, it had seemed as though they'd made the right choice. Kathleen had put her best foot forward – *if you're going to do it, do it right...* She had organized parents' mornings. She had helped out at the fundraisers. She was on the parent-and-teachers' board. Her eldest, Roisín, won the school Irish dancing competition two years running, and pretty little Cliona was invited to all the boys' birthday parties. It was Kathleen who always organized the gift for the teacher at Christmas and the end of the year, tactfully requesting only five euros per person – the rest she would chip in herself, and, of course, the teachers knew it. But there it was again – the same old problem. For even though the school professed to be Catholic (and they didn't all profess such a thing nowadays) and was situated in a good part of Dublin, there were children from broken homes in Cliona's class, there were families on social welfare, and even a little boy with long hair who belonged to a single mother. People like that couldn't be asked to chip in more than five euros. So it was Kathleen who took the hit.

The single mother bothered Kathleen somewhat. It was her brazenness. She skidded about smugly in a battered little Fiat as though it were a Rolls, and stood in clós waiting for her malnourished-looking kid. She would lean casual-as-you-like against the wall, smiling away in her skin-tight miniskirts and knee-high boots without a care in the world. The way she kissed her child as well, and tousled his hair, all sweetness and joy – you'd swear she was the world's best mum. That's if you didn't know that the poor kid had never met his father! Some of the mums said it was a married man who had fathered the child, and that was why he wasn't on the scene. People talked. The kid was bound to hear it someday, and what kind of life was that for a child?

As Graham had quite rightly pointed out, though, there were no non-nationals at Gaelscoil. At least there was that. It wasn't a question of racism. Kathleen simply didn't want her child held back because Bubba Mac Zuzu at the Educate Together couldn't understand a word of English. That was fair enough, Kathleen thought, and the other mums all agreed.

In a way, it was because of the single mother and the broken homes that the whole idea had taken off in the first place. Kathleen had been in to talk to the múinteoir about it. She wasn't hugely religious herself, she said, but she went to mass, and, well, it was worrying, the things that Cliona was coming out with. Cliona said the long-haired kid had run crying to the teacher when Cliona told him that ladies couldn't have babies until they got married and prayed for one. 'That's not true,' he had said, 'my mam isn't married and she has me.' *Mam*. Apparently, whichever múinteoir was on clós duty had said sometimes that was true and all families were different and some Educate Together, hippy-dippy, happy-clappy nonsense like that. Now, these múinteoirs were supposed to be in charge of the children's moral education as well. Cliona would be doing her communion next year, and that everything-goes attitude was totally outside the school ethos, as far as Kathleen was concerned.

Ger agreed. She said she would raise the issue at the next

committee meeting. But when the day came, and Ger asked Kathleen to outline her concerns, some of the mums looked at each other under bowed heads, chewing their lips. Ger assured her she was taking the issue seriously, but her cheeks raged puce and she kept flitting off the subject all the same.

'Show me your friends and I'll show you who you are,' her granny Kath used to say, and sometimes Kathleen thought of this when she met with the girls. It was her duty as a mother, of course, to put in the effort, but sometimes she wondered if she should really be keeping company with messy women like Ger; disorganized women who dubbed themselves easy-going, who laughed with their heads thrown back and made jokes about their weight. Kathleen smiled politely at Ger's jokes – what else could she do? – but if she looked like Ger she wouldn't be laughing about it. Ger sometimes broke wind at coffee with the girls, and then chuckled. She made Kathleen feel prissy and pernickety. And anyway it was all a façade – the easy-going thing. Ger had gone to a lot of trouble to have a new dress made up.

Well that's how it started, really – Ger and her wedding dress.

During coffee with the girls, Ger had taken a laminated wedding picture from her handbag and sighed before handing it around. 'Look what I found in the bits and bobs drawer! I'd never fit into that dress now – would I girls?'

The bride in the photo was slender with pink cheeks. A lip-stick smile neither happy nor sad but pretty with a kind of bravery. And it made an ache in Kathleen's chest to recognize – in the little creases around the eyes, in the dimples, in the small hands – big, dough-faced Ger. It made Kathleen's stomach tighten so that she couldn't finish her latte. That afternoon she had screamed like a ban sí because the kids were laughing too loudly in the back of the car. She had noticed, in her rear-view mirror, that the blue lines under her eyes were worse than ever. When she got home she pressed seventy euros into Marillia's hand and asked her to take the kids to Wagamama and Leisureplex, even though it was a school night. Then she had climbed under the duvet with a few little pieces of rose-flavoured Turkish Delight and watched the whole of *Pride and Prejudice* on the new wall-mounted flat-screen.

That night, while everyone slept, Kathleen lay looking at her husband's back. His skin was very white and there were a few sparse black hairs between his shoulder blades. He hadn't showered before bed, and his skin gave off a sour, oily smell. At 2 a.m. she crept down to the hallway and poured a glass of Chianti. She sat on the cold polished-oak floor with the glass and gazed at her own wedding snap, tastefully framed and presented on the hall table for all to see. She thought of poor fat Ger with the beautiful Thai au pair.

'Did she not have a photo with her CV?' Ruth had asked.

'I would worry,' Kathleen had said, 'about an au pair like that . . . Does she go about in her nightie?'

'Ha!' Ger had said, picking up a mini croissant and pushing it through her pillar-box lips – and she a diabetic – 'I wish she would! One less job for me to worry about!'

It was that kind of attitude, of course, that led to messy houses, poorly adjusted children, wandering husbands, but, thought Kathleen, but . . . That young, slim Ger in the photo, with the excitement in her cheeks, with her uncertain lips turned up very slightly at the edges, with the tense dimples and the disappointment already creeping into the corners of her eyes – hadn't she been a good girl, trying her best? Weren't they – all of them on the GCN Parents' Committee – good women, good mothers trying their best? Staying married, staying faithful, staying respectable? What gave her the right – the young single mum – 'she's a researcher,' Ruth had said as though she knew what that even meant – what gave her the right to swanny about in a rickety tin can and no trousers on, call her bastard Blaise, of all things, *Blaise* – to swanny about like Lady Muck as though she had no shame in the world with her wild black hair and her pert little ass?

Kathleen had spoken to Cliona. She had explained that some people weren't taught right from wrong by their mummies and that those people should be avoided. The child agreed that the kid would not be invited to her magical genie and bouncy castle party in June.

What thanks did they get, people like Kathleen and Ger, for doing the right thing? Why did they deserve to feel unattractive and useless and petty? If it weren't for people like them there would be no parents' committee, no present for the teacher at Christmas.

In her wedding snap Kathleen sat with Graham in the vintage car and they each held a champagne flute. That car had cost a fortune, but Kathleen's mother had said you only get married once, and it should be the best day of your life, and her father had said he would spare no expense for his only daughter's wedding. She had blonde ringlets and she wore a tasteful half veil. Her smile was proud, as though she was receiving a prize. Kathleen tried to remember how she had felt when the picture was taken, but she couldn't even remember the photographer. She remembered the wedding night, when they retired to the penthouse suite. Neither of them was too drunk. She had been glad of that. She had searched Graham's eyes while she undressed and when he mounted her she had smiled and thought, I am as beautiful now as I will ever be. She had smiled and searched his eyes and said, 'I love you,' with all the passion she had imagined she would one day feel for her true love. She remembered feeling a fool, because Graham's eyes were the same after the wedding as before – of course they were – flat and mild and giving nothing away, looking at her bottom and breasts like a spectator, and her voice sounded ridiculous when she said it, 'I love you,' shaking her head slightly, with too much emphasis on the word 'love', like an old-fashioned actor, and she had felt, just for a moment, that it was not she who had craftily orchestrated her destiny, but someone else. She had felt, just for a flash, when Graham's eyes shifted away from hers, when she said it again, 'I love you,' that she had been duped, that she had been made a fool of.

Ger went for the idea immediately. The others giggled but they wanted to do it as much as Kathleen and Ger. 'Just for the laugh,' Ger had said, and the others had blushed and nodded, 'just for the craic...' That was one thing Ger was good for – getting people on board. She made them embarrassed to say no. Ger talked a lot, but it was Kathleen who had spoken to the priest and arranged to borrow the red carpet from the Chapel. Ger had a new wedding dress made, and so did Becky – exactly the same as the originals, but much bigger. 'If we're going to do it,' said Kathleen, 'let's do it right!' But Kathleen didn't even need to alter her dress. Her body slid easily into the cool satin bodice. The limousine idea was hers. She suggested a stretch limo to bring each of the Brides Again to her house for the evening. Every girl must have their own limo ride. Every girl must feel special. But then there were complaints about the cost. There was a recession on, they all said. Ger had already spent a fortune having her dress remade. Then there was the alcohol, the food, the babysitters...

Kathleen's girls headed away that afternoon with the au pair to Trabolgan for the weekend, and Graham would be getting in late after a business trip. The trip had been planned for six weeks. He had bought a new suit for it, and a new razor, and it was going to involve four days away. He couldn't tell her what time his flight was coming in at – it was all organized by the business – but he probably wouldn't be there until after everyone had left. It was a women-only event. She suggested the mummies had their husbands look after the kids – 'Don't we deserve one night, girls?' She had a great solution too, to the cost of the food. Each of the girls would bring the first dish they had made as a married woman. There were nine of them coming – Kathleen would make the canapés, Ger the entrées, there were two women on starters, three on main courses (one carnivore, one veggie, one gluten-free) and two on desserts. Then the only things they needed to chip in for were the champagne and the limousine. There had been no charge for borrowing the red carpet. 'It's a good cause,' the priest had said.

But there was coughing and muttering about the limousines. It was the usual suspects – Ruth, and the other one with grey streaks in her hair who never wore make-up – Gráinne. They said they'd pass on the limo.

'I think you might be going a bit far now . . .' said Ger.

'Come on girls,' Kathleen said. 'If we're going to do it let's do it right!'

Kathleen suggested hiring only three cars. Each car could make three trips and the cost could be split . . . Then Ger had to push it. It was too expensive. It was a silly expense. Out of pure desperation, Kathleen had suggested just one, it was much cheaper if they just hired one for the evening to pick them all up. The two stick-in-the-muds grumbled their consent.

'But each bride rides alone in the limo with a glass of pink champagne,' said Kathleen. 'The driver picks one up, and drops her, then goes to get the next one . . . We can start the canapés while we wait.'

Ger said she'd collect everyone's contribution and they would balance it all out at the end.

By the time the evening came it seemed as though it was all going to tick along nicely. Marillia's friend, another Spanish au pair, came to help for the evening. She did a great job cleaning the house, and decorating it with silver ribbons and white balloons. She spread the red carpet all the way down the hall and out into the bark-mulch driveway. It seemed as though the limousine plan would be fine. Kathleen had asked all the girls to text their addresses a week before so that she could give them to the driver. Then she had called the limousine firm. She had organized a pink stretch limo. It was a little more expensive than the girls had agreed, but Kathleen would make up the difference herself. It was worth it.

While she waited, Kathleen walked about the house in her dress and make-up. She found herself wandering into the hall over and over, and gazing at her wedding picture. All day she had been thinking of something silly that upset her last year. It was the kind of one-off glitch that all marriages have; the kind of thing she knew she shouldn't dwell on, but she couldn't stop her mind from returning to it, over and over.

It was that time at the theatre. Graham was quieter than usual at the interval, staring into his glass after he had emptied it, tilting it about so that the ice swirled and clinked in the dregs. When she went to the ladies she understood. Standing in front of her was the lady from the photographs. She had, as Kathleen had rightly noted, a thick waist and pink spots under her skin, especially on her chin. She had felt Kathleen looking and she turned and smiled. She had something that Kathleen couldn't put her finger on; some glint, and from her smile Kathleen knew that this was the sort of unbeautiful woman a man could fall in love with.

97

That evening in the car, out of compassion for Graham, she pretended nothing had happened. She chatted away about the play, and about their daughters, and she saw him flinch as though her voice hurt him. Then he turned to her suddenly, and rubbed his face hard. 'Look, I'm tired, Kathleen,' he said, 'I don't care. I just don't care.' Kathleen couldn't remember what she had been saying, so she couldn't answer, but his face – the weariness in his voice – she felt a fool. They drove home in silence. When they parked the car in the drive he said quietly, 'Sorry love. I'm tired.' Kathleen looked at her nails – freshly shellacked that morning so that she would look nice for the theatre. They were candy pink and she saw now that the colour was tacky. She patted her husband's knee. 'Okay,' she said, and they went indoors.

Ruth arrived first. She and Kathleen ate canapés together in their wedding dresses for half an hour before Gillian turned up. Kathleen had asked her hairdresser to come out to the house that day. It had taken two and a half hours to get her hair right – with highlights and curlers and everything. She had contemplated getting a professional to do her make-up too. Standing by the canapés, the white paper tablecloth flecked with pink and blue confetti and spread with seven different nibbles (Kathleen had made them all herself the night before, all from the first cookbook she had used as a new wife), she was glad she hadn't gone so far as to hire a make-up artist. She had picked up a few disposable cameras in Boots, just for the laugh, like the good days – it was all cameras back when they got married, not smart phones – and she asked Ruth to take some photos of her sticking her tongue out. Two hours later three more had arrived, but they were still waiting for one of the starters, one of the main courses, and the desserts. Ger turned up in a cab with a sherry trifle.

'Gráinne texted me,' she said. 'It was taking ages for the limo to get everyone, so we decided we'd speed things up and get cabs!'

Gráinne arrived shortly after, and then Paula, also in a cab. When the limousine finally arrived with Mary, Kathleen went out to tell him he didn't need to get the others. She said it to him as though it was no great change of plan: 'Thank you very much. Don't worry about the others. They've made their own way.' He had been hired for the evening, and looked a little alarmed. But then he shrugged.

'Whatever makes the ladies happy...' He asked what time he should come to pick them up. Kathleen went back inside to ask the assembly of Brides Again.

When she entered the room they all stopped speaking and turned to face her. Ger held a champagne glass in one hand,

and a blini with avocado and salmon cream in the other. 'Oh God,' said Ger, 'the poor guy. Tell him to go home. We'll get cabs.'

Two other Brides Again nodded and took large gulps of champagne.

'He's hired for the evening,' said Kathleen. 'We have to pay for the evening.'

There was silence in the room, except for the 'Here Comes the Bride' instrumental that was still playing on a loop. Kathleen had wanted each Bride to arrive to that tune.

'I arranged to hire him for the evening,' said Kathleen, 'because that's what we all agreed.'

'I think we should leave it,' said Mary, 'we've had our limo rides now. I'd rather cab it . . .'

They all stood around Kathleen's beautifully decorated dining room and looked at her. Each of their dresses was a slightly different shade of white or cream. Mary's was almost beige.

'Perhaps he would do us a deal,' said Ruth, 'if we let him go home now?'

Kathleen touched her neck. She knew her lips had thinned into a straight cut, the way they did when she was angry. She had put a lot of work into this evening on the girls' behalf. After a little silence she said, 'Fine. Can I have the money to pay him please? Eighty euros each, as agreed.'

'I gave mine to Ger,' said Gillian.

'Oh Kathleen,' said Ruth. 'Sorry, I forgot. Can I pay you on Monday?'

Then Kathleen heard Graham's car on the gravel outside. He came into the hall, sighed loudly and threw his overnight case on the floor. That wasn't like him at all. Graham was gentle and controlled in his movements. He placed things. He was never rough.

'Oh,' said Kathleen. 'Strange. Graham is in earlier than expected.'

He came into the room and kissed Kathleen beside her mouth. 'Don't you all look great!' he said, and then: 'What's yer man doing in the pink stretcher?'

'Waiting,' said Kathleen, 'waiting to be paid as promised. But some of the girls forgot their money.'

There was a clustering about and a muttering. Ger went into the hall to get her clipboard and cashbox.

Graham smiled and shook his head, but Kathleen stood stock-still with a straight back and her hands clasped in front of her.

'I have gone above and beyond, girls. I organized the whole thing. I even paid extra out of my own pocket to get the pink one – and not for myself. I didn't even get a ride in it . . .'

Ger came in from the hallway with Ruth and Mary and Gráinne, and pushed a crumpled pile of money into her hand.

'We'll give you the other two hundred on Monday...'

'Well,' said Kathleen, touching her veil and the soft glossy curls, 'well it won't do. I need to pay the limo man. And I need to be reimbursed for the champagne...'

'Oh Kathleen,' said Graham, 'don't embarrass yourself. Just use the card. Sort it out later.'

Kathleen rarely said no to her husband. She respected his authority on these kinds of things. But she put her foot down on this one. 'No,' she said. 'No. Ger agreed to collect the money.'

Graham grimaced. 'I'm tired, Kathleen.' Then he looked wearily around the room. 'Well, goodnight, ladies,' he said. 'I'm going up. Have a good night. You all look...' Then he moved swiftly towards the stairs.

Kathleen stood looking at her friends. They lowered their heads. Ruth picked up an entrée, and put it down again.

'Well,' said Kathleen. She allowed her eyes to travel slowly over the small crowd. She looked at their hands; their ankles; their cheeks. She was sorry to notice that they all wore too much rouge, and each a different shade – some crimson, some pink, some orange. She hoped her make-up was alright, and knew, suddenly, and with absolute certainty, that they should all have chipped in for a make-up artist, instead of the limo.

Bride

TO AVOID BUMPING into her husband, they met early on the steps of the district court. A quiet rain had fallen during the night, leaving a film of water on bins and windowsills and bicycle rails. They waited in the morning chill for the doors to open. Anne tucked her fingers into the sleeves of her cardigan. Her barrister paced back and forth. There was a pregnant woman with ink-black hair asleep in the doorway, and a man from the council polishing the pavement with a noisy machine. The street smelled of rubbish and of soap.

At last two men came and lifted the heavy brass bolts of the courthouse door. Their uniforms were navy blue with silver buttons. They were unperturbed by the heap in the doorway, the mottled swell of belly peeping out under her tight hoodie.

They dealt with it by standing near her, eyes averted, arms crossed, until she picked herself up and disappeared.

Anne's barrister found them a consultation room on the first floor. A window opened onto the street below, but there was no breeze to cut the closeness of the walls and the low strips of fluorescent light.

The court summons said 10.30. Anne thought that was when their case would be heard, but her barrister said that all the cases were called for that time, and anyway the judge was late. At 10.45 there was an announcement and her barrister left the room. When he came back he said that Anne's case had been put near the end of the list. The judge wanted to get through the simpler ones first, he said.

They stayed in the room for hours, listening to names being called over the intercom. They called them by initials: K.T. and M.T.; C.B. and H.M. Every time the letter A was heard Anne felt a feverish urge to shit and the very possibility of such a thing made her eyes water with shame.

'You just relax,' said her barrister, 'I have it. It's under control. The important thing is to be calm. No hysterics.'

When their case was called, her barrister opened an old sports bag. He took out a starched white bib and a black gown that had been rolled into a ball. He shook out the creases, put his arms into it and stretched black wings over his head with a yawn. He made strange sounds – 'rrrrr,' 'llll . . . aaaaa'. Then he grinned reassuringly and smoothed the bib against his chest.

In the courtroom he was unsmiling. He called her by her married name:

'Can you tell us please, Mrs Casey – when did you begin to think that something was wrong?'

Anne shifted her chair so that she could face the judge. Her barrister had advised her to do this. It was a plastic chair, the kind found in school assembly halls. She had to lean her weight on one corner to stop it from wobbling.

She had decided not to wear make-up. 'Look like a mammy,' the barrister had said, 'don't get all dolled up. If it's the judge I think it is, he doesn't take kindly to dolly birds.' It was a different judge than expected, but by the time they knew this it was too late. She hadn't even brought lipstick in her bag. Her mouth was pale. Her hair was drawn back in a black velvet scrunchie – the hairstyle that suited her least – and she wore the office-style trousers that made her bum look wide. She had purplish hollows beneath her eyes and moist pimples on her chin. She didn't like her husband to see her this way.

She had prepared an answer: 'When they came to the door. When the guards came to the door.'

That wasn't quite right. She felt now that the knowledge had begun long before – a spindly thing unfurling itself patiently in the dark. But there were things, Anne had learned, that could not be botched into narrative.

They had honeymooned in Thailand. There were street children selling flowers. It wasn't the way he looked at them. It was the way he didn't look. It was the way his hands moved, stroking the napkin.

'Those girls . . .' he said. 'They brush up against you when they ask for change. Today, one of them slid her hand into my trouser pocket. They're not as innocent as they seem.'

They were in an expensive restaurant that Anne had booked months before the wedding. At the centre of the table there was a glass bowl filled with liquid of a luminous artificial blue. A pink flower floated on the bright surface. It moved slowly around the perimeter of the bowl. At least that is what she remembered, but how could it have been moving? What could have made it move? She had gazed into the fleshy pink folds, and not at him.

'Look,' Anne had said, 'isn't it strange that the flower hasn't been dyed blue? It hasn't sucked up the blue water and turned blue . . .' She raised her eyes to his, and he looked away.

The judge was waiting for her answer. She took a sip of water. This gave her a moment to summon her voice. She looked at the judge, and lowered her eyes.

'When they came to the door. When the guards came to the door.'

They had come on a Sunday morning. She had opened the door to find three men standing in the porch. Two of them wore guard's uniforms, the other wore jeans. He showed her some papers that meant they could search her house. 'Oh,' she said, 'oh.'

She opened the door and stood aside. Her husband came down the stairs, rubbing his jaw. 'What?' he had said. 'Anne, what's all this?'

While they searched the kitchen, she knelt over the toilet and heaved up her morning tea. When they began to mount the stairs, she followed. They entered the nursery. She woke the baby, took her down to the kitchen and nursed her, though it was only an hour since the last feed. While the men moved around the house, Anne felt her pulse steady to the rhythm of the suckling infant. She sat at the kitchen table and rocked the child the way she had in the hours after giving birth, when it still felt as though they were the one body, painfully sundered. She wanted to put the baby back inside where it could not be looked at.

Her husband was standing at the foot of the stairs, his face to the wall. The morning light was bearing in on him through the coloured glass door, casting yellow and blue and crimson shapes over his hair, his back, his flannel pyjama pants.

She heard the men enter her bedroom. She heard their heavy shoes through the ceiling. Shoes weren't allowed upstairs, not since the new carpet had been put in. She thought, They'll find the handcuffs. They had never even used them. Handcuffs with pink fluff on them and a safety release catch. She had bought them at an Ann Summers party. Her friends had all bought vibrators and beads and other things she wouldn't even know what to do with.

The guards sat them both down in the living room, where there were framed pictures of their wedding day, and their parents' wedding days, and a dull oil painting of a village church that her grandfather had left to her in his will.

The man in jeans was older than the others. He had a short beard and creases around his eyes. He told her his name and said he was a detective. The younger ones watched as he leaned towards her, his hands still, the palms softly touching.

'Your husband has something to tell you.'

She played with her rings: her wedding ring, a neat gold band, and the eternity ring her husband had bought for her after the baby was born. 'You deserve it,' he had said, 'after all that work.' There were three stones in it. One was pink, one was blue, and one was a small, uneven pearl with a soapy yellow streak. She ran the pad of a finger over the two sharp bumps and the smoother swell of the pearl. She tried to remember the names of the coloured stones. Her husband was sitting on the couch. He was in handcuffs, and Anne thought again of the fluffy ones upstairs.

While her husband spoke, the detective frowned a little, watching her face. He wanted to see if she knew. The younger guards looked at their laps. She could feel the shock play out on her face. She didn't cry. She remembered thinking, *I should cry now*.

'How young?' she had said, glancing at the door. The baby was asleep now in her pram in the hallway. The detective sucked in his lower lip, and swallowed. He looked at one of the guards, and the young man looked at her, and she knew she had said the right thing.

They had confiscated his laptop, and hers. Then they had taken the handcuffs off. After they left, Anne did some ironing, the baby slept, and her husband sat at the kitchen table. Anne wanted to ask him why the handcuffs had been taken off, why he hadn't been taken away, but she preferred the silence. She ironed things she had never ironed before. She ironed baby blankets and socks. She wanted to stay in this quietness, with the doors closed, the little sleep sounds of her baby and the soft hiss of the steam.

When the baby woke up Anne said, 'We need to get the shopping.' They went to Superquinn. When they spoke it was to discuss whether to buy penne or spaghetti. As it was eleven cents cheaper, they chose spaghetti. Her husband was trembling as he took the packet off the shelf. He steadied himself against the trolley, shut his eyes and breathed out. Watching him, Anne had thought – had she really? – *Now he will have to make amends. Now he will have to be a better husband. Now I am all he has.* The baby sat upright in the trolley and blew spit bubbles.

Nothing had happened for a few weeks. Then he was called in for questioning, and then she was questioned. She asked to see the images they had found. The detective said, 'I don't think you should, love. I really don't think you should. These are things you can't unsee. But leave him. Take your daughter and go. A leopard doesn't change his spots. Trust me. I've been working on these cases for ten years . . .'

He was going to say something more, but instead he sighed.

'Speak up, please,' said the judge.

'When the . . . When the guards came to the door. To raid the house. That's when I first knew, I suppose.'

★

They taped the interviews. Anne sat in the room facing the detective, who had seen those things her husband looked at. Anne said she knew nothing, understood nothing. When she had no answer, she said nothing. The detective's eyes were disconcerting, so she stared at the wall behind him. There was a row of empty shelves and a door with a combination lock. Beyond it was the room where all the evidence was filed. She thought of all those crimes packed together as data – flat disks, and papers, and memory sticks, and little Dictaphone tapes with voices on them. She wondered what colour the walls were in there, and whether there were windows.

Before it hit the papers, she had spent a weekend in her parents' house in Wicklow.

'Something bad has happened,' she said, 'that I need to tell you about.'

The baby was in the other room, in an electric swing that played Mozart in slow, robotic notes. There was a remote control for it, and when the button was pressed the swing clacked back and forth for ten minutes, the music played, and the baby was quiet.

Her father blinked and said nothing. Her mother spoke slowly, her voice a high, brittle vibration.

'You're not going back there. You're not taking that child back to that house.'

'I've had legal advice,' said Anne evenly. 'I have to stay in the house to keep my legal right to it. Otherwise I might lose the house.'

'The *house*?' shrieked her mother. 'The house, Anne?'

After the police interviews, nothing happened for a while. Then journalists started to phone, and they had to change their number. Some famous men had been caught as part of the same investigation. It was mostly their names in the paper, but one article gave a list of all the men, and Sophie from two doors up called in with biscuits and red eyes. 'Did you not know, Anne?' she said. 'Did you not even suspect?' Some of the neighbours stopped letting their children play on the street. It took a while to go to court, and when it did, and he wasn't locked up, Sophie said that it couldn't have been so bad, what they found. He was registered as a sex offender, so they couldn't holiday in New York as planned.

As part of the court order they had to go to sessions in the outpatient wing of a mental hospital. Her husband had to attend a programme for 'recovering offenders', and it was recommended that she meet with a support group of offenders' wives. There were eight women in the group. One of them couldn't read. Most of their husbands were alcoholics, and were in for worse than Anne's husband – they had actually *done* things, most of them; they hadn't just downloaded the wrong videos. She sat quietly at the meetings, disgusted with the weakness of these women, their poor vocabulary, their poor dress sense, the brightly coloured bruises on their cheeks. She did not belong in rooms like this, with sun-bleached curtains and peeling lino on the floor. There was a cheap green-and-white clock hanging high on the wall. It twanged dully every time the hands moved.

She was not staying in her marriage from ignorance, or because she had nowhere else to go. She kept repeating it to the group: she had a job, and she had a family. She was staying because she would never forget what the priest had said before he married them: 'I admire what you are doing,' he had said, holding their folded hands between his own. 'To choose to love someone, no matter what – a human being, a sinner. Made in God's image, but so flawed. In sickness and in health. To choose that. To make that commitment is truly admirable.'

She was staying because she knew what it was to love, and because when she saw her husband's chin tremble, his lip fold on the cusp of tears – 'Look at me, Anne. Look at me.

It's me...'–she was certain that she knew him, that she could love him, if she chose to, and that to love was a good thing.

In any case, it really couldn't have been so bad, what they found, or they would have locked him up. He told her the police had exaggerated a bit; they weren't that young.

And sometimes Anne thought that perhaps she was the same as her husband. Weeks after the raid, she remembered something. Her husband must have forgotten, or he would have brought it up – but the more she thought about it, the more certain she became that they had watched one of those films together. It was on YouPorn, a video called 'Music Lesson', about a girl and her teacher. The girl was sitting on the piano with her legs splayed. She looked Spanish or Italian – she had dark eyes and she didn't say any words but she moaned a lot. Her breasts were very small; she looked very young and at first Anne didn't like it, but she had hair there and her husband said, 'Don't be such a martinet, Anne. If there's grass on the wicket, let's play cricket.' He kept watching, and pushing his fingers into her mouth, like the teacher in the video, and after a while she got into it and they played out the roles a bit together; she pretended to be shocked, she pretended it hurt, and she liked how much that made him want her.

They got carried away that time. It was only afterwards – after the raid and the newspaper articles and everything – that she thought about the video, and she began to wonder if that was the sort of thing the guards were talking about. If they had let her see the videos, she could have judged for herself.

In that interrogation room, they sent a woman in to question her. She asked about intimate things – what her husband liked in bed – did he like it shaved, did he like her from behind... Anne had told the truth. She had been with men before her husband and she knew it was normal for men to want it bare, and all men wanted anal, though she could never really understand why. But she didn't say anything about that video, or the role she had played out, or the way he said 'good girl' every time, for she knew what they would think of her.

The last of those interrogations was more like a lecture. The kind detective kept trying to hold her in his gaze. 'As young as seven,' he said. 'Do you understand, Anne? Definitely children, Anne.' She had nodded but she couldn't quite see it. Eleven maybe, because some eleven-year-olds could look sixteen...

And if she were to leave him, what would that mean about their wedding, where they had kicked off their shoes and danced all night on the beach, heavy sand clinging to the end of her dress, her freshly waxed and tanned shins, her pearly pink toenails? What would it mean about the night they had met, the jolt in her gut when he had looked at her?

After six weeks of the support group meetings, Anne was invited to speak with her husband's psychiatrist, a long-necked man who wore an Aran jumper and had a smug, close-mouthed smile. He was a specialist, and the words he used were new to her. He talked about dissociation. The strange words relaxed her. 'Projection', he said, and 'image-mediated aggression'. Her husband, he said, would never actually *do* anything. He was only looking. He didn't even enjoy it. It was an addiction. So Anne had been right. She was different from those women, and her husband was different from theirs.

Once, there was a crash near their house. She saw it on the way back from work. There were ambulances and gardaí, and a great bloody splotch on the road. Anne's car had almost slowed to a stop before she realized what she was doing – she was peering out her windscreen, hungry for a glimpse of horror. Sometimes terrible things could be compelling. Perhaps that's what it was like for her husband.

The judge looked at Anne for a moment, and then there was a silence during which he glanced through the papers in front of him. He looked at her again, and then at her barrister. Then her barrister looked at her. Anne felt so absurdly looked at that she was afraid she might cry, or laugh, or throw something, to destroy the terrible muteness in the room.

It was a family affair. That's why the hearing was in camera: no one was there but her barrister, her husband, his lawyer, and the judge. Her mother had said she would come with her to wait, but Anne preferred to go alone. The wide eyes, the trembling, the constant threat of tears would only make things worse. Women's Aid offered her a court accompaniment, but Anne declined. She knew what other women thought of her.

In the silence of the courtroom, Anne suddenly wondered had she spoken at all, or were they still waiting for her answer. She said it again:

'When the guards came to the door. To raid the house.'

Her barrister's face didn't change. Her husband's lawyer began to cough. At first it was a small, suppressed cough that sounded painful, but then it caught in his throat as though it might choke him, and he hocked wetly. He drank some water, and said to the judge, 'I apologize, your honour.' He spoke with impossible correctness, no accent to betray his origins, as though he had sprung fully formed from a law book. He was middle-aged, with dusty grey hair and full, pink cheeks. She wondered had he a wife, or a child. Did he think her a liar, or did he pity her, even a little? Did he pity their child?

Her own barrister cleared his throat.

'That's when you discovered about a previous incident. But we will not refer to that today as it is no longer on the register.'

Anne breathed out. He had explained that he would have to say that. No one could stop her from saying anything, but he was not permitted to use it. He continued:

'When did you first suspect something was amiss with your daughter? What made you deny her father access? Take your time.'

'Well, I began to worry when the school... when the principal of the school called me in and they said they were concerned. Some teachers had noticed unusual behaviour. She was obliged to mention her concerns, she said.'

In the headmistress's office Anne felt a child, blissfully helpless. It was the smell of the leather chairs, the stillness of the room and light cutting in through the venetian blinds. The woman had soft, clean hands and pink, unpolished nails. She asked Anne to sit and poured her a glass of water. She wore a perfume that reminded Anne of her grandmother. While the woman spoke, Anne wept and said nothing. The headmistress handed her a soft, thick tissue that smelled of eucalyptus, but still she wouldn't look away, she wouldn't stop speaking. When the talking stopped, Anne opened her eyes, but she couldn't speak.

The bell rang, and the headmistress handed Anne a cup of sugared tea.

'I have a class,' she said, 'but you're welcome to stay in my office. Take as long as you need.'

Anne stayed there until it was time to collect her daughter. She looked out through the window at the games pitch, and at the cars filling up the car park.

She didn't like to go home to an empty house. Sometimes when she came back from work in the afternoon, a terrible fear took hold of her. It usually began with a nagging sorrow, brought on by the silence of the house, the indifference of their little dog, who didn't like her, and the smell of the clean floor. She would have to sit down with her head between her knees and concentrate on breathing. She didn't think anything when this happened, only waited it out. But she felt that something had reached up from a terrible place, something with no beginning, half-formed, a spine too soft to snap, eyes like black buds, claws sticky as fish scales, fingering her neck, pulling her down under her life.

When the next bell rang the children were brought out to the yard and released to the minders and mothers. She saw her daughter waiting for her, chewing the inside of her cheek, but Anne stood watching from the window.

The child was pretty. Everyone said it. Only last week Anne was sitting on the steps of the porch, keeping an eye on her daughter, who was having bicycle races with another little girl. One of the new neighbours came out with a mug of tea, and sat beside Anne – 'She's grown so pretty, hasn't she?'

Anne shrugged, but it was true. The girl was changing very suddenly, though she remained tiny in size. At the age of seven she already had little bumps under her nipples. Her cheekbones were starting to rise. Her hair had grown to her shoulders, where it hung in ringletted clumps. It had never lost its baby blondeness.

'Sometimes I think she is very pretty,' said Anne. 'Other times I look at her and I think, You know what, you're not all that gorgeous as you think. I had blonde hair like that until I was sixteen. She gets that from me. It will go mousy when she's sixteen, like mine did. She has my thighs too,' she said, punching her own legs, 'fat thighs like her mother.'

Anne watched the children run to their mothers. She bit her lip. *Why do they love us like that?* She watched until her daughter was the only child left. Then she walked out to the yard, nodded at the teacher, and took her daughter's hand.

The child's eyes were heavy. She hadn't been able to sleep the previous night. She had lolled in the doorway while Anne did the ironing.

'What nightie of yours does Daddy like?'

Anne hadn't replied.

'Daddy likes me in all my nighties. Isn't that right Mammy?'

'I don't know,' Anne said.

'Daddy says you know. Am I like my daddy or am I like you?'

'I don't know.'

'Daddy says you know.'

Sometimes he lost his temper with the child for no good reason at all. He took her off to visit friends on a Sunday afternoon, to give Anne a break, and more than once, when the little girl came down the stairs he would shout at her for wearing clothes that he didn't like, or for not having combed her hair. He would make her return to her room and change, and if he didn't like what she was wearing then, he would shout some more, drag her into the room, and pick her outfit himself. Some Sundays they had to force her into the car. Her father held her in while Anne shut the door, and waved them off, her daughter sobbing in the passenger seat, 'I hate you. I hate you. I wish you weren't my mammy.'

But they had a good life. They had built a conservatory out the back, where they sat together in the evenings, and drank wine, and read books, and he no longer put her down in front of his family, who had never liked her, but who had refused to speak to him for a year after the thing had been in the papers. He knew who loved him now. It used to anger Anne, the way his mother said his name, 'Noel', a reminder of his birth on Christmas Day, of her authority as his mother. But his mother was meek around Anne now, grateful.

At night their daughter asked for stories, and Anne told the story of how they had met, or the story of their wedding day, the way Aunt Myra's chair had collapsed beneath her, and Anne, unable to contain her laughter, spat her champagne across the table. She told her what cravings she had when she was pregnant, and all the kicks she'd got, how the baby had come out looking like her father, only older, redder, more wrinkled.

One night her daughter asked, 'Does the daddy or the mammy own the baby?'

Anne had laughed. 'They both do.'

'And who owns the mammy and the daddy?'

'They own each other, love. Go to sleep.'

It had pained Anne to take the wedding dress from its fragranced box, to see the slim shape she had been back then, the luxurious fabrics her body had merited. It hurt less than she expected to take scissors to the dress, to pull out the ribbons from the corset, to rip the stitches from the waist with an old cross-stitch knife. She had worked through the night to create the little communion dress. She had done a beautiful job. She had fashioned a littler veil from her own long train. She had given her daughter a crown of tiny crystals and satin flowers. She had even used the roses off the corset of the wedding dress to trim the hem. The skirt fell to just below her daughter's knees.

'I don't need to shave my legs, do I Mammy?'

'No, love. Not yet.'

The children all sang as they walked up the aisle to receive for the first time the little disc of holy flesh. There was incense and a blonde lady with thick lipstick playing the harp. Each little girl wore a white dress, white gloves, white veil, and white satin shoes with the soles already blackening. The boys wore miniature suits.

Anne had been watching her daughter's shoes on the polished floor when she noticed that one of the white socks with the little pink bow on it had fallen down to her ankle. She thought of her daughter's skin, the talcy smell, the warmth of it when she slept, and the pale soft hair on her legs. Then she understood. At first it cut like a chink of light, like relief – to understand at last – but then it settled in her mind, took weight there. She left the church and vomited quietly onto the gravel outside. Her husband followed her. He touched her elbow, and handed her a tissue.

★

Her barrister had warned her to concentrate on the concrete. 'No hysterics,' he had said. 'Concentrate on what was said, what you observed, what the school observed. Look at the judge. Don't cry. If it's the judge I think it is, don't cry.'

Anne told the judge what her daughter had said on the evening after her communion, with the car pulled up on a grass verge, on a side road halfway between their house and Wicklow. Anne didn't say how hard it was to like her daughter, how hard it was to look at her, how she had almost turned on the radio, turned back to their lovely home with the stained-glass door, and a dog in the porch, how she had watched the clock as her daughter choked up her confession, knowing there was still time to turn around before she said too much.

The judge wrote slowly with a fountain pen for a long time. Everyone had to sit quietly in the courtroom. Anne looked at her barrister, but he made no response, so she looked at her hands. She had put her wedding ring in her handbag for the day. She turned her eternity ring around. It was loose now. She must have lost weight.

They had to stand to hear the court order. Her husband stood and looked at her, blank-faced. Anne didn't under-stand what was said. The judge's voice seemed far away, overlaid with the throbbing of blood, her heartbeat pulsing in her ears, in her throat, louder and stronger until her hands and cheeks lost feeling and all she could hear was the steady push of her blood like waves hitting the shore. She held the chair to steady herself. Her barrister helped her to sit down.

When they were back in the consultation room, her barrister explained that the case was adjourned until June. This would give time for the doctor's report to be prepared. She could withhold access until then. Her barrister said she had done well. 'It's a good outcome,' he said, 'it's what we want.' He patted her awkwardly on the shoulder.

On the way out he recognized a colleague. 'Well done,' he said again, and wiggled his fingers in goodbye. Anne walked out alone into the wet afternoon, down the steps and out onto the street. She needed a drink, she thought, then she would take the bus to Wicklow, where her daughter and her mum were waiting. She didn't switch on her phone yet. She shook her hands out, closed her eyes tight and opened them again and kept walking. She found a wine bar. She ordered a glass of red. She had never done this before – sat alone in a wine bar. She had never sat alone in a cafe, or on a park bench. She had never been the type.

She sat outside on a metal chair with her cardigan and no jacket, sweating in the cold, and looked at the glass of wine and waited for the throbbing to stop.

A girl approached the table, or a woman. It was hard to tell. Her bare arms had the skinniness of a child's, but her face was lined in odd places: tight ridges straining down her cheeks and neck. There was a bandage on her arm, wrapped too loosely. She wore tracksuit bottoms that clung to her small, round bottom. It was the black hair Anne recognized. The girl had lost the hoodie she had been wearing on the steps of the courthouse.

'Excuse me,' she said. Even in the dim light, Anne could see the hardness of the girl's face, the hollow cheeks, and the dry lips, the eerie beauty of her want.

'I lost my purse,' said the girl, 'and I need to get home to my mother. I need to take the train home to my mother. The ticket is twenty-six euros.'

She unfurled her hand, the spindly fingers, the clean, rough palm.

'Please,' she said. She tried to look Anne in the eye.

'Sorry,' said Anne, doing her best to neutralize her accent, 'I can't help you.'

'Please, miss.' The girl's thin face changed. Her eyes widened as though in pain.

There were two boys with old faces standing on the corner, watching. They had large, hungry shadows for eyes, like smudges of ink in the half dark. They watched and they didn't speak to each other. The girl's voice became hoarse.

'Please, miss. I'm having a baby. I just need my mother, miss. I just want to go home to my mother, miss.'

Then one of the boys shouted, 'We're going, Jen.'

'Please, miss,' she said. 'Please, I only need twenty-six more euros.'

The boys began to walk away, cursing, unsteady, leaning their weight on each other's shoulders. The girl turned around and bolted after them. She roared from her raw throat, from her gut, 'You promised, Kevin. Don't fucking leave me, you fucking liar! Kevin. Please!'

She ran with her legs slightly apart, a gentle lurch. She never put her hand to the tight swell of her belly, the something-like-life that must be turning there in the dark and the water and the blood. Anne watched her round the corner. She sat and drank her wine slowly, and as the evening closed in she heard the girl howling wordlessly, somewhere in the dark streets.

Terraforming

A GROUP OF men applauds the landing, their claps and whistles drowning the grumble of the Earth as it passes beneath. Caitriona lifts her face out of the cup of her palm. Wet. There is drool down her neck, drying to a tight crust along her jaw. Beyond the window, only a syrupy yellow mist. She wipes her hand on her leggings and uses the end of her sleeve to rub at her neck and face. She knows there must be marks on her; chalky tide lines mapping the shapes where the saliva has dried.

The plane sighs to a halt, but over the speaker comes an announcement that the doors can't be opened yet and phones are to be kept off. Some of the passengers come out into the aisles, removing bags from the overhead lockers, pulling coats out from under haunches and feet.

It's been years since she was in London. She remembers only the dark veins of the underground, deceptive landmarks made by cafe chains, brisk men who did not offer to help with bags. She stayed a night – no, two – with her sister, before either of them was married. They shopped for clothes and Boots cosmetics, saw a musical, ate chocolate cereal in their hotel room and talked in a way they hadn't done since.

The man next to her leans into the aisle, trying to tug something out of the overhead locker. In the twist and stretch of the effort, his T-shirt rises over the khaki canvas belt. Billow of flesh; oblong navel; neat thatch of hair that cleaves the belly in two as it runs from umbilicus down to the neon blue band of his trunks.

Caitriona looks away. She does not want to glimpse the knot that once tied the stranger to his beginnings. While she dozed on the flight, she was thinking about her son: the delicious creases at the back of his neck, his incongruence with the adult world of airport lounges and foreign currency.

'Sir, please remain in your seat until the seatbelt light goes off!' It is the air hostess who tore their boarding passes at the gate. She has turquoise eyelids and big crunchy hair. When they boarded she was calm and smiling, but now a dangerous shade of red is rising from beneath her powder complexion.

The man produces a long rucksack with many straps and flaps. He turns to the air hostess.

'There now,' he says.

She snatches the bag from him with two hands and pushes it back into the overhead locker. 'Wait for the seatbelt light to go off!'

The man sits down, muttering. He shakes his head, turning towards Caitriona, his palm flat on the empty seat between them, but Caitriona keeps her face towards the window. Her hand luggage is at her feet, and she has the directions written out clearly on a piece of paper. A bus, one Tube stop and a three-minute walk. She will find a bathroom and remove the signs of dried drool from her face. Then she will go straight to the hotel and check in. She has packed a sandwich. There will be no need to leave the room until morning.

It was after her father's death that the dreams began. They arched up like a nest of waking cats, all purr and acid hiss. They licked at her ears, tongues at once gentle and scouring, and with their claws they tore deep stars into her night.

She has followed them here to this compact hotel room, clean and cool with a bed hemmed by a wall at the head and foot. There is a flat television, a row of green and red lights glowering up its side. The screen shows a picture of stones on a beach and a bubble with the words 'Welcome Ms C. Dawson. We hope you enjoy your stay' moving about the screen like a wandering buoy. She should have used a different name. There is a small desk with a block of Post-its, a pen, a phone and a card with the numbers for Reception and Emergency and Room Service. Fixed to the wall, a monitor shows her how much energy she has used, and how much water. A green smiley face says she has been energy efficient so far. Caitriona has never been in a room like this before.

She sits on the side of the bed, takes her mobile from her handbag, and squeezes the power button until it blinks to life. She has to wait through a series of texts as the phone acclimatizes to the new location. Then it settles down and she can call. As the ringing begins she can feel her eyelids twitch; a kick of panic when she hears his voice.

'You made it?'

She smiles and nods as she speaks, because she read once that people can hear the expression on your face. 'Yes,' she says. 'Eleanor picked me up. Flight was fine, you know, as you'd expect. Get what you pay for... But anyway there you go. Is my little man all right? We're going for a bite to eat now... God, yeah – so good to see her... A girly night, yeah. But listen babe, I'm on my mobile... they don't have a landline, no. No, don't upset him... I'll be back before he notices. Don't forget the eczema cream when you're getting him into his jammies. Yeah.'K. I'll phone you tomorrow . . .'

Afterwards she takes a shower, and the monitor on the wall becomes an orange face with a straight mouth. Then she sits at the desk and unwraps her ham sandwich. Not hungry.

She wakes in a gaspful of sand to the low whirr of churning air. Red and green prickle the dark. She couldn't turn off the air conditioning. It has dried her skin taut to the bone, and her lips taste of blood. There is an en suite, but on the mirror a sticker saying not to drink the tap water, and the message: 'Did you know? All our toilets flush with greywater!'

She knows there is Coke and mineral water in the little lobby at the end of the hall. She saw the vending machine on her way to the room, but she was too keen to get in and shut the door. She will nip out quickly. A cardigan over her pyjama top. Remember the key card.

Round white sensor lights click on one by one overhead. The hallway is painted a clean shade of eggshell. There is a charcoal carpet underfoot, and along the walls, tall sprigs of straw in slate-black, pyramid-shaped vases. Her feet are bare. No slippers, and no clean socks for tomorrow either.

There they are. Too late to turn around. Two of them sitting right there on a black wicker couch beside the machine.

Deep in conversation, they dip their heads together like a pair of swans. Caitriona recognizes the girl from the cover of the bright magazine that comes with the Sunday paper – an oval face set in a perfect bob. In the picture she wore a red jumpsuit, metallic powder shimmering on her cheekbones, a space helmet under her arm. Her hair looked set in plastic; peroxide white and mortis stiff. In real life she is smaller, her colouring muted, her hair alive with a haze of frizz and a stubborn cow's lick. Her feet are folded up beneath her, and one of the couch's silver cushions is nestled on her lap. Caitriona doesn't recognize the girl's companion – a narrow-chested man with a vague beard – but he is one too. She knows from the T-shirt, red with black letters: *MISSION MARS – Let's Get This Future Started.*

The two lift their eyes as she passes. Fat sag of pyjama bottoms. Naked feet. The vending machine is a big old beast with lots of empty metal swirls where packets of sweets and chocolate bars once were. It glows coolly, illuminating its stock: lots of water; aloe vera juice; only a few bottles of Coke.

She reaches into her cardigan pocket. No money. Key card and no money. She presses a selection all the same. The two candidates resume their conversation. 'The training will be hard,' says the girl, her speech quiet and moist, the confident, winding vowels of fluent second-language English. 'We can remember it is ten years away. There is much that can be learned in ten years. We will not be sent unless we are capable. We will not be chosen unless we are right.'

'The radiation,' says the man. He is English. 'I want to be sure there is medicine with us up there – painkillers. I don't mind dying up there, but it's being without access to the right medicine. Euthanasia, even. If it comes to it. I mean, it'll be new laws there, won't it? Or space law?'

'Space code,' says the girl, 'strict space code.'

Caitriona pushes her hand into the vending machine flap, then into her cardigan pocket, hoping to conceal the absence of any bottle. She shuffles away quickly and this time they do not pause as she passes.

'Somehow I'm not scared,' says the girl, leaning in close. 'It's like it's my destiny, you know? It feels right. I have told them already I want to be the first mother on Mars. Mother of the first Martian. It will happen. I know it.'

'They'll send you in one of the later groups, then. Not the first group anyway . . . There's bound to be teething problems. And who knows what the radiation will do to our fertility?'

The corridor is still lit. It takes three swipes before the key card opens the door. In the dark, she puts her mouth under the bathroom tap.

★

Settled into oblivion in some cave of her mind, bypassed for years by the circuits and synapses that keep things going, is a pool of facts that her father left for her:

Mars is a wandering planet.

Jupiter is a ball of gas dense as water.

Pluto – Pluto, which was once her favourite planet, a pretty little orb out there at the end of the sequence, Pluto is all ice and rock, a cool marble mottled blue and yellow like a bruise, and it orbits the sun, spinning faster and slower as the aeons pass in a cycle that takes millions of years.

'Imagine all the lives that pass in one cycle,' her father said. 'Imagine all the work that goes into each of those lives. All the harvesting and skimping and counting to make ends meet and keep food in mouths and coats on backs, and bring babies to adulthood. You can't imagine it, can you? Me neither. You would have to be God.'

There are infinite possibilities, life on Earth is all a coincidence of gases and heat and time that could as easily never have been.

They were rare moments when her father would sit with her and point out all the planets in a large, coloured hardback. He had bought it with the help of tokens saved from Blue Moon biscuit packets. It stayed in the small good room with the *Reader's Digests* and the grand china doll that her mother had been given as a child. Her father drove a bread van and when he wasn't doing that he cleaned the gutters or windows of wealthier houses. He resoled his children's hand-me-down shoes with strips of leather he had soaked overnight, teeth clenched while he worked, lips drawing back to pull tight the stitches. Then, with his tongue between his lips, he positioned the glue and firmed down strips of old tyres for grip.

Ashamed of living in a council estate, he wanted to own a house. When Caitriona was fourteen he had managed it.

'You can do anything, Trinny,' he told Caitriona. 'My Trinny can do anything. Don't let anyone do you down. Not for being a girl or a bit heavy – don't mind that. Hold your head high.'

It was her sister who was with him when he died. She phoned from the hospital, voice like a paper bag tossed hollow in the wind. Caitriona said, 'Okay,' as though consenting, and got off the phone as quickly as she could. She was surprised at how little she minded. While she waited for her husband to get in, she finished the washing up and checked on the baby and made a cup of tea to sip on the couch and wait. As soon as she sat it reached up from her gut, a small, sore cry. She thought of the empty house and all the carefully shelved *Reader's Digests* with the slippery pages and wondered if there was a way to make them mean something.

That night sleep came easy. She slid into the gas planet; surface as thick as liquid; nothing hard to kick at. She recognized the feeling – a place where contact is impossible because nothing is divided. All yield and push; her self dispersed into all matter and all of it in her. She woke in a sweat, ears and toes rippling with a queer nostalgia. She knew she must have dreamt it before.

Jupiter is the god of everything.

Sometimes she is on the red planet itself. Blood-tinted sky and the heat pressing like flesh against her face. Wind and sand ahead, wind and sand behind, and no way of knowing which way to go. Stretch of dark. Blind hand looking for touch. Spear puncturing the surface and she feels the hurt of it in her breast somehow. A little flag but with what name on it?

She made the audition tape alone on her laptop. It felt strange to declare her name. 'I am Caitriona Dawson. I dream of exploring space.' She must have expected to be chosen, some blessing from the dead, perhaps, because when she received the email she wasn't too surprised. She knew she would pass the Skype interview. 'There'll be plenty of interest in you,' said her liaison officer. 'Out of one hundred chosen candidates across the globe, you are the only mother. You'll get a lot of coverage.'

'After the next round,' she told him. 'If I get to the next

round, then okay. Then I'll tell my family and I'll do all the interviews and stuff then . . .'

There were qualities they saw in her, the liaison said, qualities that a new world would need; the honesty and the compassion and the fire that they were looking for.

She knew then that yes, this was what she was for. She could do anything, and no one was to do her down.

When morning comes she discovers that there is a way to unplug the television, by reaching in behind. It is a relief to see the little lights blink away. The sliding door by the desk, which she thought was a wardrobe, in fact conceals a second sink, with a sticker saying *Potable Water*. Beside it there is a small kettle, and two black teacups, a black wicker basket with teabags, sachets of instant coffee, individually packaged biscuits and thimble-sized portions of UHT and soya milk.

She makes a cup of tea, the wrong colour, and pours a second dose of milk in after the first slides to the bottom. She eats two counterfeit Jammie Dodgers, sitting at the desk, dipping them in the tea while it cools. As it turns out, the tea is not too bad. The cups are rather shallow and the conference is not for another two hours, so she makes a second cup.

She had an outfit picked for today. She bought it specially – a smart blouse and a waistcoat – but she knows now that she cannot wear it. It is a costume for a circus master. She will blush all through the day, squirming the clothes to comic crookedness. She brought a grey jumper dress for the flight home. The dress she wore on the way over is better – a quiet green colour and a way of cinching the waist – but she won't be able to remove the smell of plane and her own frowsy sleep from it. The jumper dress then. She sponges the stains from her leggings. There is nothing to be done about the socks.

According to the website the first talk is called 'Why It's Time to Go'. The event page showed a picture of Earth with patches of blue and red and black, the surface blistered and peeling like scorched skin – something about the ozone layer. She tried to read about it at work, but she was so afraid of being caught that the blood started to pump too quickly behind her eyes and she couldn't string the shapes into letters. She knew how they would all laugh at her; the open-mouthed guffaws of her manager, the stiff snorts of the front-of-house girls.

The e-vite said to come early for a chance to chat with experts and meet the other candidates.

The front entrance opens into a round room with many doors in its curved walls. Slim women with ponytails meander slowly through the crowd, offering something hot from large silver pots. There are more people than she expected. Some are talking in tentative pairs, but most are standing apart, flicking through pages in red pocket folders, trying to avoid the terrible quietness of the place. There is a pillar in the centre and all around it a ledge where miniature bagels, and miniature Danish pastries, and bites of marmalade-glazed toast the size of postage stamps are presented on silver platters. The walls are lined with information stands displaying bits of rock and large glossy photographs of the galaxy.

'Excuse me,' a man no older than twenty with very yellow hair touches her elbow, 'you need to register before you can enter.'

'Oh . . .' Caitriona says.

'Are you here for the conference?'

He points to a banner reading *Mission Mars Orientation and Registration*. Below it, a second young man with an identical hairstyle is sitting at a long table. He is a little broader than his colleague, but he has the same look: disconcertingly symmetrical features set stiffly in an unlined face. They are both dressed impeccably: black suit, black tie, wound-red shirt and, on the lapel, a red enamel disc ringed with gold.

'Welcome to the first European Mission Mars Candidate Conference,' says the broader man. 'Can I see your ID?'

A machine no bigger than her phone prints her name onto a rectangular sticker. He peels it off and hands it to her on one fingertip. The other man hands her a red pocket folder fat with stapled papers, a *Mars One* pen, and, wrapped in a clear envelope, a pin like theirs, the sharp gold point poking hopefully at the packaging. The object has a pleasing, tight weight to it, like the smooth old bullet her father kept in a tobacco box over the bookshelf. Caitriona hooks it into the fine-knit dress, worrying immediately that she has placed it exactly where her nipple is and that people will notice it jiggling stupidly. Too late.

The two men open their palms in tandem towards the room. 'The conference will begin in two minutes,' says the slimmer one. 'Good luck, Caitriona.'

The first half of the day is made up of a series of lectures that Caitriona struggles to follow. There is quite a lot of science, but the lecturers repeat that candidates mustn't worry; they don't have to understand it all yet. A big projection shows the houses they will live in – a row of silver domes on a crimson terrain. There is one lecture called 'Our Galaxy; Our Neighbourhood', where they are given brief summaries of the other planets in the solar system.

Someone puts their hand up. Caitriona can't hear the

question but the lecturer repeats it through his microphone. 'This lady is asking about Pluto, about why it is no longer a planet . . .' He explains that it never really was, but it is a good question because soon they – the men who do these things – will send a probe to take measurements and photos and find out more about Pluto. So there might be some hope for Pluto after all, thinks Caitriona, to have a place in the galaxy; to be remembered again. A colour picture of Pluto is projected onto the wall. The lady murmurs again, and the speaker repeats her question for the audience:

'Would it be possible for them to find something that would make Pluto a planet again?' He laughs. 'No, sorry, that's not how it works, I'm afraid. Right, any more questions before we wrap up for lunch? . . . No? Okay, chosen candidates go with Pearse. Make sure you have your ID. All other stakeholders please come with me.'

Pearse is a tall man with a whey complexion and long, blueish fingers. He stands at the front of the hall while the candidates form a flock. He counts the heads: twenty-five. Then he leads them out into the main auditorium and off down a corridor to a smaller, cooler room with a whiteboard and collapsible chairs pushed back against the walls.

There are three cardboard boxes on a desk, and a water dispenser sitting awkwardly in the middle of the room. Pearse stands by the boxes and congratulates them all on being chosen. He warns that this is only the beginning of a long and harrowing quest for a new world.

The boxes contain their lunch – a selection of protein bars. These are samples of what they will be living on for the seven-month voyage. Pearse says there are three flavours – strawberry, chocolate, and vanilla. All three are the same muddy colour and wrapped in the same red greaseproof paper. They smell like rotting wood, but the taste is inoffensive. 'Some people find they taste like pineapple,' says Pearse. While the candidates eat, a nutritionist called Camilla explains that the bars are made from tiny green sea vegetables and contain a full spectrum of vitamins, proteins, and trace minerals. They will need to take fat supplements on board too, and lots of water.

After lunch the water cooler is wheeled into the adjoining room, and they are asked to help fold the chairs properly and stack them in a corner. Then they are told to form a circle. One by one they must announce their names and tell the group something about themselves.

'I am Caitriona Dawson,' she announces, 'and I work in hospitality.' She can feel the heat in her face and she can't figure out what to do with her hands, so she fiddles with the Mars pin, taking the back off and pinching the little wings to open the hole and put it back on. She has an urge to push the point into her palm. Her response isn't the worst, though.

One woman tugs fiercely at her cuticles with her teeth and when it comes her turn she says, 'I am Delia, and I have three cats and six goldfish.'

Somebody sniggers and Pearse says, 'No laughing at other candidates please. Anything at all about yourself. Thank you, Delia.'

Next they are organized into groups of four. Caitriona is asked to choose a group name and she says 'Pluto,' before she has time to think. They are each given a big round blue sticker and they write their name on it, and the name of their team: *Caitriona Dawson – Pluto*. There is one man in the group, a skinny fellow from London who says he works in a hospital but doesn't disclose his role there. She noticed him earlier because he has been wearing the black version of the *Mission Mars* cap all through the day. The more merchandise you buy, the more Mars points you get. You get points, too, for blogging, more if you give interviews to journalists, and there will be a documentary with the chosen candidates. They explained all this in the interview. They need publicity for funding, they said; the mission depends on it.

Also in her group are the oval-faced girl from last night, and an older lady from Scotland with big jewellery, very small hands, and an enormous bosom. The lady touches Caitriona's elbow and winks warmly. 'Good name,' she says. 'I've always had a soft spot for Pluto.'

Pearse sits on a high swivel chair at the top of the room; one foot tucked in his crotch and one dangling. He rotates slowly from side to side, making the hinge yelp. Their first task is to explain to each other why they are volunteering. 'Be completely honest,' Pearse says. 'This is only amongst ourselves.'

Caitriona huddles into her group. The hospital worker says his name is Eric and that he will speak first. He removes his cap to reveal a slick of thinning hair. Then he flips open a sleek black wallet to show a photo of his son, a round-eyed child with a frightened mouth.

'This is Howard,' he says, 'my son.'

He slides the picture out and passes it around his three teammates. There is a pause while they each take a moment to look at Eric's son. 'How sweet,' says the Scottish lady, and Eric nods sadly. He takes a deep breath and returns the cap to his head. Then he begins to speak very fast, eyes pecking at the faces of his audience. His ex is a psycho, he says. She is always cutting access, always trying to make him do all the running around. Now the courts have ordered him to pay her maintenance. 'I'm going to show them all I am a dad to be proud of. He'll be able to say "My dad is a spaceman," and then she'll be sorry. Boys love rockets.'

When he is finished speaking Eric looks exhausted. There is a silence into which the Scottish lady sighs, 'Well I might as well go next . . .' Then she gives a deep, sad chuckle. While she speaks Eric lowers his head, but his eyes still dart about as though he wasn't quite finished. The woman rocks on her heels, hands clasped at her belly. She punctuates each utterance with a little laugh, like relief after pain. 'I just want to be remembered. That's all. That's all really. To make a mark.'

The white-haired girl quickly takes over. She makes Caitriona nervous. She says she is an astrophysics student and she lives in Stockholm. She began her studies in marine biology, she says, but she soon decided that the answers were not on this earth. She is either mad or extremely clever, with lots of words that Caitriona has never heard before, spoken with strange authority in that alien accent. 'The next war will be the end of life on Earth,' she says. 'Someone has to find a new planet or human life is finished.'

Caitriona doesn't know what she will say but then the words come very quickly. 'My dad died last year. He wanted me to do something extraordinary but I never knew what it should be. So . . . yep. That's why I'm here.'

The groups are assigned tasks; a number of computer-simulated crises which they will have to manage together. At first Eric has a lot of opinions – 'Look girls, what we need here is to think outside the box. Who's to say plants can't pull the water from the atmosphere?' – but he soon lets the astrophysics student lead.

★

On the e-vite it said the conference would finish at six, but when six comes, Pearse asks them to follow him. They arrive in a dimly lit room where there is a scattering of fine black dust under a long glass case. The case is in the centre of the room and they are allowed to walk around the exhibit and peer in through the viewing panels on the side. This, he says, gesturing with both hands to the stretch of glass, is a new metal that copies itself over and over, and when it copies itself it creates a gas. One of the purposes of the mission is to take this substance up to Mars. Once it begins, the stuff will keep copying itself until, after millions of years, it has created an ozone layer around the planet. Then they will start filling the atmosphere with air. This is called 'terraforming'. 'Imagine all the lives that pass in those millions of years,' her father once told her – but did he? Or are these the things she is inventing now, to make him real, to remember a person about whom there is very little to say?

After they have looked for a while at the metal, Caitriona expects that they will finish up, but instead Pearse says that each group has half an hour to come up with a presentation on the best way to multiply the metal on Mars.

She waits until seven before slipping out of her workshop group. 'Sorry Pearse,' she says, 'I'll have to excuse myself...'

For a moment Pearse's face loses all expression. He keeps his eyes on her while his voice goes up like a siren. 'Excuse me everyone. I need your attention for a moment!'

The room falls silent. They are all looking at her now, with pity or disdain, perhaps. She doesn't know. She keeps her gaze focused on Pearse. She will not lower her head.

'A candidate . . .' he peers at her badge, '. . . *Catreeownna* . . . has just told me that she needs to leave to catch a flight. That leaves her team down one member. For this mission you need to be dedicated. You need to be able to deal with the unexpected . . . Well. Let's all say goodbye and get on with our work.'

Dark, despite pipes of light running cool as drains overhead. The air is thickened by the earth that must be muffling against the concrete, dulling the faraway chirrup of the trains. Cram of bodies teeming down and up the stairs and keeping to one side for the sake of order. Which side is it she should be on? She keeps veering to the wrong side. She needs to find a bin to stuff the conference pack in. Her badge, too. Remember to take off the badge.

If she misses the flight it means using the credit card. It means inventing some excuse. Already she will have to explain the conference fee. As a chosen candidate, she was given a special rate, but it was enough to make a dent. Barry will notice it and ask and she still doesn't know what she'll say. When she squeezes between the sliding doors she is still holding the red folder.

'Mind the gap.'

So many people. Blank faces but she can tell their types by the way they dress and the things they have; a tall woman in an awkward blouse knitting with purple acrylic amongst the crush of passengers; a bearded young man with a checked scarf, hugging a rolled canvas.

Wobbling at his mother's knees, hand squelched tight in hers, is a little boy in a camouflage jacket with a crest saying *Army Man*. He looks like the child in the hospital worker's photo. Huge eyes and mouth shut small until it opens wide and lets out a shriek. 'Look Mummy!'

He is pointing at the floor. Some of the conference pack contents have slid out, Caitriona sees; they are sprawled down amongst the feet.

'Look! SPACE, Mummy! SPACE!'

The mother's face is flattened with a thick layer of dust-dull make-up. She rubs her son's head, pulls it to her hip. 'Shhhh . . .'

There is no use trying to squat and pick them up. She will only drop other things if she tries. Panic starts in her lungs. What is it that they are breathing in and out down here? What is keeping them all standing, making the blood move through, and how long will it sustain them? She clutches at a loop overhead to steady herself, jiggles to the pulse of the carriage. Only one Tube stop and a bus. Then the plane and then her little boy's face slotting into her neck, ears like the singing tunnels of seashells, fragrant scalp, the rippling cable of his spine.

She tries to tidy the papers a little with her feet: the pictures of the galaxy and of the machine that will make the oxygen, and the strings of words she could not understand. She should have thrown them out right there in the conference centre. She has probably failed anyway. Of course she has.

The child is on the floor now, trying to pick up one of the pictures he has seen – the solar system, which is not a sequence of eight as she once believed, but a blur of stars and planets too vast for her mind to map. Fat sticky hands like her boy; her boy who exploded from a tiny nook; a surge of blood thrusting her body into a new space and then his birth that threw open her sky. But she will close it up neatly again, as she suspects all mothers do. She will grow away from him over the ten years it will take to train for Mars, and that is right of course. A curling beat inside her and then a cord. A breast and then a head in her neck; a hand in hers and then no hand because that's how it is with time and space. Wider and wider the distance; the journey that began in her, and who will he be out there with no touch left between them?

The door slides open.

'Mind the gap.'

She pours with the shoal of passengers out onto the platform and the crowd is gone, moving blind as maggots on the steps. At the top there is only a dull light; it is evening now. She has almost reached the open.

'Hello lady.' The child has grabbed the end of Caitriona's dress. A little shut mouth again, a little chin. Big bug eyes.

'Shhh,' the mother says, 'sorry about that.'

'Oh no,' says Caitriona. 'No, I have a little one myself. . .'

'So you know how it is?'

And the woman's smile is like the swell of a dying star, the disappointed climax and the heavy joy, and the relief because Caitriona knows it too – the awesome detail of accidental being.

The child is thrusting a bundle of papers towards her: three sheets stapled together and on the front the picture of the home on Mars – a row of huts like silver polyps on the rust sand.

'You keep that,' she says, but the child shakes his head. The pin then. She pinches the back and pulls it from her chest.

'Look,' she says, 'do you know what that is?'

'Space,' the boy says.

'You keep that, okay?'

*

.On the plane she allows herself a sigh of relief. The smells she carries are of packed bodies and recycled air, a sweet, fruity broth of panic – but she has made it, and the evidence has been disposed of. The only thing she has kept is the big blue sticker: an innocuous thing, the kind of thing they might give out in playgroups for children's names. But that too should go. She folds it into a half moon, sticky sides together, and then into smaller and smaller wedges, before tucking it into the pocket in front of her with the onboard shopping magazine. No one will ever open it to see what is written there: *Caitriona Dawson – Pluto.*

'Oh yes, Pluto. That used to be a planet, didn't it?' Barry touched the hand-painted mobile, making it wobble clumsily above their sleeping child. The mobile was a gift from her sister. It has a sun and an Earth and seven other planets, but no Pluto. She didn't notice until the day she returned from maternity hospital.

Pluto was the precious livid piece in her solar system jigsaw, and she always slotted it in last. Today she saw the planet projected huge against the white parchment. It was exactly like the jigsaw; an unfathomable full stop spinning out in space, its surface blotched brightly like the skin of an unburied corpse.

Right to Reply

HIS LATTE WAS tepid when it arrived, grease marbling on its surface; but Louis wasn't going to make a fuss.

When the phone trilled he was standing by the penthouse window looking down on Galway Bay, rolling the wiry tassels of his moustache between thumb and forefinger. His face felt tight and sore, as though exposed too long to the elements. Lola wanted to walk on the beach today, and his skin had already registered the drudgery of it – the heavy sand; the salt-sharpened wind; the scribbles of crusty bladderwrack before the tide. And she would want to drink in a typical Irish pub. It was all such a waste of time, barely worth the pleasure of her unzippable pencil skirts and long, callow throat.

'Your phone,' said Lola.

She laid her fruit salad in a nest of bedsheets and unfolded her legs, curling her tongue over a bloated grape as she reached towards the bedside table. She brought the phone to him and rubbed his back too softly, pressed her lips to his shoulder. The girl was as clingy after sex as he was squeamish.

Louis held the phone to his ear and took a quiet mouthful of the latte. He always let the caller speak first. It was a technique he had learned at a seminar once. It was called 'Keeping the Reins'.

'Louis,' said his sister. He pinched the milk scum from his moustache and stepped away from Lola, lowering his head. *Mammy*, he thought, and in an instant he could see his mother's cheeks fall and flush with shame for him, the disappointment in her voice, *Are you not ashamed?*

'Bertha.'

'How are you?'

'Fine.'

'You haven't seen the paper then.'

It was a Sunday. Dine woke late to find eight missed calls on her phone. Sitting up in bed, her head knocking for caffeine, she rang back.

'Bomama did you call me?'

'Dine,' said her grandmother. 'Darling. When can you come?'

Her grandmother was never good on the phone. Her calls were generally just a summons, or a transfer of information, and she shouted down the receiver as though to cross the great distance between them. Before her husband's final stroke, she often made calls like this, with no greeting, just 'When can you come?' For there were days when he was 'very down', and 'it would do him good to see you.' But by now Dine's grandfather was two years dead.

'Are you alright Bomama?'

'Just come darling will you please? When can you come?'

'I'm getting dressed now. I'll get the next bus.'

'Take a taxi.' Her accent was agitated, clipping her English into a succession of hard, quick taps; *tickataxi*.

'What's wrong?'

'They are saying things about Bompa. Disgusting things.'

They should have known him. If they could have known him they would be ashamed to say these disgusting things about her husband.

Where did they get that photo? Well he was handsome there: his lovely mouth with the lower lip that brimmed to a cliff before the swoop of his chin; his fine neck; his freshly razored jaw. She knew what his skin must have smelled like when that photo was taken – sandalwood shaving

157

soap spiced with morning perspiration, scent of his blood running close beneath. Where did they get that photo of her beautiful husband, and what did they think they were proving, the newspaper men, by overlaying the picture with a grey swastika? 'Shadow from the past,' said the headline, and the swastika was cast clumsily over her husband's face. They would fool no one with a trick like that.

She had been there – this past they thought they could assemble from murmurs and frigid scraps. They could ask her how it was. She could tell them how it was, if they wanted to know.

In school she sat beside a friendly girl called Livina, who holidayed in Germany every break and made fat whirling swastikas all over her copy book. To save water, Livina used a powder that her mother bought in Germany, sprinkled it on her feet, patted it under her arms and worked it through her hair. 'As effective as a good scrub,' she claimed, but she smelled like flour and like bone broth.

They were all Flemish girls in her class, and most had families in the Legion. Grietje remembered the thrill of the Easter play. They went to the school that evening to dress. The nuns had kept the fire in, and the girls huddled at the back of the class, shoulders and hips prickling with cold, tang of warming wool and unwashed feet, and Livina offering around her German powder.

As a child, Grietje was stout with dark brows that met in the middle, and it must have been for comic effect that they made her the devil. Her aunt loaned them the black cape and Sister Thérèse fashioned a headband with squat red horns. She fixed the horns onto Grietje's head, rubbed coal into her brows and pinched her cheek. 'A devil with dimples,' she said. Dressed as angels and lambs, and Grietje as Satan, the girls walked two by two, their amber lanterns brushing slow smudges into the dark. What did they sing as they made their way to the town hall? A church song or something for the Legion? What she remembered was linking arms and singing at the top of her lungs, frost grazing the back of her throat raw.

Like most Flemish children, Grietje was raised Catholic. As a girl she gazed at a white-faced Christ and tried to warm to him, but by the time she put the first baby Louis in the ground she had seen enough of life to mistrust the tender embrace awaiting him. This first child was still a stranger, hardly pulled from her own flesh, when he ended. It was a thing she could choose to bear, like losing a limb. But the second Louis lasted longer. He had already weaned to words and steps, and had nine teeth when he died. And though the third came out here in Ireland, piglet-backed, red-faced as the natives with thin, dangling legs that would carry him up through the years, this solace did nothing to renew for her any meaning beyond the needs of this world.

Until her husband Theo died, the afterlife had seemed to Grietje a horrifying prospect – a world overpopulated with clamouring dead. It was for that reason that she wanted them both cremated – no flesh through which a soul might inch back to sensation, no worms or gases or facial hair growing like grass in the rotting muck that time would make of them. But now she felt him sometimes. He could be beside her, in the chair that sloped to the shape of his sore back, or at her shoulder while she knitted a sampler. Sometimes he was there in the morning, for bed was the worst part – sleeping alone, only her own heat to draw from, no Theo folding his knees up under hers; and waking alone, no breath in her hair, no feet to help into socks. She had said it to her granddaughter Dine – 'Am I getting mad, Dineke? I feel him like he is just here. I can almost hear his voice.' But Dine had just kissed her brow, and then her hand. She had smiled in that sweet, bewildered way that childless women smile at babies.

Theo had lovely feet – long, spare toes lined up in perfect gradients, silky light skin, soles plush like puppy paws.

Grietje left the newspaper spread big on the kitchen table and moved to her armchair to wait for them to come – her children and her grandchildren. One way or another they had all been summoned.

Louis's wife had said he was away for the weekend, 'golfing or something'. She had said it in a stringy voice that let Grietje know what she meant. Well, Bertha would track him down.

Where did they get him from? Her third Louis – round-backed and scald-pink when he came out, indignant squeal from him, then soft suckling as he worked fiercely on his own fist. Grietje had lifted up on her elbows, peered over the Sister's shoulder and she saw the shape of the child and she heard the sound of it and she knew that this time she could not dredge up enough. That was in the clean Coombe hospital where women laboured quietly in close rows of beds, smoked and gossiped between contractions. By the time that happened Grietje was nearly twenty-three. Her heart had shifted and tightened. She held the baby to her skin and tried to believe in him, but her milk turned to pebbles. A kind Sister said she understood, told her to mix an egg yolk with donkey's milk, gave her a glass bottle to take home, and an address for a donkey keeper, and that's how Grietje fed this Louis. He was what they called a 'long baby'. His legs would always be skinny, but he lived, and so did the fat little girls that came after him.

That Sister wrote 'Liam' on the birth certificate, instead of 'Louis'. Theo had to sort it out afterwards. It was a terrible mess, but the Sister meant to be kind, 'For the child's sake, love,' she said. 'You don't want him going through life foreign.'

When Louis was four there was a fire that ate their house to a husk without even licking her children. That was because she bundled all three of them into a buggy, threw a wet blanket over it and pushed it through the door. That was a clever thing to do, but there was also a kind of miracle to the four unblemished corners of the blanket. Afterwards on the scorched lawn an itinerant woman in a white-and-blue shawl said, 'Your troubles are over now.' Theo thought Grietje was tootle-loot when she told him about that woman. She didn't tell him that she thought she recognized her way of peering up from her cowl like something hunted.

Grietje sat with each hand cupping an armrest, her back straight. Into the silence she said, 'Theo,' and the sound embarrassed her but she said it again, 'Theo. Pouske. Theo.'

Theo would have known what to do – such sharp lines he could draw up with words, building them easily into clean logic. But her mind pulled up only a wild, mute grief. The face of a mime she had seen once on Grafton Street – a painted face, all oily white except the eyebrows, and an expression of outrage so comic and sorry it made her eyes sting.

She remembered the journalist, Tiernach, because it was

an unusual name and one she didn't like, and because they had talked so much about him after he had come to the house. She was not tootle-loot yet, for she remembered his face across twenty years, and she had only met him once. He was young and sure of himself, with a triangular little head and pale, fidgety eyes and a smoothness of brow she had only seen on zealots of one kind or another – Jehovah's Witnesses, Christian Brothers, Livina DeSmedt – a sloped brow polished like a shield against uncertainty, salmon scalp clashing under yellow-orange hair.

It was a Wednesday morning when Theo received him. It had been agreed with the editor – the boy could write what he liked, so long as Theo had a right to a written reply. He asked Louis to be there – Louis who was sullenly beginning to learn the ropes. It was a sensitive time for Theo, passing the business on to his son like that, and he could be bossy. Theo sat behind his desk and the journalist on the other side of it, a big flat tape-recorder whirring between them. Louis was given an armchair off at the side. She could remember her son's face lost beneath all that hair, nose perched like an inquisitive bird on his moustache. He had winced when the journalist sneered at the tea she brought in on a tray with buttered biscuits.

'Tea with tea biscuits,' the journalist said. 'Do you Belgians always take things so literally?'

After the Tiernach fellow had left, Theo's neck stretched tall with anger. 'Where are Vincent's standards,' he said, his head jerking as he spoke, 'sending me an ignorant *pestkope* like this? I had to explain him everything – he didn't know a thing about the Flemish – and he accuses me of all kinds! *Got verdomme!* The boy doesn't know where Flanders is on the map. He thought the Flemish Legion was *started* by the SS. *Started by the SS!* Idioot. Idioot. Idioot! He has not even done the smallest research. After all we worked for, all we have given this country, to have some ignorant *pestkope* come in like this . . .'

Louis left with hardly a word. 'Useless boy,' Theo had muttered, 'brainless little cockerel, sitting there with his furry lip saying nothing. Where did we get him from?'

She and Theo talked into the night and in the morning she had typed up Theo's letter to the editor: 'Dear Mr Bell, I do not know my blood type – do you know why? I have no letters tattooed beneath my left arm, nor my right arm either. You are very welcome to check me over . . .' Vincent Bell had pulled the article. He had phoned Theo: 'I appreciate,' he said, 'that in his over-enthusiasm, our young journalist may have jumped to unfounded conclusions. He is not a historian, you see. He does not know the ins and outs perhaps. In any case I do not deem it responsible to publish material that may be slanderous. Let us forget it, Theo. No hard feelings.'

'*May be* slanderous, Vincent?' – Theo's voice travelled all the way down the hallway. From the kitchen she could hear him – '*May* be? I will come to your office right now. I will raise my arms above my head and you can look me over and tell me if you see my blood type written there for that is what the SS did, Vincent, or must I be tattooed as a victim now to prove my innocence?'

Vincent and Theo had patched things up. But Vincent Bell was dead now, and so was her Theo, his voice strangled by the stroke and burned to ash; now the Tiernach fellow could say what he liked.

Schijterd.

Her Theo could never suffer fools or cowards and he was never a hypocrite.

He never lied, even when it was convenient, but Grietje did. Grietje could tell white lies and darker ones too. At the beginning, when they came here and had very little, she could say that she had eaten when she had not; she could lose an early pregnancy and call it a spot of women's trouble. Once she had buried a miscarriage at the back of the garden. She had taken the tea towel from around it so that it would crumble quickly into earth. It had a wizened, long head and frog legs and a tight little penis like a pea shoot. Theo had never known how she could fib. More than a fib was the betrayal about the letter – a lie she still squirmed beneath,

165

but one she knew, all the same, to be a right thing. He was very down when he wrote that letter to Louis. Her poor Louisje. Even if Theo meant what he said, he would not have written such things if it were not for the stroke that was storming his brain, hooking his lip up, stiffening his neck and sending the anger crackling out of him.

She didn't open the letter immediately – the first lie was the nod she gave when he asked had she posted it. She held her breath as she nodded, for the letter was stashed in the lining of her handbag. The second betrayal happened a few days later, after his final stroke. The envelope was sealed with Theo's trusting tongue, but she could not destroy it without reading it first. There were no surprises in the ugly things written there. He was ashamed of his son, he said – Louis had no integrity, he reduced their life's work to profit margins, he went with the herd in everything, had no conscience of his own, he was to be cut out of the will . . . It was true that the pretty teas and massage oils that the firm produced now were not of Theo's standards, but how could they be? Louis could give no more than himself.

Her son had always been a strange child, awkward with people, clumsy with words, given to sickening silences and cold-faced tears. It was a misfortune that Grietje attributed, sometimes, to her petrified breasts and the way that for many weeks after the birth she found she had difficulty looking at the baby's narrow red face. As he grew his shyness hardened to look like arrogance, so that few people ever saw her Louis for who he was.

She had dropped the letter into the fire, so she would not have to think on those things again.

She could remember walking Louis home from school one afternoon. He was clodhopping beside her with his frizzing dark hair and those skinny legs – she knitted him thick, long cotton socks, trying to bulk him up beneath his clothes – it was raining and he was under the umbrella with her, and then he was gone. When she looked back she saw him crouching by a bush. He put his fingers to his lips as she approached, and nodded to a little robin only a foot away, beneath a shelter of leaves. His face then – black, close-set eyes and that queer upper lip; too long and peaked as though it hurt, quivering with awe at the speechless world; the brazenness of the bird, the smell of rain calling worms up from the earth, and his own silence. After a pause she called to him and he began to run, his limbs clattering like a puppet's. All the way home she was warm with the rush of relief, and she said it to Theo that evening, 'There is something in Louis you know. There is something in that boy that people don't often see.'

Her son liked freesias – their scent, and the way each stalk trickled down from a simple bloom to pearly buds. They came from Africa, he told her, and magpies came from India. When he was studying for his finals – poor boy, cramming so painfully on a subject he was not made for; he would have been happier flying an airplane or fiddling with car engines – she would wait until he went downstairs for elevenses, and then she would arrange bouquets of white freesias in his room, angle a bowl of seedless green grapes beside his desklamp. His smile then, a secret smile that made his moustache fan out. 'Thank you Mammy.'

When the phone rang, Grietje cursed, '*Got verdomme,*' because the sound startled her and because, although they had done a wonderful job with the hip replacement, she had pain again – pain standing up from her chair. In any case she didn't like to discuss things on the telephone. 'Just come,' she had told Dine. 'Just come,' she had said to Bertha, who hung wailing at the other end of the phone, 'Mammy. How dare they print a picture of my daddy like that.'

'Just come,' Grietje had said, 'and telephone to Louisje too, will you please? He is off somewhere.'

'Mammy . . .'

'Just telephone to Louis, please Bertha. And pull yourself together darling.'

Yes, it must be Bertha again, calling from her car that way that made her voice sound all alone down the bottom of a well. Before lifting the receiver Grietje settled a kitchen chair up beside the phone. She braced herself for more tears. Bertha would always pull on her like this, she could not be trusted to release Grietje into old age.

'Yah.'

'Nazi bitch,' said the voice – not somebody's real voice, someone speaking in a lower, rougher voice than their own – 'Rot in hell with your Nazi husband.'

'Oh!' Grietje let a whoop that could, in other circumstances have been mistaken for joyous surprise.

She left the receiver springing at the end of the cord while she checked the back door and the front door and set the house alarm. Then she sat in her chair to wait for them to come, her children and her grandchildren. She felt her pulse too quick and hard for her veins, dredging too much excitement from a stock of weary hurt. She thought, *I am an old woman now*. She would not weep, not for some cowardly *schitjerd*, but she covered her face and spoke into her hands, 'Theo.' Death was soon and it was a time for closing, not for opening, and explaining, and assembling and reckoning with the world for all the fragments that time tossed up.

Her granddaughter Dine came first, tapping timidly on the window, her skull pushing blue under colourless skin.

'Poor Dineke,' whispered Grietje, kissing her, for Dine was neglected-looking, hair uncombed and the pouches beneath her eyes tinged with kohl.

'I am sorry to worry you, Dineke.'

'Let's get you some coffee, Bomama,' said Dine. 'Coffee. Let's have some coffee and I'll butter some biscuits.'

Grietje felt brave with her grandchild there, for Dine had Theo's thick, shapely lips and his seriousness... but then Dine showed her another paper. 'What Brews Beneath?' demanded the headline – 'The Belgian herbalist who founded Ireland's leading natural remedy brand may have been a member of the SS...' It was not the headline that startled her, but the picture beneath it – it was a building she had not seen in over sixty years – that building in Brussels that would make you cross the street and take the long way around, because of the cold that came off it, and the terrible things that might have happened there, and the secret Jewess upstairs of their flat, who disappeared so silently that by the time Grietje noticed she could not remember the last time she had heard her slip out by the basement door. To think on her made Grietje's throat block, a drowning feeling in her breath.

There was a documentary that her grandchildren watched and wept at one evening in the living room, and when Grietje said, 'Could it be true, such disgusting things? Don't you think they exaggerate?' they snapped at her and were ashamed of her and said yes and everyone knew it Bomama, you must have known it, and she said she never saw such things, not in Brussels, but she did know that there were small children in factories all day making the clothes that they buy cheap and negroes in slavery for their diamond rings. 'You know that don't you?' she said, 'but also you don't know.' And then even little Dine was ashamed of her and went to vomit in the bathroom. But that was many years ago now.

That upstairs ghost was a quiet old woman all alone, her head always cowled and dipped, a grief-stricken face and no story and never even a *bonjour*. *On the run*, is what they thought, and so they didn't speak of her, even amongst themselves. Not until after, and even then – well, where was the point in going over it?

Was she forgetting something now, now that she was old? Sometimes now, in the night, light silvered like rips in the dark, pelvic curves moving slow, slow – is that a man? Not a man nor a woman. Those are other shapes they plant now into her dark. Those are nightmare shapes and why do they pull her into their nightmares like this? Railway tracks and everybody walking and sorry sorry, but the sorry feeling can come to anyone for there is so much in the world to be sorry for. The sorry feeling does not mean it was she who saw or she who was there on the bone-slivering nights they show now on the television. Some people want angels and all that but all Grietje longs to know is a black night at the end.

They were for a free Flanders, but not for the ugly whispered things. And though they had once been in sympathy with the Germans – though they did not resist when their houses were occupied, though they were obedient and polite with the soldiers – on her parents' street everyone left their back doors unlocked at night, soup and bread on the table, warm blankets ready by the stove and a basin with soap and washcloths. Would they have done it if the first Louis was still alive? That was a thing she sometimes wondered. The difference between sacrifice and suicide, Grietje knew, all lay with the right witness. She could have been more curious about that building, and about the whispered things, but Grietje did not think so much of herself to believe her curiosity could veer the course of history.

'They are saying Bompa worked there, Bomama. Do you know anything about that building?'

Grietje was cold from remembering that building and the whispered things, and the way it could suck the voice and the heat from you just by standing there so tall above the pavement. She laughed to push out the insult, but the anger made it come out wrong; a snicker.

'Why are they inventing? You have no idea...' she said,

'what that building was. We none of us could bear to walk that street, for the shadow of that building...'

Grietje heard her own voice tremble and trip. Was Dine not ashamed to ask such things, she who was born so far from it all? She who once loved to sit on Theo's belly with her bottle, head nestled back in Theo's neck and her legs crossed at the ankles? As a little one Dine brought her grandfather wounded things – snails with cracked shells, earthbound birds – as though he could heal all. There was a time she wrote him poems about endangered species and acid rain. Theo had kept them in a blue folder.

'What about the Flemish Legion, Bomama? That's what they say... that the Legion joined with the SS and that Bompa was in the Legion and that's the connection, you see, that they are making,'

'*Connection*, Dine? The *connection*?'

'Well... or the leap. The leap they are making. They think that means he worked there...'

'Ha! Suddenly the communists were a fine people?'

'The communists? No, that's—'

'They have the time of things wrong. With the Legion he was on the Eastern Front,' she said, 'against communism. That was much before occupation – though then, you know, we were in sympathy with the Germans then. The communists wanted to take over the world and there were things that came out about them too you know, you know what gulags are, don't you? You don't blame the communists for that, do you? You think they were so much better than the Germans?'

'No Bomama, I'm not saying that. No one is saying that . . .'

'It was only right to fight against Russia, doesn't matter with who – the things that were happening. You know about it, Dine, Bompa must have told you? And when they hear he fought the communists they say he was a Jew killer? You think the communists spared Jews?'

'Don't say "Jew killer", Bomama. If you are talking about this, please don't say that. It might sound – people might take it the wrong way.'

Grietje wrapped her fingers tight over each armrest and looked at her granddaughter. Dine had the moon-bright skin of an early baby, and it seemed to glisten now, slicked over her temples like something less solid.

For this she had carried herself away from Belgium, her hair bleached lurid rust to match the passport, the third Louis pushing her old stretch marks fresh, so that all the flesh she sent out after that would be new, all her children and her grandchildren. She had named him for his lost brothers, but she never spoke her mother tongue to the new Louis. She wanted no way back to Belgium, the rotten gendarmes or the girlish nonsense of nationalism.

She could have slapped Dine, she could have torn up the paper. Instead she nodded and clicked her tongue against the roof of her mouth.

'Yah. Don't say this Bomama, and don't say that Bomama, but who was there, Dineke – you or me? I can say how it was. I hide nothing and I tell how it was and they can check it and check it and make their stories but it was me who was there, not this little *schijterd* with his inventions and not you my darling! Oh after the war you could not speak. No one had an opinion on anything – how is it possible? No one saying a word about anything. And we mixed together in the evenings – a great big Russian with bullet wounds in his back and shoulder, and when he drank he would open his shirt and show us and tell such stories you wouldn't believe; and a woman with the painted red lips of a gypsy and no one giving their real name . . . All the Russians were called Richard and every word we spoke was salted. They locked me up, you know. They locked me up for three months – threw me in a van with abortionists and all sorts – disgusting women – and my sister too, because the postman said we had a picture of Hitler over the piano – of all the stupid things. That was the kind of stupidity and spite that was happening. For three months I waited to hear what I was accused of – and it was that Walloon postman, saying I had a picture, framed, over the piano . . .'

Her granddaughter drank coffee and let her speak, squinting sometimes as though trying to make her out from a distance. Such a terrible glow from her skin.

'It was not for fun that your Bompa fought on the Eastern Front. Theo who could not see a rabbit shot in the field, you think it was for fun or for murder he went to the front? There is no shame in it and he never lied about it. He was there two weeks. It made him so sick he passed blood and they let him home for stomach ulcers and is it for that they say these disgusting things? I will answer. They said he could reply and then they wait until he is gone to spit at us. Well I will make my reply for them.'

'Okay, we'll give an answer. Let me write it down, Bomama . . . or maybe we should get a journalist to come. What do you think? To hear your reply? Will I get someone to come, Bomama, and write an article with your side?'

'Would you? Yes. Yes, that is what you do, Dine. Do that will you please?'

She would tell them how it was, but how could she begin? They wanted a story that ran glossy and clean as ribbon like their own, not the convoluted knots of sixty years ago.

It was like when she first arrived here, nodding and frowning to facial cues, unable to shape her mouth to the new language, saying only things she had the words for because what she meant would take so many unknown sounds.

'You know, don't you, what they did to us? The Walloons? You know when our baby boy was sick, how the gendarmes laughed at us? They laughed at him burning up in my arms, the eyes nearly popping with pain, his arms slapping out, and they would not allow us to call the hospital, they laughed and said, "No loss, we do not want more Flemish muzzles yapping at our heels..."'

'Don't think about that now, Bomama.' Dine's face seemed to shrink to the frame. She smiled a sore smile, her Irish-blue eyes edging shame. Such terrible white skin, like Theo's sister. 'Don't talk about the Walloons, Bomama, if they interview you, or the evil Russians!'

'Dine, you are pale darling,' said Grietje. 'I hope you are getting enough sleep.'

And was it the ream of morning light that beaded along the bones of her face, but Grietje thought she saw an unhappy laugh ripple over the big, sad lips of her frowning grandchild.

When the bell rang, Dine gave her grandmother a kiss for reassurance, and left the room, closing the door quietly behind her. The front door of her grandmother's house had a rectangular hatch set at eye level. It opened onto a window of diamond-patterned bars. As children, Dine and her cousins used to stand on chairs either side of the door, opening and closing the hatch, exchanging secrets and coded notes through the diamonds. Like a church, or a hospice, the house had fixed her into tiptoeing slowness, and she almost put her finger to her lips as she unlatched the little hatch. Through the bars she saw Billy standing on the doorstep, jigging in the bright cold. There were patches of dust-coloured hair daubed across his face and neck. Billy was a stocky man, all mild angles, wobbly throat, kind grey eyes and clean, blunt fingers. He wore his knapsack secure over both shoulders, each hand clinging tight to a strap.

'Hey,' Dine whispered, 'hang on till I get the alarm.'

He nodded. He was trying to look solemn, she could see, but the excitement twitched in his cheeks. Billy's father had once been a very successful journalist. At university Billy was president of the History Society, editor of the college paper, a leading member of the LGBT society, a great debater, but since graduating he'd had only a few articles published – dense, essayish things that, he complained, had pivotal chunks clumsily cut at the last minute. This could be a proper story for him.

She opened the door only enough to admit him.

'It's warm in here,' said Billy. He gave Dine a brief hug before tugging off his scarf.

She nodded. 'I like the beard. When did that happen?'

'Oh . . .' he rubbed a palm back and forth across his jaw,

'it's not quite there yet. I – Paul likes it so . . . But how are you doing, with all this? Disgusting, isn't it? I would have thought the paper still had some standards. Things like this have their own momentum, it only takes one irresponsible journalist . . .'

Dine shrugged. 'She's upset, Billy,' she said, 'and shocked. Just see what she wants to say, that's all. Don't push for a story, okay?'

'Can I see this right-to-reply letter? They will only publish if we have that . . .'

'It's not here, but we have it. I'll have it by tomorrow . . .'

She led him into the kitchen where the fire's heat swelled viciously and blocks of yellow sunlight cut the tablecloth. As Dine entered she saw a private frown pass over her grandmother's face. Her eyes moved from Dine to Billy, and she touched her hair briefly, smoothed a hurried finger sternly along each eyebrow. A painful impulse kicked in Dine – she wanted to wrap herself over her grandmother.

'This is Billy, Bomama,' she said, 'he's going to hear your side of things.'

'Yah.' Bomama's lips closed small, her cheeks tightened. 'Hallo,' she said. She pushed herself to her feet, one palm flat on the table as she leaned to shake Billy's hand. Dine's grandmother had big, bony hands. The pads of her fingers tapered flat to the strong curve of her nails.

'Sit down, Billy,' said Dine. 'Tea or coffee?'

'Oh tea please, if you have it.'

'Dineke darling, get me my hand cream will you please? It's in my handbag.'

Dine flicked the kettle to boil and rummaged in her grandmother's handbag, 'Sit down, Billy,' she said.

Billy rested his bag on a chair and unzipped it. 'Mrs Tack, do you mind if I record this?' He removed a silver contraption the size of a small wallet.

'Oh. Well. Dineke, what do you think darling?'

'It's up to you, Bomama. It's handy for Billy, so that he can remember exactly what you say.'

'Yes okay. Whatever you think.'

'Don't worry, Bomama. Billy is here to help. Two sugars, Billy?'

'Just one now,' he said, 'I'm trying to cut down...' Then he turned to her grandmother. 'Don't worry, Mrs Tack. I'll explain what you tell me. I'm a historian really – my thesis was on twentieth-century independence movements... Just to say, you know, I am aware of the complexity of these things. My father says Tiernach Mac Mahon is a notorious ignoramus... He says his name has no place on a broadsheet...'

Dine set Billy's tea in front of him, and sat beside her grandmother. 'Drink your coffee, Bomama,' she said, kissing the large hand which scrunched her fingers in an oily grip of rose-scented hand cream, leaving only Dine's thumb to rub back and forth, back and forth over the raised veins, the waxy skin stretched thin as a drum across the bones, and a single brown age spot, raised like the blisters on the flat-bread she used to make.

'We will sort this out, Bomama. We will sort this out together.'

Billy pressed a button on the recorder and placed it in the centre of the table.

'Do you want me to put some questions to you, Mrs Tack? Or do you know what you want to say?'

She shook her head and straightened her back, released Dine's hand and grabbed it back again. After a silence her voice came thin. 'You should have known him.'

It sounded guarded and hard. She took a breath to say something, but swallowed instead. Dine rubbed her hand again, and her grandmother repeated the words as though to herself.

'You should have known him.'

'Well,' said Billy, 'well, I am here so that you can tell me about him, Mrs Tack. Tell me why Mac Mahon is incorrect? Mr Tack was listed somewhere as a translator. Mac Mahon is saying that translator was code for interrogator, so maybe if you tell us about his translating job . . .'

'He got a job, for a few months, translating local papers

into German and French. He needed a job... they were gossip papers. We used to laugh about them – advice on how to manage your wife and so on...'

'Okay,' said Billy.

'You know, Dine will know this – when Theo was nineteen, all in the Legion swore allegiance to Hitler, but he refused. We didn't think all these ugly things about the Germans then – that wasn't why – it was just because he had already sworn allegiance to the King. "How can I swear to both?" he said, and he was quite right. "It is not logical," he said. Nobody took it in bad part. Theo could be particular like that. That was the kind of man he was. He would not lie. You know, Billy, it is important to say it – that was a terrible building. He was never inside that building...'

The phone rang again and her hands flew up like a flurry of startled birds. 'Oh – don't answer it, Dine!'

'But Bomama—'

'Leave it. Don't answer.'

Billy looked at the table.

'It's probably Mammy, Bomama, or Aunty Bertha. They'll worry if you don't answer.'

The ringing stopped, but just as Dine drew breath, it began again.

'If it is some halfwit you just hang up, Dineke.'

'Okay, Bomama.'

'Hello?' There was silence on the other end. She tried to sound nonchalant. 'Hello?'

'I'd like to speak to my mother.'

'Hi Louis.'

Uncle Louis was always uncomfortable. As children Dine and her cousins were afraid of him, for he was one of those rogue adults with the demeanour of a slighted child. He would scoop children up by the ankles and hang them upside down for too long, his face set in a sardonic scowl until one of his sisters found an excuse to retrieve them from his clutches. The other thing he would do was rub balloons on their hair to make it stand up. Sometimes, when babysitters did that it was funny, but there was nothing light-hearted about Uncle Louis; that was the problem. He rubbed so hard that their heads burned. Even when he smiled there was a shadow pressing on his brow. Instead of putting them at ease, the sense that he was not actually grown-up under the moustache, but another awkward child like them, was cut with danger.

'Bomama,' said Dine, 'it's Uncle Louis.'

'Oh Louisje!'

With her daughters and her granddaughters, Bomama was clucky and bossy, but Louis brought on a sort of cheek-flushing heartbreak in her and she stood now, as though in honour the caller. When Louis came to the house the

children used to disappear to the back of the garden, and
Bompa retreated to his study, but Bomama bustled for tea,
hung on his every word. Uncle Louis liked to stay standing
while everyone else sat. He had a proud way of delivering
a small piece of information, or a statistic that he had
gleaned from the daily news. Straight-backed at the kitchen
table, each hand lightly touching Bomama's embroidered
tablecloth, looking straight ahead at no one, he would kick
all sorts of banalities out from beneath his moustache, while
his mother nodded. 'Oh yes you have it, you are right Louis.'
When Dine got older she learned to sit in the kitchen and
pretend to listen to Uncle Louis too, because it hurt Bomama
that Bompa never gave him much regard.

'Move my chair up to the phone would you, Dine?'

Her grandmother settled herself in the chair and spoke her
son's name like a sigh, 'Louis.' She clutched the phone to
her head with both hands, nodding. 'Have you? Well if you
think so, Louisje . . . Now I need you to get something from
Daddy's files, Louis. You will find it in his letters from 1985, I
think . . . the right to reply, yes, that is important, Louis . . . No,
only Dine. The others will come. And a friend too. A friend of
Dine's. A journalist . . . Oh well he seems very nice you know.
It is a friend from the university.' Then she cupped her mouth
with her hand, and lowered the pitch – but not the volume –
of her voice. 'I think he is of a *special kind* if you are with me.

Nice to his mother I would say, but they can be very nice too, those fellows, you know. He is writing down the real thing, explaining what Theo did in those years, and all about the Legion, you know... Oh do they? Well I don't know, Louisje. Do they yah? Well you know best... But he seems to know a lot about the history. We have the right to reply, Louis – Daddy made sure of it so you find that letter, yah?'

Her grandmother stopped speaking then. Red patches blossomed high on her cheeks. The sag beneath her jaw began to tremble, and she lowered one hand onto her lap. Dine mouthed, *Okay?* and her grandmother rolled her eyes theatrically, but she lodged the phone between cheek and shoulder and began to rub hard at the age spot at the back of her hand, harder and harder, as though scrubbing at a stain. After a while she held the phone at arm's length, her face spattered red as fresh burns. 'Dine. Your uncle wants to speak with you.'

Dine took the phone, leaning her back against the sink. 'Hi Louis.' After a silence she said it again, 'Hello Louis, would you like to speak to me?'

She was about to hang up when his voice came low and steady. 'Dine. Get that journalist out of my mother's house.'

'Billy is a friend, Louis. We are helping Bomama to write Bompa's reply.'

'There will be no reply.'

185

'Well Louis, Bomama would like to write a reply, and we are helping her.'

After a pause, he pronounced, 'I am the head of this family.' Some loyalty to her grandmother stirred with embarrassment for him; the steadiness in his voice, and each word spoken deadpan like a magic spell that might conjure him into greatness. She could hear him suck a breath before he said it again, 'I am the head of this family.' This time he said it in protest and yearning and bald insistence, like a brave child, '. . . and you, Dine, are way down the pecking order.'

'The pecking order, Louis?'

Dine remembered it suddenly – one summer when Uncle Louis shaved the moustache. She saw his naked upper lip, a wavy, hurt-looking thing, flinching like a snail.

Billy was looking up at Dine from his downturned head. Her grandmother was moving her gaze eagerly from Dine's face to her own hands, to Dine's face, and back to her hands where she had drawn blood by scratching at the thin skin of the age spot.

'Dine,' Louis said, 'I am giving you twenty minutes to leave my mother's house, with your faggot friend. I am coming now and if you are still there when I arrive . . .'

'Yes, Louis?'

'You will regret it.'

When Dine hung up, her grandmother said, 'Well. Louis is

a special one. Many people do not understand him very well. It caused Theo to wonder a lot, you know. Where did we get him from?'

She would often say, 'There is something in Louis, that people don't often see...' Her favourite proof was, 'You know he built half an airplane, once?'

For Dine this had once added an exciting dimension to her strange uncle. He was a teenager when he built it, and it was still in the shed. 'Ask him to show you,' Bomama would say, but Uncle Louis had a way of raising his eyebrows if anyone spoke to him, as though to demonstrate how unimpressed he was, how unsurprised he would be by anything they might try on him.

On Dine's phone a text came up:

Dine this is Bertha. Do not be flattered and tricked by that journalist. Do not be naïve and lured into a trap. We have hired the most expensive PR team in the country. Please stay out of it or you will regret it.

With a surge of pride Dine wrote,

Is naked propaganda really the way to go?

When Bomama spoke of that plane, the grandchildren

imagined baked-bean cans rolled out and soldered together to form the body; skeletal bat wings covered in parchment, Uncle Louis an unlikely genius, twiddling tiny cogs and bolts, fashioning an engine from old bikes and bits of oven. When they finally snuck to the garage to look, they left quickly in silent disappointment. It turned out he had bought the parts and assembled the plane like a very expensive Lego kit; no wings, just the nose.

Billy looked into the bottom of his mug. 'Mrs Tack, would you like to leave it for today?'

'Leave it? Oh no. No I will reply. I have the right to reply, you know? Theo made sure of it. But we should be quick you know, my son Louis has some funny ideas. Always buying. Theo said we gave him too much money. You know he has a fish tank that makes the wall of his kitchen? Tropical fish in it. Poor Louisje.'

Billy rewound his tape and placed the recorder back in the middle of the table.

'Okay,' he said, 'remember this is a reply, so try, if you can, to answer each of the suspicions that Mac Mahon has raised.'

'You should have known him.'

Lola had offered to come to the office with him, but Louis dropped her at the crossroads near her house, ignoring her pout and sigh. He would put an end to all that Lola nonsense soon. Not today – he hadn't the energy for it – but soon.

He swiped his ID card at the staff entrance and made his way across the lobby, head down to avoid the gaze of his father's portrait. An old, slow-shutter black-and-white picture taken in the garden while he sniffed at some knobbled twig, his eyes serious and his lips breaking a smile, it was a thing Louis regretted the moment he first saw it installed. He had done it for his mother, though, because his father had died only six months before the new lab was finished. Perhaps it was also for the sentimental nagging that came with his father's death, the guilt at the perfect revenge that fate had wrought on him. That the man who could never suffer fools should be reduced to a kicking infant had given Louis more satisfaction than he could reckon with. The portrait was as high as a man, each pixel impregnated in plastic resin. It was mostly for her that he had done it, but when his mother saw it she had said to him, 'Well *Got verdomme* Louisje, where did you get such flashy taste from?'

As he mounted the stairs, Louis ran his fingers along the metallic wipe-down walls. He was proud of the impersonal functionality of the new building – the faintly green walls and the hospital smell that meant business.

His parents had started their firm at home in the back room. They maintained a desperate intimacy with their staff

– loaning them money, cooking them lunch. His mother even cleaned the house of the handyman when his wife was ill, and when the itinerant girl whom they hired cheap as a lab assistant said she was moving to Liverpool, his father made his way to the caravan site, dressed in his brown suit, head high on that skinny neck, believing, like some fool, that he could talk the family into letting her stay. Oblivious to his thick accent and foreign head, his father always thought he could set his own rules, deaf to snickers and blind to sneers, and retreating always into a sterile stoicism. These were the humiliations that had punctuated Louis's teen years, but by then his family name was known all over the country, and being a Tack was something to be proud of. It got him onto the rugby team, and they had so much money that he had his own car to drive to school in.

His sisters didn't remember what it was like at the beginning. Their parents worked all day and much of the night and Mammy went without medicine sometimes, because an order was worth more than her own health. At first it was just them: Mammy mixing and typing and posting and filing and delivering; Daddy weeding and planting, writing advertisements and phoning, visiting the pharmacies and coming home with a grin for every tiny sale. Bitters was the thing they had started with – a complex goo of twenty-two herbs and roots. It was fermented for eight weeks and every day his mother turned each bottle at a certain angle according to the moon. For years, the hotpress was full of bitters. The smell of it, solemn as bile, thickened the air of that windowless back room. They got a secretary in first, and a delivery man, but still his mother did all the disinfecting and chopping and mixing. The palms of her hands were scratched and yellow from powdering roots.

There were colleagues who thought Louis had been handed a golden goose for nothing. There were those, Louis knew, who sneered at nepotism and his graduate degree, but they did not know how he had paid. Louis had taken nothing from his father that he had not earned with his mother's absence and exhaustion, with the strangle-ache of those nights he woke to find her downstairs with a single lamp, still in her house frock, still crushing and chopping and measuring according to his father's instructions, her hands fluttering up when he startled her. 'Oh Louisje darling . . .' kneading the cold from her hip as she kissed him, then knitting while she watched him drink his camomile, the fine grey needles clacking softly and the socks towering down around and around beneath her hands. The stench of flax seeds boiling to molten glue on the camping stove.

And he'd laboured for his inheritance – all those afternoons he'd spent harvesting herb leaves and scraping the dirt from the roots – never quickly enough, and never cleanly enough for his father. Then the quiet days in the living room with his little sisters, a jigsaw that spelled CAT, paper airplanes made from old invoices to shush the girls because Daddy was researching, or Daddy was angry over a spoiled batch, or Daddy was showing the garden to a client. Louis's father may not have been a Nazi, but he was certainly a tyrant, and Louis had paid for his life's wealth in his mother's flushing cheeks, her pushed-down tears, the sneaking she did, back then, to make it seem she had enough when she did not – dandelion salad for her supper, water in the milk, the dregs of the teapot to bathe her eyes.

He had not told his mother – there was no need, she need never find out – that they would be discontinuing their signature Tack Bitters. The concoction must have worked at some time, for some reason, but along the way they had tweaked it here or there, and at last the mixture had lost its power. Few bought it now, and those who did sent letters to say that it tasted like tar and stained their teeth and did nothing to cure them.

His mother had given everything to his father's name. All of this stuff in the papers would upset her terribly, he knew, and she should be kept out of it. He had warned Bertha not to get hysterical, and he had tried to speak to Mammy on the phone – 'Yes yes Louisje . . .' – it was the voice she used to respond to his father's rants, not listening but only soothing,

'Yes Theo, yes,' the blush climbing her cheeks, the way she hurried the conversation closed – 'Yes, yes Louisje . . .' It was as if his father was at her shoulder, for it was the same yessing she did always for Daddy, smoothing things over, tucking things away, agreeing with everyone.

On the second flight of stairs Louis wondered why he hadn't taken the lift – he was eager to find the file and get that troublemaker out of his mother's house. The eldest grandchild, Dine, had always been an attention-seeking, interfering little bitch, but somehow she had his mother wrapped around her finger. She was his sister Josephine's. Josephine had her young, and it was his mother who ended up minding her. As soon as she was born her picture appeared all over his parents' house. This was followed by lumps of clay, rocks painted like ladybirds, framed certificates for one thing or another. The two often spoke intimately together, heads bowed, and at his father's funeral it was Dine who rocked his mother back and forth, back and forth as she wept.

His sister Bertha told him that she had often seen their mother pay for Dine's taxi like she was some sort of princess. She was always giving her gifts, she even gave her his father's pen after he had died, and once, he found them at the dining-room table, leafing through a small photo album of his mother's first child.

Now the girl was studying pharmaceuticals – of course she was – and his mother had told him already that he was to give her a job at the firm.

Louis had put on weight. His breath was sore when he reached his office and he had to sit for a moment and take a drink from the water cooler, before searching out the key for the file. The water was so cold it hurt his teeth. That was another thing his mother objected to – the water cooler. She said it was a waste of electricity, and that it was healthier to drink room-temperature water.

After his father's death, he and his sisters had cleaned out the office. Bertha had suggested, and probably she was right, that it was best to clear out their father's things now, and do the room up. They had agreed already that they would sell the house after their mother died, and it was best not to have too much work to do on it when the time came. It had given him pleasure to take a blank cardboard box and jumble together all those papers that his father had kept in painstaking order, that careful, slanted handwriting. He told his mother he was keeping them safe, and he had driven straight here to his new, clean office, and pushed the box onto the highest shelf of his file room.

He remembered exactly where the box was – at the very

end of the room on the cold metal shelves, a spot labelled 'Private'. He was panting when he set it down on his desk.

The item at the top was a shock – he had forgotten about that. It was a hardbacked book with lemon-yellow pages and pink lines. There was a white label stuck on the front, and in soft, knife-sharpened pencil his father had written, *Louis (III)*. He did not need to open it, for he knew what was there. His mother knew too. He had seen her peering around the kitchen door as he left his father's office with the ledger in his hand. He could see by the droop at the corner of her eyes that she knew, but whatever she thought of it all, she would never say.

His father gave it to him the day after his graduation – a miserable event at which his father complained about the uncomfortable chairs, the 'pomp', the cold, the vanity of graduation photos, and his mother kept her jaw shut tight, for she had left school at fourteen, and she felt her accent and her knowledge and her dress all wrong for the setting.

Over breakfast the next morning, she told him, 'Daddy will have his elevenses in the office today, you are to join him.'

When he arrived the tea tray was already there on the desk – an almond finger for his father, some buttered tea biscuits, the metal teapot and the two cups, their gleaming white interiors gaping in their saucers. His father beamed at him.

'Now, Louis,' he said, 'you are a man.'

In the book, his parents had logged every penny they had ever spent on him – new shoelaces, piano lessons, the car.

He did not know why he had kept that book. He pushed it at his wastepaper basket, but it was too wide.

Next in the box was a blue envelope folder made of thin card. The sticker across it said 'DINE'. It had been written in the same smudging lead, but with a child's hand. The backwards D had been rubbed out and rewritten. Louis had expected to find the same thing in there – all the taxis and the school fees which, he knew, his parents must have paid for her. But the folder saying 'DINE' contained objects of her own authoring: splodgy paintings, handmade birthday cards, scribbled rhymes. There were other folders too – for Bertha and Josephine there were bits of paper that amounted to love letters. His father had written out the funny things they said as children, he had collected photographs of places they had been together: 'Theo and Bertha a nice day in the Park'; 'JoJo falls asleep in the Camomile'...

Louis stacked all of these useless things on his desk. He had taken them all from his parents' house in a post-funeral trance, and now he did not know what to do with them. He should find that letter about the reply. His mother was getting herself all worked up about it.

He hadn't mentioned all that to the PR team. He would be

meeting them later that day, but on the phone the assistant had advised that today's newspapers were the fish-and-chip wrappers of tomorrow. Often, said the expert, the best thing to do with a scandal was to do nothing – particularly where a business was concerned. People wanted to buy and they wanted to forget any reason not to. Why remind them of something they were already forgetting?

But his niece was there working his mother up into a fret. By the time he arrived she would be all set to go with her reply and there would be no talking her down. He knew how it would go. 'Yah,' she would say, 'yah you are right Louisje.' But she would go ahead and do what she wanted anyway, and what she wanted was whatever that bony-arsed little bitch told her.

The letter was in its very own folder with 'TRIBUNE' written across the front. There were three letters inside, and a clipping from the paper, a picture of Josephine cutting a ribbon. It was the opening of his parents' first lab. 'Tack Herbals to Employ 150 Staff Members', said the headline.

The important letter was there. 'Right to Reply 1985 Me/ Vincent Bell' was written along the top in his father's hand.

'Dear Mr Tack,' the letter began, 'I hereby confirm that, should the upcoming interview with our journalist, Tiernach Mac Mahon, result in an article of any sort, or quotes of any sort, this article will first be read by you in order to allow you the opportunity to reply as you see fit. I hereby agree to publish your full reply, notwithstanding . . .'

Louis did not have much time. His mother would be waiting for him to come, moving to the window with her sore hip, and back again, sitting and standing and rubbing her hands. She would phone him soon, he knew, wondering where he was.

He piled them back into the box and brought them down in the lift. Several times he had to set the box on the floor and swipe his card – to activate the lift, to access the lobby . . . He crossed his father's giant portrait which was – his mother was right – in poor taste. He balanced the box in one elbow while he swiped himself into the photocopier room. Inside, the air was caustic with paper fibres, toner dust, the eye-tingling ozone from all that photocopying and scanning and faxing. He glanced up at the air vent before letting the door swing shut behind him.

There was a plywood table in the centre of the room, and the walls were lined with grey and white machines – the sleek new colour copier, the laminating press, the humpbacked shredder. Louis set the box on the table and removed the lid. He began with the ledger, and he was surprised how little it hurt as the shredder ate and spat, ate and spewed. One by one the yellow pages went quietly into the great machine.

Dolls

SUZANNE STUCK THE plastic bottle under my nose and said something. A question, but I couldn't understand it. She sniffed at the open neck and spoke again, her eyes steadying on mine to press at the meaning.

I understood the last word – *puew* – just because of the way the sound shot out and made her mouth pull high and round as though readying to spit, but I wasn't going to make that leap of effort.

She had forgotten our appointment. Instead of the ritual sliced apple, pencil and paper that drew me daily from the slippery riversides of that summer, the table held the kind of useless trinkets left over after a car boot sale. For a moment I thought Suzanne was preparing for the *vide grenier* – attic clearing. My cousins had told me all about it – the day when the neighbours would bring their unwanted clutter to sell in the half-used car park of the village train station. It happened every year, they said; there would be candyfloss and we would be allowed to buy some, and if we went back at the end of the day people would give us things for free. Last year, my cousin Annie had been given a flowering cactus plant, a stag beetle preserved in a cube of resin, and a cheese board with real horn trimmings to give to her mother. She had shown me the insect – a thrilling thing to hold in your hand and turn about under the lamplight. You could see the sorry frailty of its underside and the spectrum of pigments mingling in the black of its shell. I had been hoping to obtain something like it when the time came.

But the items set in careful clusters on Suzanne's kitchen table were things touched too intimately with another's ownership to ever become a prized possession. There was an upholstered jewellery box, its folds clogged with dust and a woozy pallor across the lid where years of sun exposure had pulled the colour from the once-pink satin. A small plaster-cast dolphin emerged pompously from crumbling waves. A wax octopus held an unlit candle in each tentacle. In the centre of the table lay a heap of plastic dolls, twisted and naked but for one Barbie's tiny glittering heels.

Usually Suzanne was considerate with me, speaking slowly, miming with a dedicated zeal the words I couldn't catch.

I was her *petite fille irlandaise* – little Irish girl, and when she said that my cheeks went hot and sometimes she hugged me to her loose throat. But she was speaking too fast now and I couldn't unpick the phrase into its component words. To show incomprehension I shrugged, stuck my lower lip out and pushed a fart sound through my mouth. It was a gesture I had learned since moving here. It could be used to mean 'I don't care' or 'I don't know' or a range of negatives in between. Suzanne pushed the bottle at me with hurtful impatience, and when I continued to stand dumb she gave a reluctant sigh and used that deep, slow voice she had for speaking English: 'Dez eet smelle?'

I sniffed the bottle and shook my head, but she took it from me anyway, sniffed it and scowled and turned towards the sink. As she waited for the bottle to fill I thought I saw her taut form fold against the draining board like a lapse in concentration. Then her neck stiffened and her shoulders squared, and her parts were pulled back in together by a deep, loud gasp. She turned the bottle upside down and let the water glug out. Still with her back to me she gave the explanation: '*Brigitte m'a envoyé un SMS.*'

I tried to wipe the sting from my face before she turned around. It was the way she spoke her daughter's name – the *Br* and the *gi* plunging down into her gut – depths impenetrable to me – and then the pretty, sorrowful inflection at the end;

the lovely sounds she had given her daughter to know herself by: *Brigitte*.

My name was Alison. These days it is Ali, because the French have a particularly ugly way of pronouncing the full name: *Aleezun*.

I had no memory of my mother speaking my name. She called me 'her' – 'I can't stand the sight of her.'

I had used gestures and a dictionary to tell Suzanne this and she had not cocked her head in pity. She had written the new words out for me, and made me conjugate the verbs. '*Et voilà*,' she said, '*les mots pour raconter votre histoire*' – the words to tell your story. Suzanne said I was lucky to have an uncle with a kind wife, and my warm, unruly cousins. My father had done the right thing. I would settle in fine.

Most days I neither thought nor spoke of my mother at all, but sometimes, while I was working, Suzanne would look at the table and push a question into the silence, a hint of incredulity in the tilt of her brow – What did I mean about my mother's nails? What was I trying to say about her nails? It pleased me to think that Suzanne mused over such things. It made me light and giddy, to think that she must have been playing my story over and over, fleshing it out for me with her adult mind and strange words.

The nails – I told Suzanne about my mother clawing for my face and being wheeled off, and me standing to let her do it, and disappointed then when the room was empty – and I wondered if she believed me or if she suspected I was leaving certain bits out, if she knew, and was too polite to say, that it was some dark, jagged thing in me that made my mother the way she was. I tried to lend plausibility to my story by telling her the medical bits, but it all slipped into moments and scenes – my mother's voice, or the slide of her jaw, or the way my father's chest would swell with sucking in his sighs. I knew that my mother hadn't always been ill and I knew I had heard, over and over, the name for what was wrong, but the word – even the English word – wouldn't come to me. So I told Suzanne instead about how my mother's hands shook more and more. I tried to describe how pain twisted her face and shrank her hands to the curling gristle of chicken feet. I had some vague idea that she was expected to die soon; the conclusion to a chain of broken neurons that my birth had set going, but I didn't tell Suzanne this.

Once, while I was conjugating *aller* – to go, Suzanne, who had been gazing attentively at the moving pencil, suddenly looked at my face and puffed out through soft lips – a dignified version of the fart sound. '*Mais*. . .' Her head made a gulping dip, as though drinking in some sudden information. She spun a pencil between her fingers and watched it as she spoke. Motherhood is a strange thing, she said. The birth of her Brigitte had made her mad, '*une tsunami de sentiment*'.

She had been afraid of drowning in it; the love was too much. Sometimes it just goes wrong, said Suzanne, and there is no one to blame. Things go wrong. '*Et voilà.*'

Suzanne placed the washed bottle on the draining board and bent to the cupboard beneath the sink. She took out a tall, pale green bottle with a cap on it as big as a cup. It was the same fabric softener my aunt used for the baby's blankets. The label showed the hand of an infant, fingers open in sleep and a feather resting on the puff palm. She unscrewed the cap, poured some of the softener into the empty bottle, and topped it up with water from the sink. Then she screwed on a spray-pump, shook the bottle and shot a spritz at the air, releasing the sweet, sleepy musk into a room more familiar with the odours of bleach, cigarette smoke, and perpetually stewing coffee. Suzanne used bleach for everything – a blocked toilet or an infected toe. The merciless smell of chlorine still sends a thrill of love into me.

I wanted to ask about our lesson. She had told me to come at half past ten and not to be late, and I had left a promising snake hunt and rushed to her flat, afraid of disappointing her. As she came towards the table I prepared to speak, but her mouth was set in a hard, distracted silence that sent my mind scrambling and slipping on the vocabulary that she was keeper of, and the questions collapsed in my mouth.

She picked up the jewellery box and made several twists to a key on the side. Eyes all expectation, she pushed it bluntly towards me: '*Ouvre*' – open.

When I didn't move, she nudged the air with her chin: '*Ouvre.*'

The inside smelled neglected and unclean, like the dirtier corners of basements. There was a removable shelf in a darker pink satin flecked with mould. It had little clefts for the rings and rectangular compartments for earrings. A tiny plastic ballerina twirled to a weary melody. She had a tutu made from gauze and a hurriedly painted mouth, slightly off centre.

'*Belle – eh?*' said Suzanne. The music began to fade and blur as though the box was slowly drowning.

Suzanne took it from me and wound the key again. She put it to her ear. '*Ça marche?*' – does it work? She was going deaf. The doctor had told her she had twenty-five per cent hearing and it would get worse. He wanted her to have an operation, but Suzanne could read lips and hands and faces. She said she got along fine so long as she had her sight.

I nodded, '*Ça marche,*' as the music began to sink again. She lifted out the insert to show me the snarl of jewellery beneath, and untangled one of the rings – a bulbous thing made from glass in a jelly-sweet shade of blue. She put it on her pinkie and sighed wetly, and for a moment I was afraid that tears would bubble up from her throat.

'*Voilà.*'

She couldn't hear the scraping sound her phone made on the laminate, as she slid it across the table to me. Brigitte's message was simple and formal. It said only that she would be coming by this afternoon to collect her things. I looked at Suzanne who nodded, took off the ring and tapped a steady beat on the table, her hand clenched so stiffly that the blood shrank from her bulky knuckles, showing them in all the white violence of bone beneath tired skin. '*Voilà. . .*'

She spoke in quick, careless French now, and it was up to me to follow. We had to sort through the things, throw out what wasn't needed and pack the rest in boxes for Brigitte. It was final. She would be marrying '*ce mec. Son musulman*' – that guy. Her Muslim. She would make a child for him, Suzanne said, '*c'est sûr*' – for sure.

Since arriving here I had learned to speak some French, and how to tell a harmless snake from a viper. My cousin Annie had taught me how to set a flea trap by placing a candle in a pan of water, how to change a nappy and how to tell if a melon was ripe, and a week earlier I had found a painless scrap of blood in my gusset – promise of a long-hoped-for puberty. From Suzanne, though, I was learning exciting things that belonged to a different sort of order. I had learned that a woman could become pregnant by accident, and that this could mean many different things. There were options other than the molten sea that drowned my mother, or the rowdy waves my aunt bobbed cheerily along with in her daily effort to keep drawing breath. A few months before I came here, Brigitte had found herself pregnant. The father was a stupid man obsessed with fishing and Brigitte, though loneliness had driven her more than once into his bed, did not want to marry him. 'C'était pour la sauver de lui que je l'ai poussée. . .' Suzanne explained – it was to save her from him that Suzanne had driven her daughter to the clinic and had the thing undone. It was an act I had heard alluded to by older girls at school back in Ireland, but only as a mythic horror involving perverse midwives in backstreets. It was a simple thing, Suzanne had explained – a little tablet to stop a thing before it started – but it had been a mistake. Brigitte was old enough to make up her own mind. She had taken the abortion badly, and falling under the influence of son musulman was the ultimate punishment for her mother.

I had learned all this steadily over the course of our lessons, and in the last six weeks I had seen the chubby, too-adult daughter grow sullen and hulking as she passed from her bedroom to the kitchen and back again. The brave skirts that had once stretched across her shuddering brown thighs were replaced with longer ones, then loose trousers, and finally floor-skimming curtains. And as her daughter seemed to shrink beneath increasingly opaque layers of fat and fabric, Suzanne in her brightening rage began to unwrap for me all sorts of knowledge I had never thought to look for.

Sometimes she got up from the table and disappeared into the small room which in the other houses served as a pantry. She would emerge with a book or a pamphlet. It was books that had made her reject her *bourgeois* upbringing, she said. She didn't always open them, just ran her hand over their covers, as though pulling strength from the object itself. I thought of the words as little bricks, the pages as walls; structures that held her up when her straight spine seemed so close to tumbling. Suzanne told me about a socialist colony she had once lived in with Brigitte's father, where shitting in private was discouraged. The thought of it sent a guilty tremor through me. She had been injured at protests, Suzanne. She showed me a little dent that ran crooked along one shoulder. Her flat was like a dusky cocoon in which my mind worked clearly and more than it ever had, the links connecting, the channels opening to life. Ideas sparked like forest fire, catching branch after branch as I munched the apple that she had peeled and cored and cut into clean wedges, until my brain was a mighty thing, fierce and crackling.

But this business with the *musulman* had only become

more and more serious. It was starting to make Suzanne quieter, less sure when she spoke. Now, Brigitte had stopped coming home – she was living with her boyfriend's aunt. Over the past week Suzanne had been shaking her head a lot during our lessons.

'*Comment peut-elle trahir ses sœurs comme ça?*'– how can she betray her sisters like this?

I was sorry to see Suzanne's cheeks white with grief, pink blooms of rage on her neck. But she was all alone now, and I had started to wonder about the empty room. I knew my aunt could have done with one less mouth to feed. And in French *fille* can mean daughter, as well as girl.

Suzanne asked me if I had any interest in the dolls. I shook my head. She asked me if my little cousins might. I did not want to touch the smooth limbs and tiny, hinged waists so I shook my head again, and she swept them into a black sack with sudden brutality.

She did not give me a choice about the jewellery box.

'*Pour toi*' – for you.

When we had folded Brigitte's clothes carefully into boxes, stacked her books into crates and wrapped her small porcelain figurines in newspaper, Suzanne said she had a special job for me to help her with. From a high shelf she brought down an old doll with a cloth body, stiff limbs, and friendly plastic head. It was as big as a real baby. It had lively painted eyes, a pretty nose and a clumsy knot for a navel, but the hair was an obscene mat of yellowish strings and there were red felt-tip swirls all over its face. Suzanne cradled it in the crook of her elbow, her gaze tilting down like a lamp, in the same way as I had seen my aunt watch the baby at her breast. With balls of cotton dipped in nail polish remover, Suzanne worked away at each of the chicken pox. Her eyes stayed fixed on the doll's face while the spots were erased one by one, and she explained the next step of our project. She was running out of time, she said. She needed to sew up the dress she had knitted for the doll, so she would finish that while I untangled the hair. It was Brigitte's favourite toy when she was a child, and it would help Suzanne, to know her daughter would have something to hold.

She used a green-backed sponge to clean a workspace on the table, opened her knitting bag and laid out the parts for the dress: the back, the front, a daisy-shaped button, a coil of yellow ribbon and a small ball of extra yarn for the collar. It was a beautiful, simple thing all in fine white cotton yarn with pearl stitching along the hem.

Suzanne showed me how to spray the hair with her

fabric softener mixture and work out the knots with a wide-toothed comb. She sewed up one of the shoulder seams, watching me the whole time, and began to pick up the collar stitches, hardly glancing at her hands while she worked. She had a clever way of sewing up her knitting from the outside so that no seam was visible. She used a thick, blunt needle with a little bend at the tip.

I set to my task with meditative concentration, taking a small section at a time and starting at the ends. It was not easy – some of the knots seemed only to tighten to lumps, and more than once I was tempted to snip them with scissors, but Suzanne gave me a sharp knitting needle and showed me how to stick it in the centre of the knot and wriggle it out. My neck began to ache from hunching over the doll on my lap, but I didn't raise my head until I had worked the hair into a syrupy slick on the table.

By then the completed garment was hanging on the back of a chair and Suzanne was smoking a cigarette at the open window.

She took her time with the cigarette. Then we began to dress the doll. The dress fit her perfectly. There were little eyelets along the breast-line, and Suzanne put the yellow ribbon on a darning needle and threaded it through, so that the two loose ends met in the centre of the doll's chest. She asked me to tie a small bow at the front. The flower button closed the dress at the back of the doll's thick neck, just covering the sequence of tough, dark stitches where cloth met plastic. Then we sat her on the table. I held her upright while Suzanne parted the hair, squeezed out the excess liquid and wove each side into a tight plait, which she closed firmly with brown rubber bands, her lips small with concentration.

Brigitte did not arrive in a hijab as Suzanne had feared. A thick black band kept every scrap of hair from her forehead and temples, but before entering she had let her scarf fall down around her neck. Her hair was tied in a loose plait at the back and we could see that she had dyed it a glaring shade of beetroot.

She avoided facing her mother, locking eyes with me as she kissed Suzanne on each cheek.

Brigitte's skin looked lighter, and her eye sockets had retreated deeper in her face and when her eyes met mine I felt a tantalizing chill. She moved differently. Her body seemed more agile now under the loose camisole and thick long skirt and her mouth was set in the sort of dignified, closed smile I had only seen in old portraits of princesses.

Suzanne had warned me about this. She had told me Brigitte had been brainwashed by the *musulman*, and to her, we were all dirt. We did not count and she could not hear

212

anything we said. She had used the word *gentiles* – we were gentiles to Brigitte. I didn't know what that meant. I thought of fancy ladies with long gloves and complex hairstyles, the *bourgeoisie* that Suzanne so despised.

'*Alors, le mariage?*' – so you are marrying him?

Brigitte said nothing. She rolled her eyes, and her lips made a slight twist at the edges, which I could not read. She began to lift things out of the boxes and put them back on Suzanne's round kitchen table. Suzanne lowered her mouth to my ear. '*Ce sont des représentations de personnes. Ils sont interdits*' – they are representations of people. They are forbidden.

As I stood before Suzanne, watching Brigitte gently remove the dolphin and the figurines, and many of the books, I thought I could feel Suzanne's weary hurt pulling heavy in my limbs. I could sense her throat tremble behind me. I would not be able to hold her if she fell, but I pressed the back of my head to her shoulder to steady her. She took a small, high breath as Brigitte lifted out the doll that we had lovingly groomed. The neat red oblongs of Brigitte's nails tightened on the soft body, but her face didn't change. She brought it to her lips for a moment, and smelled the hair.

Suzanne turned away, moving to the other side of the room, which had an old couch in it and a TV. She sat on the couch and flicked blindly through a newspaper, her face angled away from us. I stayed and watched Brigitte.

213

Brigitte glanced at her mother, and when she thought she would not be seen, she pulled some towels out of one of the boxes, laid the doll gently inside, and tucked the towels back on top.

I helped to bring the boxes downstairs and pack them into the car. On reaching the street, Brigitte lifted the scarf up over her head and arranged it deftly, an expression of serene resolve on her face, all her features settled into an effortless symmetry. We loaded the boot in silence. Suzanne stood watching us from the bottom of the polished concrete steps that led up to her flat. I kept thinking she would speak. As Brigitte reached up to pull the boot closed, the words came forward without any search, and so loud that I shocked even myself. 'La poupée?' – the doll?

I didn't see Suzanne's face because she was standing behind me, but I was glad that Brigitte stiffened. I had caught her. Her eyes widened and I thought gleefully that her face looked puckered by the black scarf which even covered her neck, squashing in the big sloppy features from all sides. I said it again, 'La poupée' – the doll, trembling with a kind of victory now, at having spoken, 'elle n'est pas interdit?' – she is not forbidden? I wondered if Suzanne could hear how well I was pronouncing the words.

Brigitte smiled again, put a painted finger to her closed lips, and winked. Her mother suffered the two farewell kisses with a face hard as bark, wobbling softly at her daughter's touch like a sapling unbraced against the wind.

Brigitte nodded at me, *Merci Aleezun.* She installed herself steadily into her rickety orange car and drove away, head lowered prettily towards the wheel.

When I looked back at Suzanne, her face shot terror down through my limbs. I wanted to run. She looked like someone else; someone bad and cold.

'*Elle a la poupée?*'

I nodded, and smiled; Brigitte had something to hold; Suzanne might be pleased. But all expression had dropped from Suzanne's flesh, the way a dead person's does, and it stayed that way, her mouth dripping down off her bones; her eyes flat. She gave a single, curt nod and turned.

Back upstairs she said something that I was too frightened to understand, so she wrote down a word for me in English: 'integrity'. Bewildered by the change in her, I didn't speak.

'She eez empty, my daughter,' she said, 'Brigitte. She eez nat true for what she belief. She belief in nothing. *Rien.* She eez no person.'

*

215

That night on my attic mattress, I wound the jewellery box and watched the ballerina dance by the light of the flea trap. I turned the key again and again until the drowning melody finally died, and she twirled there in silence with her wonky mouth.

Manners

THE FIRST TIME Adrian had seen the girls he thought they might be prostitutes. They both had crusty sores on their lips that had been dabbed with flesh-coloured paste, then glossed over many times with candy-pink goo. Their nails were long and flaked with silver polish. One of them had a purple bruise on her neck. They wore thick gold earrings, tight sequinned jeans, and running shoes. They were his daughter's age, just turned women – buttocks full, hips pressing intently through the chafed denim. They had tight waists, bony wrists, wide, clear eyes and tough little jaws. He had expected them to get off at Stoneybatter, where a businessman could buy a lunchtime blow job for twenty euros. They might have been wearing flimsy nylon tops under their hoodies. They might have had slippery armpits under there, brothy sweat, more bruises, bites. But they had stayed on the bus until Grafton Street. As they disembarked one of them took the other's hand and whispered into her ear, grinning with the giddiness of a mischievous child. Then they waited quietly on the pavement for an older woman to get off the bus.

Adrian hadn't noticed the older woman until then. She was round, zipped into a too-small fleece jacket. She had the same jaw as them, the same dark, itinerant brows, but her skin had the look of granite, dense and pitted, and her coarse black hair was twisted into a plait that tapered all the way down to the cleft of her ass and swung there like a tail.

The girls weren't prostitutes. He should have seen that by the way they curved their shoulders – they didn't know they had two pairs of beautiful breasts in there under those hoodies. His own daughter knew only too well. It made him uncomfortable, the way Carla's clothes increasingly resembled underwear – bits of designer lace to decorate her cleavage and the tops of her thighs – and the way he paid for the privilege of seeing her walk out like that. He was having a new credit card issued soon. He would keep the numbers from her.

He had been taking the bus to work for two months now. It had embarrassed his wife at first, and she had insisted on dropping him to the stop lest he be seen walking. Last weekend, though, he had heard her on the phone. 'Oh yes,' she had said, 'well, we're in the same boat. My Adrian sold the '07 . . . who would have seen it coming? Grown men like ours, professionals, trudging to the bus stop . . .' She still had the four-by-four. One car for a family of three was no great hardship, he told her, but Margaret savoured her horror at the loss of the Merc. He hadn't got much for it, but keeping it was an expense, he had explained – why pay insurance and petrol and parking fees, when he could as easily take the bus?

There were a few things that hadn't worked out. His girls needed to understand that.

He owned a vacant penthouse apartment in a half-built development surrounded by acres of flattened wasteland, a motorway without a pedestrian crossing, and the promise of a tram stop. Out of laziness or optimism, the large billboard saying *HoneyHive Village: Work. Live. Succeed!* had never been taken down. There was a crèche on the ground floor called Oxford Junior. It had a heart-shaped crest with a book in one chamber and a teddy bear in another. He had also bought one third of an unused warehouse.

Recently, in a cafe, he had overheard a conversation between a middle-aged man and his young lunch companion. The man spoke loudly, showing off. He told the girl that the word mortgage came from the French *mort* – death. It was a debt till death – that was the literal translation. That was why the French rented, the man had said.

He recognized the regular commuters now. Sometimes he found himself nodding at familiar faces, and they nodded back. It was nice, in a way, to see faces other than that of his secretary, the usual clients, and the man who worked at the coffee dock. There had been no new clients lately, no new stories, just follow-on cases – access reviews, maintenance reviews, fines for broken court orders.

He saw the girls once or twice a week. They always got on at the same stop – the Spar on the Foxborough road – and he reckoned there must be a council estate around there. There were always skinny men loitering outside the shop. The woman with the plait usually chaperoned the girls. This time she sat beside Adrian at the back of the bus, facing them. She crossed her feet and folded her hands on her lap one over the other, like a lady. She pursed her lips, trying for pride, perhaps, or displeasure. It made him think of Margaret when she was young. When she was nervous she would straighten her back, fold her hands on her lap, survey the room, and swallow.

It was startling how easily he forgot what his wife had been like then – the way she pinned her shoulders back, the curve of her spine. He'd met her at a dinner party and wanted her immediately. It was the way she allowed her chair to be held for her as she seated herself at the table, the way she held her knees together. He had thought of making love to her, calling her 'good girl', the polite little moans she might make. They had driven him wild, those impeccable manners.

It took him two months. It was much as he had imagined it. She was sweet and mock-demure, hesitating with a grin before parting her legs. When prompted she sat daintily astride him as though riding a horse, brushed the hair from her eyes, left her underwear on with the crotch pulled aside, made small, dignified sounds and smiled triumphantly when he came. What made him start to love her a little, even on that first night, was the way that all of those manners fell away when she slept. She snored like a man, and muttered and scratched and kicked and drooled and fought with the pillow. In marriage he had hoped to access that part of her, to lose the politeness of words and waxed legs. He had looked forward to seeing her face scrubbed bare, to all the gore of pregnancy and birth, to sleeping curled together like animals.

Lately Margaret had taken to wearing an eye-mask to bed. He would come home some nights to find her lying on her back, her hands in cotton gloves to get the most out of her hand cream, and the black mask over her eyes with the word 'sleep' embroidered on it in silver thread.

One of the girls had tried to bleach her hair, but the peroxide had been no match for the thorough blackness of her mane.

The hair had come out orange-pink, like a sunset, with two inches of roots. The other girl, slightly taller, with hair greased back in a tight ponytail, was beautiful. Her face was flat like so many of those traveller girls', with high, dented cheekbones like a form carefully beaten out of bronze. Her thick lips were both stoic and accidentally sensual, raw as a wound. It was the upper lip – the way it swelled a little over the plump lower one – that made her beautiful: the hurt she wore in her mouth, and the resignation, and something else as well – the wince at the edge of her eyes, as though she were tolerating something, resisting an urge to roar. He had noticed the colour before – emerald green shot through with glistening yellow shards like a shattered bottle.

The girls were each sipping a bottle of Lucozade and the sugar was already doing its job – they were becoming jittery and hyper, giggling and whispering. That must be their breakfast, he thought: a high-calorie drink designed for sportsmen, rich in glucose. He thought of Carla, battling already with her weight. Throughout sixth year she had been eating egg whites for breakfast, an apple for lunch, and turkey breast or white fish for dinner, grilled by Margaret on special fat-absorbing paper. Mother and daughter were both on the Special 8 diet now, which, as far as he could make out, meant that they ate nothing but bowls of cereal with fat-free organic yoghurt. If they could see this –

two itinerant girls with perfect figures drinking Lucozade for breakfast. . .

Because she wasn't cooking for herself or Carla, Margaret had taken to filling the freezer with high-quality ready-made meals. She left one to defrost on the kitchen table for Adrian every afternoon. In the evening he was supposed to come home and put it in the microwave, but he was never hungry by then. He ate a lot during the day. Business had been quiet lately. Middle-class separations, with all the mess of joint bank accounts and properties, had kept Adrian in work for two decades, but things were different now. There was less money to fight over than there was to lose on legal costs, and no one could afford to live alone.

After greeting his secretary in the morning, and opening his post, Adrian had taken to sitting in an Italian cafe for an hour with coffee and a pastry and some folders. Sometimes he sat there until the afternoon. It was easier to deal with paperwork there, amongst walls of wine bottles, than in his brightly lit office. There were PhD students with laptops, women with babies, lovers with problems, ex-politicians. There were low-hanging amber lampshades and cheap paper placemats. There was good coffee. There was never such silence that you could hear the waste of energy hum in the plug sockets. At lunchtime he would order a plate of vinegar-drenched antipasto and eat it slowly.

He tried to tell Margaret what a waste of money the ready meals were – he ate so often during the day, he said, so many business lunches – but she insisted that since the recession had hit there were great deals on all these things. Marks and Spencer wasn't even making a profit, she said. They were loss leaders, the three-for-two ready meals that she bought for Adrian. It would be a waste *not* to buy them, she said. She loved that expression, 'loss leaders'.

For the first years after they had married she had cooked him elaborate dinners every evening. She went through phases. First everything was done in the pressure cooker, then the slow cooker. Then she began to grill things. For a time it was their main topic of conversation – her cooking, and his eating. She always asked him what she might improve, and was there enough salt on it, and every Thursday she tried something new from the *Living* supplement of the Sunday paper. It had gone on like that for – how long? And when had it stopped?

Margaret took seriously her duties as wife. She had given up her job at the hotel. She had run the house like a good business, constantly striving for improvement. In the eighties they had needed a conservatory and an antique oak floor. In the nineties they had needed the conservatory taken out; in its place they needed decking, and a gazebo. Margaret had designed the gazebo herself, and had it custom made. That was her way of loving him. He knew that. He was no better.

He had started buying her chocolates and flowers. On her birthday he had bought a card that said 'To My Lovely Wife' on it. On the front was the outline of a woman. There was red silk stuck over it in the shape of a dress, and a string of tiny pearls glued at the neck. There was a time when she would have made a joke of that. Now, she was grateful. She kept the card on the dresser for six weeks. He was not the worst. There was no one who knew quite how to love anyone else. If family law had taught him anything, it was that. How many times, right before a settlement, at the end of a vicious dispute, after the poisonous accusations, the financial ruin, the custody battle, had he watched a client collapse in tears – 'I tried my best. I tried so hard to love . . .'

A few years ago he had paid a girl to piss on him. The girl was thin with brassy yellow hair. He could smell alcohol off her piss, and after it was done he couldn't remember why he had wanted so badly for Margaret to do it, why the thought had turned him on like that.

A boy sat himself down behind the girls. He had bum fluff on his chin – a colourless foam, like the mould that sprouts at the bottom of discarded tea cups – that nauseated Adrian. The three teenagers were talking in low, excited mumbles. The woman with the plait was scolding them continuously in that half-English language they spoke. Adrian couldn't decipher her words.

His grandmother used to bring dinner and worn blankets to Mrs O'Connor, a traveller woman with nine children who settled in a nearby field every summer. One day she had taken Adrian with her to the caravans. Bits of broken things lay discarded amidst patches of long, parched grass – half a bicycle, a crushed washing line and, in the black aftermath of a bonfire, a cluster of smashed bottles, green and brown and yellow. Adrian had seen a little boy with no trousers or shoes on straddling a shaggy horse, and Mrs O'Connor had shouted something at the boy in that language. Inside, the caravan was very clean and neat. There was a bedspread with large red flowers on it, and a skinny baby sleeping face down on a sheepskin. The sons had grown into thugs, his grandmother had told him, which was a terrible pity, because Mrs O'Connor had been a lady in her own way, and her long, black hair was always clean and glossy.

The woman was talking to the boy now. Adrian thought he could understand. 'When you get back don't go straight to sleep,' she said. 'Go for a walk first.'

Adrian checked his watch. Then he verified the time by checking his phone. It was 9.05. Carla would be picking up her results. How did it work? he wondered. Did the students all queue up, the way they had when he was that age, and file into the principal's office to hear, after a summer of waiting, how they had done? Or were the results posted on a board, the way they were in universities? Or were they each handed a sealed envelope with their name on it? She wanted to do law like him, poor child. For a year the exams had taken over everything. Carla had tacked a study plan to the back of her bedroom door. Margaret had woken her every morning with a black coffee, and poached the egg whites while Carla did an hour of morning revision.

Was it he, or Margaret, who had chosen that crèche when Carla was tiny? The only one in Ireland to start Montessori classes at two years instead of three, which had a uniform that made the toddlers look like Victorian dolls, and taught them the violin when they could hardly walk. It had seemed to him, back then, that it would protect Carla to be armed with that education, that class. That's how it had seemed then.

Throughout sixth year he and Margaret had been invited to the dinner parties of parents from the school. One night a father had cornered him in the kitchen.

'I hear Carla's getting straight A1s in higher maths? Martha says she's the best in the class. That's an advantage alright, isn't it? They get extra points for higher maths.'

'Yeah. I think she is. That's what she tells us anyway, hah! You never know, though, she says the girl who got the maths prize last year only got a C in the leaving. It all depends on the day, doesn't it?'

The man eyed him suspiciously, and moved in closer.

'What grind does she go to? I won't mention it to anyone else. Please. Martha wants to do science. She needs a B in maths or she won't get into her course.'

He had told Carla yesterday, 'You know it doesn't matter how you do? Things will work out for the best. Your mother and I know you've worked hard. That's what matters.'

Things will work out for the best – what did he mean by that? He hoped she wouldn't get all those points. He hoped her fat-necked boyfriend would dump her. He hoped her life would be thrown off course now before it was too late. He wanted her to enjoy herself in college, to miss class sometimes, and get a job in a bar. He wanted someone to fall in love with her for real, not as an aspiration. He wanted her to sit on grotty couches and argue with other kids as though they all knew everything, and just talk, for God's sake, and laugh stupidly, and not keep striving into the future, as though there was something there for her.

Besides, Margaret had promised Carla, without consulting him, that she could have her own brand-new car if she got over 550. He couldn't afford that.

His phone was flashing and vibrating. He had forgotten to take it off silent. Six missed calls. Margaret and Carla had both been phoning. He picked up and Carla shrieked into the phone – 'Five-sixty-five, Dad! Five-sixty-fucking-five!' In the background her classmates were shrieking too.

The itinerant girls were looking at him. They could hear the shrieks. The green-eyed one had dimples twitching in her cheeks. She wanted to laugh at him. He was aware, suddenly, of his briefcase open at his feet. He hadn't closed it after taking out his phone. His wallet was lying mouth open on top of some thin files. There were two fifties and a five clearly visible, sandwiched between layers of fine Italian leather and silk. The girl saw him look at the wallet, and then at her, and he was too embarrassed to reach down and tuck it away, buckle up the briefcase. Carla was still screaming. He didn't want to speak. The girl would hear his accent, and she would laugh. What would he say anyway?

'Well done, Carla. Well done, darling.'

'I have to go, Daddy. I have to ring Mark! Ahhhhh!'

The girls had lost interest in him now. They were messing with the boy behind them. The boy's ears were red. They were leaning around the seat, reaching into his pants with their lovely young hands – the rough palms, the filthy nails, the cracked metallic nail polish. It was electric blue today. The boy was hunched over his crotch, shrugging them away with increasing humiliation and anger. Poor kid. Adrian had the impression the boy might hit the girls if they didn't stop. The mother leaned over and slapped them each on the knees. 'I didn't raise you to be doin like that.' The girls turned around and sat on their hands, but they couldn't stop laughing. Then the taller, beautiful, green-eyed one said, 'Come on, Mammy. We're to be gettin off.' As the woman passed the boy she clipped him on the ear. 'Go for a walk first,' she said.

Before dismounting, the mother took an old buggy from where she had left it by the side door. On the pavement she assembled the buggy with a deft flick of her foot, arranged some blankets to resemble a small baby, and covered the bundle with a rain protector. Then she handed each of the girls a paper cup, and fixed their hair.

Cords

WHILE DONNA STANDS in line she thinks about her feet and the floor beneath them. She tries to keep herself planted steadily on the squeaky lino, to fix herself there, in focus, long enough for the lady to get all the details she needs. The registration booth is beside the pedestrian entrance and there must be a fault with the doors, because they keep snapping open unprompted and sliding slowly closed, admitting the night air every time; a gust of frost to relieve the frowzy vacuum of bleach and instant coffee and unwashed skin.

The lady sits behind a yellowed plastic screen that has scratches and smears on it, and a little cluster of round holes for her to talk and hear through. She leans back, twirling a pen between her fingers, pulls her chin into her neck and peers at Donna over small glasses. 'Right, what's the patient's name?' As Donna tries to speak the lady squints, turns her head to the side and pushes her ear closer to the screen:

'Sorry, you'll have to speak up. He's how old?'

A blurring feeling is starting in Donna's hands. She touches the tips of her thumb and forefinger together. She thinks about the border of her body – the outline of her hair, the scuffed toes of her trainers – the points where she ends and the space around her begins. She has to repeat the things – his name, the spelling of their surname... and she stumbles over his date of birth, never very good with remembering numbers. There is a couple standing behind her with a limp, pink-faced child in the father's arms. Instead of her own words, Donna can hear only the man saying, 'Ridiculous. There's people here with kids. Ridiculous standing here.'

When the lady is finished with her, Donna turns to go. As she passes the couple, the mother rolls her eyes at her, and the father shakes his head. It is only then that Donna realizes it is she who is ridiculous. It is she who was standing there.

The doctor's smooth, clean hands are younger than his eyes. A single frown line cleaves his forehead; 'You don't have the name for what he took?'

'Sleeping tablets I think, but—'

'—but you don't know which ones, and you don't know what else. Yes?'

Donna nods but she has missed a beat, the response coming too late; a ridiculous nod to no one. The doctor has already turned to her brother. The words come loud and distinct from his sturdy frame:

'What did you do here?'

When there is no response the doctor leans over him: 'We are going to clean your stomach, okay?' Her brother closes his eyes and Donna wonders at his eyelids; a metallic mauve sheen on them – were they always that colour? And the skin so thin. She remembers a punctured butterfly dropped from the cat's mouth, the way the wings had dulled to dusty flakes, the ugly rind of its centre, black blister eyes. She wonders at how bodies keep so well intact; how eyelids don't tear with wear, how all the liquid and heat of insides stay ordered and contained beneath the skin.

'What is his name?' asks the doctor.

'Kyle.'

'Kyle, we are going to give you a blood test to see how much damage you have done. We are going to put some charcoal into your stomach now to clean it and you will feel sick. Okay? Kyle, would you like us to do that? You will feel sick and then you will feel better.'

Kyle rolls his head.

233

'Say yes, Kyle,' Donna says. She talks loudly, as though speaking on the telephone, trying to communicate over a long-distance call with a crackle in the line.

'He has to accept treatment,' says the doctor, 'otherwise I can't—'

'Say yes, Kyle. The doctor has other people to see.'

Sore sounds strain through from far back in his throat: 'Fuck you,' then, his lips barely moving, 'slut.'

He turns his head on its stiff neck, in the doctor's direction, his voice easing out. 'Yep—' he opens his eyes, a sardonic kink in the line of his lip, '—I'll have the black stuff.'

The doctor asks Donna to leave them. She leans to kiss her brother but there is the nausea again, burning up into her throat, so she has to stand up straight and exhale. She goes into the corridor and pulls the curtain behind her.

This is a makeshift ward because the hospital is full up tonight. There are three other beds in the corridor, separated by sheets of green plastic hung from rails on wheels. Strips of milky light run along the ceiling. There is no traffic outside, only the occasional whine of an ambulance.

Donna rubs the small of her back and walks up and down and the rhythm of it soothes the urge to vomit. There is a woman in an oversized jacket pacing outside the curtain opposite. She is talking quietly into her phone, hand cupping her mouth. When the call ends Donna makes eye contact. She needs the lady to smile but her eyes slide away.

It is the force of the vomit that knocks her down, or the force of suppressing it; a thud from the base of her spine, filling her throat, stopping her breath and she can hear, past the drumming of her pulse, the lady's irritation, her posh accent, 'Do you need a nurse? Here, have some water... oh for Jesus' sake... hello, can you fetch me a nurse please for this girl?'

When she can speak again Donna says sorry. 'Sorry. I just need to get sick. I'm a bit pregnant.' She didn't mean to say that.

The woman is kneeling beside her. She has ropey hair held up in a scrunchie, and a down-turned mouth.

'Put your head between your knees. Will I get a nurse for you?'

'I'll go to the toilet. I'll be fine once I've been sick.'

'Do you want a ginger biscuit?'

'No, no. Thank you.'

'How old are you?'

'Eighteen.'

'Sorry to ask, just you look younger. You with that boy?'

'My brother. I'm alright now. Thanks.'

'Well. Congratulations.'

*

The doctor is still there, his hands sheathed in a thin white sheen, holding a bucket to Kyle's chin. Kyle retches weakly, and tongues out the last strings of charcoal.

'He has done this before?'

'Yes.'

'Do you know why?'

'I'm going to London. I was supposed to leave today. My granddad's not well and stuff so, you know . . . it's only me and Kyle and my grandma really and he doesn't think I should go.'

'He has had help?'

'He was in St Pat's for six months last year.'

'Maybe you should call them. Let them know anyway. It would be good, I think. They may have advice for you.' He peels the gloves off, revealing hands the colour of biscuits, pale nails. The latex fingers hang shrivelling in his grip.

Her brother has collapsed back down on the bed. There is a thick silicone tube coming from one of the machines beside him. It is draped over his face and disappears under the blue blanket. There are other, smaller wires tangled about the sheets and stuck at his wrists.

'We will get the results in an hour or so,' says the doctor. 'You should go home now. You are no use to him here.'

★

There is no chair. After the doctor has left, Donna squats beside the hospital bed, hands gripping the metal frame, cheeks pressed on her arms.

'I'll go so . . . Will I go, Kyle?'

When he doesn't reply she stands over him.

'Answer me. Will I go? Is that okay? I've missed the flight now so . . . I'll go home.'

'Fuck you,' he says.

Her brother's mouth twists to a sneer, or is it pain making those shapes?

There was no need to panic the way she did. There never is. There is no need for their grandmother's lips to wash livid, for her old hands to tremble, and her face drop into palms full of breath and tears. Kyle has never been as close to death as he would like. Their mother did it quietly and efficiently and only once; she did not feel the tug of life's cord, anchoring her here beyond purpose. Kyle is not made the same way. Like Donna, he is compelled to follow each breath with another; like her he is wired with alarms and trip switches and can never make the leap to meet their mother where she left them. Donna is the only one who knows it. She can see how shallow his wrist scars are, and in the wrong direction.

'Do you have any money?' says Donna. 'I left everything at home.'

Kyle closes his eyes.

'Kyle, answer me. Do you have a phone?'

Her cousin Ailbhe will be on her way to the airport to pick her up already. She will watch everyone filing in from the Dublin flight and when there is no one left she will think Donna has backed out of the abortion, remembering the placards of dead babies they saw that time on Grafton Street; mangled corpses with putty limbs. There was one she would remember often; a human shape with a dent for a mouth, belly purple and veined and a jelly tube fleshing out into a bloom of blood. It was a woman her grandma's age who held that picture, mouth closed, cheeks puckered as though dissolving holy paper, one hand gripping a stick while rosary beads worked like ants through the fingers of the other.

'It's not what they made us think,' said Ailbhe. 'It's fine, Donna. It's really fine. And the ladies are so nice. They understand...'

Kyle's hand twitches. The tube that was across his face has caught in his mouth and he opens and closes his lips slowly, trying to make them meet. He frowns through the drowse and his taut cheeks crinkle, as though he might cry. Donna leaves him struggling weakly. She can feel how blank her face is. She puts her hand to her belly; a hard swell like something inflamed. With the same dumb compulsion that makes her brother breathe in and out, makes his heart suck and spew, her body is throbbing at a little capsule of fluid and tissue, bringing it blood and protein and whatever else is keeping it growing. If no one interrupts it will keep chugging steadily away until it has filled another being into life, and the thought of that secret mutiny, tucked with something like pleasure in her womb, makes a laugh bubble up into her throat, but then no sound comes.

Her brother puffs, indignant at this small discomfort. She watches him snorting, his head swaying slowly, hand lying still now under the glare of small wires thatched with the miraculous intimacy of veins over the wool blanket. He is unable to identify the thing that is bothering him and his head rocks from side to side with increasing distress. She stands over him and checks herself for any sympathy. Nothing. Only the backache, the weary ankles. It takes an effort – a moral effort, to move the drip away from his mouth. No one will ever know.

Donna rests by the bed on her haunches, her head on her arms and the bars of the bed cold in her grip. She has missed it now; the kindness of an adult woman with a dainty voice, the gentle efficiency of painkillers like her cousin described. If you're from Ireland they won't give you the pills, Ailbhe said, they do the hoover instead, but at least that means it's over and done in one go. Ailbhe paid for the flight and booked the appointment. She might refuse to pay for another one.

She wants Donna to stay in London. 'Granddad wouldn't want you to throw your life away now,' she said. 'We'll find you a job. Don't stay in Dublin for Granddad. It's not what he'd want.' But there was the time Granddad talked about the British throwing their half-baked children into buckets; there was the lady on the helpline, whose voice sounded so wobbly with hurt. She said there were always better options, her granny might understand, and if not she could stay in a special house until the baby was six months old. 'A new baby is always welcome in the world,' she said.

But Grandma wouldn't throw her out. She would just heave more burden onto her shrinking frame, the same way she carried Donna and Kyle even after her hips were too old to be resting children on them and her lungs too wet with grief. 'Don't do something you won't be able to live with,' said the lady, 'not unless you are one hundred per cent sure...' But time is moving only towards one outcome. Every moment she is becoming more pregnant. She can already feel it washing in; a current steady and mesmerizing and powerful as the sea. She knows how easily it could loosen her grip on herself; the relief of surrender, the way it could wash through her and take her with it into a world of its own making.

Her brother makes a spluttering sound and Donna pulls herself up on heavy legs. His face is expressionless. It's his eye sockets and his lips, when they're sapped of everything like that and the skin eerily bright. That's what's reminding her of Granddad.

For years their grandfather has been hooked up to machines the way Kyle is now, his legs shrinking from disuse into the skinny pegs of a boy. He can't eat so they have unstopped his belly button and pegged a tube to it, for pumping the food in. Every few hours a nurse comes in and pours grey liquid into a bag that hangs from a hook at the top of a three-legged metal bar. The liquid sloshes into the plastic and it heaves about like an old cow's udder. For two years all he has tasted is his own mouth. The gums must be hollow where the teeth used to be. If he ever puts his tongue in them he will feel little caves of scarred flesh; little hollows of stone-hard blood.

When Kyle was little Grandma sometimes wondered quietly who his father was, because of the alien cut of him, all cheekbones and warm skin and the large blank eyes, and because he was so tall compared to the rest of the family. Granddad didn't let her talk like that – it was only alone with Donna that Grandma said, 'You know I wonder, sometimes... was it that boy with the tattoos...' as though there might be clues written on his father's biceps that could help them with the riddle of Kyle. Now, though, with his lips stiff and drooling, his body limp, surrounded by metal and flashing lights, Kyle looks like their grandfather. It's the shape of the bones with the skin scraped back, the muscles lax, the hopeless mix of assent and concentration along the crinkle of the brows and, pumping him alive, the ugly cord like a battered twist of meat.

Because of the stroke, Granddad couldn't move at all for months. Then he learned to control his left hand, lifting his puffed fingers slowly, one by one, like a heavy fan. These days he can hold them up for a moment, pointing his forefinger, poised as though about to land one of his reassuring facts, opening his mouth, taking a breath, gagging to speak. Then he looks disappointed, and sighs, and his hand drops. In the jaundice of his eyes death makes its undignified appeal.

Whatever Donna should feel for her grandfather has dissolved now into an abstraction of love; a duty. But her grandma is in love still. She spends her days sitting, massaging his arms, talking. Every morning he is dressed in a crisp white shirt that she has washed and ironed. Every evening he wears matching cotton pyjamas. She irons those too. At the end of her visits she packs his soiled clothes into a pillow case, plucks out the dead flowers from the vase, and puts his favourite album on repeat.

Donna waits until day, crouched outside the curtain, rubbing her ankles. The morning light washes in through the plate glass like a hospice watercolour; the pigments strained to weak pink, pastel purple.

The posh woman comes out from behind one of the curtains, still wrapped in the large grey sports jacket. It reaches her knees and is folded over itself at the front, pinned to her body by tightly crossed arms. Her face is stern, her lips straight. Tiny red veins cover her face like filigree. She nods at Donna's belly.

'When are you due?'

'Oh. No. I'm only thirteen weeks...'

'That's my son in there. He took an overdose.'

'Oh. Same. My brother.'

'It's the third time.'

'Fifth time,' says Donna. 'He never takes enough...'

'I remember being pregnant,' she says. 'You getting lots of kicks now?'

'I don't know. I think sometimes, maybe. Maybe I am imagining it.'

'Enjoy it. You never forget your first pregnancy. I'll never forget the first flutter. They're so tiny, aren't they? They sort of tumble in your tummy. I remember thinking it was like having a little fairy fluttering around in there.'

'I saw the scan and it was curled up, scratching its head. The doctor said it was only that big.' Donna shows her how big, making a two-inch gap between thumb and forefinger.

'I don't love him,' says the mother.

'Your son?'

The lady nods. 'Isn't that terrible?'

'Yeah.'

'I did, though. Just not now.'

'That's okay,' says Donna.

'You don't have to stay here. You should go home,' she says. 'It's not good for your baby.'

'Oh. No, well. I left my purse and phone at home. I panicked. The ambulance men were really nice. They kept the sirens off and everything. My granny is asleep. She'll be up at seven. I'll find a phone and she'll come and get me when she wakes up.'

'Oh. My phone has died,' says the lady, 'or you could use that.' She roots in the pockets of the big jacket. Donna can hear keys and hard things bumping each other, and bits of paper crackling. The lady produces a fifty-euro note, and folds it in half over one finger, as though this might make the gesture more discreet. She passes it to Donna silently, at hip level, and disappears behind the green plastic curtain. Donna can hear a chair squeak, the creak of the big jacket as she shifts about.

She crouches on her heels and closes her eyes. She cannot go back behind the curtain to where her brother's face pulls her blood to water.

There is a rustle as the mother opens a packet of something; crisps or crackers, Donna thinks, or ginger biscuits.

With her knuckles squished into her eyes, Donna sees yellow splotches and the veins in her eyelids like red cables winding into dancing shapes. She sees her grandfather lift his finger and open his mouth, the big breath in and the toothless cavern, tongue heavy like a grey oyster: her grandfather about to make his last point.

Playing House

BECAUSE SHE HAD nowhere else to go, the woman told the movers to carry on. The one in the cap crinkled his face, but he continued up the stairs anyway, pieces of her son's cot under each arm.

To occupy herself while the men worked, she hung her clothes in the wardrobe, which was white inside and out. She did it slowly to fill the time, shaking and smoothing each garment, dipping her head in and out one hanger at a time. There were pale hairs curled in the corners and disturbed dust crisscrossed the base like shadows on a forest floor. She had planned to clean the room before unpacking. She thought it might look rude though, now, if she was to get out the hoover and the polish.

Officially, she was renting the place unfurnished, but the

bedroom wardrobe was built in. There were fitted cabinets in the bathroom too, which she was glad of.

When the clothes had been unpacked, she began to lift books out of a cardboard box and stack them against the wall.

A passing sunbeam lit the room, heating the woman's face and exposing a sparsely woven cobweb strung across a corner of the ceiling. Before it left, she noticed the friendly shape of a small, splayed hand clouding the windowpane. It was made of something sticky, she thought; a jelly sweet that had been sucked and mauled, folded into a hot palm and dissolved to make a paste of spit and sugar and childish sweat.

The removal men heaved her headboard into the bedroom. She turned to face them and, feeling called upon to make some comment, she said, 'Can you believe it?' The outrage in her voice surprised her. Emboldened, she said it again, 'Can you believe it? I don't fucking believe it. I've checked the email. It says it very clearly: the property will be vacant from the third. Today is the third. Any time from the third, I can move in, it says. I just don't know what to do. This is ridiculous. It's unacceptable.'

The older of the men, Mick, knelt down by a bedside locker and began to pick delicately at the wide brown tape she had used to keep the drawer closed for transit. He glanced up at her and shook his head. 'You should be careful, chicken. Something not right there. State of his nails . . .'

He lifted his cap and shook it, hooked it at the back of his skull, and tugged it forward over his crown. A trail of sweat swelled at his temple and ran a bright path down his cheek to his jaw. He wiped it away with his shoulder. Turning to the younger man, he said, 'Did you see them, Carl? Did you see the nails? Polished like a girl's. Not right. Puff or something.'

Carl was plugging a heavy tool into a socket positioned high up on the wall. He took a breath to speak, but then he looked at the open door and exhaled.

The woman's landlord was leaning against the frame. He had an elbow cupped in his palm and with heavy eyelids he was examining his nails. The edges of his lips curled wide in an expression of quiet amusement. His chest was bare and so were his long, bony feet. He looked past the men, directly into the woman's eyes.

'Look,' he said. 'It's just a mix-up. It doesn't need to be a problem.' He moved to fill the doorway, putting a hand on the frame, and the other in the pocket of his loose tartan-print trousers.

'I don't mind if you don't mind, basically. I'm sleeping in the top room, but you can move the furniture in now, I don't mind. And you're welcome to sleep here. I mean, unless you're afraid of me or something . . . I'll be leaving tomorrow and you won't see me again.'

249

*

When the men had left she opened the bedroom window to let out the smell of their sweat and their boots, and looked out onto the dim scrap of yard below: dark paving, dead grass, brilliant blobs of evergreen shrubs. It was evening already, the sky had hardened to a grey tarnish over the russet housetops. She liked all the matching roofs; the lines they made on the horizon, the soft colour of the tiles and the blunt peaks like lids on all the neat lives they closed.

She made patterns of the view; stuttering configurations of walls and windows and slopes riffling closer and smaller as they wound into the thick estate. Her new home was hidden in a maze of cul de sacs and traffic circles, Glades and Groves and Crescents and Courts – hers was a Court. There was a green at the centre, with railings around it and a swing set. Her son could play there, perhaps. That was somewhere to go on a Saturday morning.

She used her sleeve to clear the dust from the windowsill, and arranged some books on it. Her bedroom was painted baby-girl pink, and there was a large picture of a blonde princess glued to the wall. The lampshade was also pink, the shape of a genie's lantern, with white ribbons and beads hanging from it like dewdrops. There was a nightlight in the plug socket with three yellow ducks on it. As the room darkened, the ducks began to glow.

Down in the kitchen her landlord was eating a bowl of cornflakes. He had closed the curtains and switched on a dim cylindrical lamp on the sideboard. The woman stood at the door wearing mismatched pyjamas and folded her arms over her nipples.

'Thank you for letting me stay,' she said. 'I'm sorry about the mix-up. The estate agent said the lease started today. She gave me the key . . . I would fuck off but I have nowhere to go.'

She sounded foolish when she cursed; she knew that. She rubbed her shoulder and looked around the room instead of at the man.

'No,' he said. His skin was a queer, even tone she knew as burnt sienna. The eyes and lips shone unnaturally pale and disconnected, like objects too carefully arranged.

'Honestly. I don't mind, if you don't mind. You couldn't have chosen a better person to . . . I don't give a shit, believe me. I'm not doing anything tonight. I have nowhere to go either, or I would fuck off.'

The woman wished she hadn't worn her glasses. She could see everything – the moistness of his eyes, the small, sparse blackheads and the angry stubble struggling up through his cleanly shaven skin.

She was ferociously hungry.

'Is there a Chinese takeaway around here? Or an Indian?'

'You're welcome to have some cornflakes.' Her landlord waggled the box of cornflakes, and put it down again.

'Thanks but I haven't eaten in two days. I'm starving.'

'You should have cornflakes if you haven't eaten yet, and a cup of tea. Then we can order a Chinese.'

It was too late to remove the glasses. There would be embarrassing red marks on her nose now. They sat opposite one another, spooning cornflakes into their mouths, looking at the stained Chinese menu that her landlord had unpinned from a corkboard on the wall. The options were numbered and there were black biro rings around no. 4 – Vegetable spring rolls, and no. 17 – Chicken chow mein. The woman and her landlord agreed on six starters instead of two main courses, and maybe a portion of duck pancakes between them.

'Why haven't you eaten?'

'Oh, you know . . . stress, rushing with the move and organizing things and stuff. Things ended very suddenly, with my husband. It's been hectic, moving out and everything.'

His phone began to trill. He picked it up, looked at the screen, and placed it face down on the table to ring out.

It vibrated as it rang, and each time it did it moved a little towards her across the table. The woman folded her glasses and placed them on the table. Minutes later the phone rang again. Then again. The vibration made the glasses tremble. The fourth time it rang she asked him, 'Don't you want to get that?'

'No,' said her landlord, 'it's my fiancée. I'll call her back after.'

She poured more cornflakes into his bowl, and then into her own. She rubbed at the sides of her nose where she knew the glasses must have made their mark.

'Do you mind if I smoke?' he said. 'I'll open the window. I know that maybe with the child you might prefer...'

'Go ahead.'

He put a cigarette between his lips, stood up and walked towards the stove, moving around the two giant suitcases that he had left lined up against the sideboard. They were identical suitcases, expensive and brand new. He started the gas and bent his face to the flame, frowning as he lit the cigarette. The way he did that opened a sore muscle in the woman's throat. She strained for that memory like a muffled tune; a night last year, when she went to a party with her husband. He had left through the back door to smoke, and she had followed him. He had frowned like that as he lit up.

Her landlord came back to the table and sat opposite her.

She kept watching his hands. It was hard to pull her gaze to his face.

She said, 'Whose is the little girl's room?'

'It was my little girl's room. She lives in London now. With her mother. With my wife.'

'Oh.'

The ducks, she thought. Should she remind him about the nightlight? Perhaps he meant to pack it. She would clean the room tomorrow; the gluey handprint, the blonde hair and all the dust between the floorboards. The dust was dead bits of the little girl; her skin cells and the dirt that had once been on her. If her landlord didn't want it, the nightlight would do for her son's room.

'I have a son too,' said her landlord. 'He lives in LA with his mother.' He pointed to the phone where it lay face down on the table and added, 'With my fiancée.'

'Oh. What age are they?'

'She's nearly five. He's three.'

'Oh. My little boy is two. He's staying overnight with his daddy.'

When she said that something tripped in her voice. She looked at her hands.

Her landlord rubbed his temples, then his eyes. 'Yep,' he said, 'that's the way things are.' He looked her in the face. 'What did you say your name was?'

'Lily.'

'Lily. Lillian. Yes, that's right, Lillian Murphy. Yes, I knew I recognized your face. We are so ordinary,' he said. 'That's what I'm realizing now, Lily. This—'

With one palm he motioned grandly to the room around them, as though their lives were here in the kitchen, the estrangements and love objects lined up on the Formica alongside the toaster and the kettle and the naked banana tree. He said, 'This is all so normal.'

He used a saucer as an ashtray. It already held two shrivelled tea bags. Their juice fed a dark pool into the centre, and the ash dispersed prettily when it hit the liquid; a burst of silver.

Lily knew what she was remembering – or was she inventing now? Her mind snatched at it; a catchy tune that hooked into her, playing on and on but the words were half made up. At the party there was that woman with careful make-up and very nice shoes, who her husband immediately noticed. He had followed the woman outside to smoke with her. When Lily came out after them, her husband looked hard at the night and frowned as he lit his cigarette. The woman smiled at Lily with closed lips and finished her cigarette quickly. She dropped it on the slippery decking and with a languid tilt of the hip she ground the butt hard with the toe of her lovely shoe.

Her landlord flipped his phone over. 'Let's order.'

He left the phone flat on the table, using one finger to tap at the digits. His nails were very clean, very even, the same pink as his lips. The mover man was right – they were polished. Her own hands had stained cuticles, blue paint stuck under the nails, and some of them splitting from all the turpentine she had used to scrub at them. Over the last few weeks, she had started to bite her nails again. She picked at her torn thumb nail, trying to remove some of the dried paint and shredded skin. She clenched her hand into a fist, tucking in the stubby finger ends. Each person's clenched fist is the size of their own heart. That was something that had a lovely ring to it. The first time she had heard that was from a drunk boy in a nightclub. He had shouted it over the music, and made a fist to demonstrate. When she nodded he said it again, as though it proved something.

When her landlord had finished ordering, he stretched an arm's length between himself and the phone, and placed it face down on the table.

Lily wanted to talk about herself. She said, 'That must be your luggage in the hall. You have a lot of pictures? Are they paintings?'

'Some of them,' he said. 'Yes, a lot of paintings, and a lot of photos. So many bloody photos . . .' He gestured to her fingers with his chin. 'You're a painter.'

Lily nodded.

'I've seen your stuff.'

'Oh.'

He smiled then, as though in triumph. His teeth were small, extremely white and straight. There was exactly the right distance between his eyes; the space of a third eye.

'You don't remember me?' he said. 'I was at an exhibition of yours. I didn't buy, but I stood at a painting for ages.'

'Oh? It's been a long time since I've exhibited.'

'I was trying to figure out what it was that made your work so . . . maybe that's what you are going for? I'm hardly an art critic but . . . I wondered why you painted, and whether you painted differently when you were younger. I did think you had great go, though.'

'Oh.'

'They intrigued me anyway . . . so that's something.'

Her landlord gave that queer smile she had seen when she had first stepped through the front door and stood, startled, before him. It might have been a smirk.

'What do you do?' she asked.

'I'm a photographer, Lily.'

He pronounced her name confidently, as though laying a claim.

'I do some good stuff, and I do some crap. Mostly I photograph ugly families and edit them to look good and they pay me. But let's not do this. I'm not going to start unwrapping my photographs to show you . . . They're bubble-wrapped now anyway. I spent a long time bubble-wrapping them.'

'Okay,' said Lily.

'It doesn't matter.'

'Okay.'

'So are you sleeping in my daughter's room?'

'Yes.'

'And your little boy is sleeping in our – my room. I saw the cot. They haven't assembled it right. Will I fix it for you in the morning? I have no plans.'

'Sure. That's kind of you. Thanks, if you don't . . . mind or whatever. I knew they hadn't done it right. I thought that.'

Her little boy would be asleep now. Today was nearly over and tomorrow she would bring him back here. But he was sleeping in the travel cot because she had taken the proper one. If he woke in the night he could climb out and make his way to the big bedroom. He would feel around for her on the far side of the bed, and would he notice the different shape, the different smell, or would the heat and softness of another woman's body be enough to send him back to sleep?

Lily stretched her arms out in front of her. She noticed her landlord glance at her lips and her loose breasts, and she looked at the curtains that covered the window; duck-egg blue, a colour too solid for the wobbly curves the fabric made.

'So your girl is in London?' she asked.

Her landlord pulled at his jaw.

'That's where her mother moved to. My wife. We had a short marriage . . .'

He sucked a long, ragged breath and began to speak. He spoke reluctantly, as though she were coaxing him.

Lily replaced the glasses quickly. She had been wearing contacts for years and had forgotten how useful the glasses could be. When she wore them, an onlooker would see only her finely arched brows and the dark of her sockets. No one would notice that uncertainty she had always worn right there under the sweep of lashes, the little nook where things like eyeliner and tears gathered, the place her husband used to kiss to calm her when it seemed uncertainty itself was a force that might burst her like a dam.

Her landlord was looking at her intently. His story held no surprises. His wife, he said, was a nag, was a psycho, was a control freak, and his new fiancée was too good for him, and too young to be dragged into all of this . . . In the dull light his pupils had swelled to black blotches. He was looking at her face, at her lips moving, her ruined fingernails. He was looking as though he didn't know he could be seen. He wanted to touch her lip, she thought, or he wanted to slap her. He wanted to put his fingers inside her mouth.

'Such bitterness,' he said, 'and sexism. Who says a mother knows best? I'm a better parent than she'll ever be. She's a psycho. But anyway I've given up. It's not fair on Alannah, dragging her over the sea every fortnight, and it's not fair on my son. He doesn't even know me. I'm going to LA and I'm going to marry his mother.'

He was rubbing his face, looking at his hands, then rubbing his face some more.

'Bitterness. She's bitter now, my wife. When we got married we were never going to split up,' he said, 'no matter what. Because my wife came from a broken home, and so did I and it's not what we wanted... I never thought... if I had known—'

Lily hoped he wouldn't cry. She interrupted him by yawning loudly. 'Oh well,' she said.

He frowned in a way that made her want to touch him between the eyes, smooth the deep crease he made there.

'I was smug about being in love,' he said, leaning forward. 'You shouldn't be afraid to let life change you.' Then he clenched his hand, turned his fist in the space between them, looking at it. 'Did you know that your heart is the size—'

Lily heard herself laugh, another woman's laugh. She threw her head back, showing the inside of her mouth.

*

The food was delivered by a teenager in a car. He apologized for being late; he had trouble finding the house, he said. He gave her a six-euro discount off her next order.

'Don't worry,' said Lily, 'easily done. They all look the same, don't they?'

Many of the doors here were painted a muted shade of teal, like Lily's. When she arrived today she had almost tried her key in the wrong front door.

Lily took out her purse, but her landlord came up behind her and pushed three folded tenners into the boy's hand.

They laid the steaming cartons out on the table and two plates and a roll of kitchen paper. Lily kept her glasses on. Her landlord was wearing some scent like grass and the sea. It mingled with the delicate fragrance of fresh sweat, and sweet-and-sour sauce, and flavour enhancer. He had taken some beers out of the fridge, and she opened them using his key-ring.

'Anyway,' he said, and winked.

'Anyway,' she said, and closed her lips around the cold mouth of the bottle.

Tasteless

THE SEATING PLAN was obscured by a cluster of guests. His wife rubbed his chest briskly, as if to warm him.

'Here Eoin, mind my glass,' she said. 'I'll find out where we are.'

She slipped into the jostle of lacy hips and elbows. It was a spring wedding. Sheets of pale light shook in through the windows, casting patches of lint and heat over the gathering. The women wore crocus colours; clean, creamy purples and muted yellow. There were wayward ribbons and awkward hats and silk shawls sliding over shoulder slopes.

At the edge of the group, a big, lumpy man scowled and pushed, huffed and shook his head. Eoin vaguely recognized him, though perhaps he was thinner before, or perhaps he had more hair. Flapping the other guests aside with large palms, the man began to wade steadily towards the plan, peered and frowned, then turned with an antagonized snort and loped head-first into the dining room. Eoin had lost sight of his wife. He watched instead the ranks of satin-bound buttocks, glossy, warped curves like shrink-wrapped fillets.

'Eoin!'

It was the father of the bride, buttery curls of silk down his throat and a frilly carnation at his heart.

'Well. Steve,' said Eoin.

'I'm glad you could come, Eoin. Glad you could come.' Steve slapped a hand down on Eoin's shoulder, pressed a thumb hard into his collar bone.

'Lovely ceremony,' said Eoin. 'Lovely. Congratulations, Steve.'

Steve was swaying with drink or joy, but his chubby mouth puckered in a sorry pout. He patted Eoin again, squeezed again, shook him by the shoulder. Holding a glass in each hand, Eoin was unsteadied for a moment, but Steve clutched him tighter, and bent his head in close. His lower lip cupped the air as some words reached his mouth and were dismissed. After a pause he said: 'Glad you could come, Eoin. Good to have you here.'

'Good to be here,' nodded Eoin, and he turned back around to face the crowd. 'Pam is just checking the table plan.'

A tall feather wagged over the huddle of head-tops. One Halloween his daughter had dressed as a flapper. She had a feather like that strapped to her head with a gold-sequinned band.

His wife scurried towards him with her face down. Her pearly nails dug at the clutch bag that she had bought for the occasion. It was good for her to get out. He was glad they had come.

'*The Kiss*,' she said. 'Table 4 – *The Kiss*.'

The girl – he corrected himself – the woman seated beside his wife had a sloppy sort of face, loose on the bones. She wore a disc of lavender felt tilted precariously across her brow like a misplaced skullcap. When she asked how they knew the couple, Eoin could utter only the word, 'Our . . .' followed by a guttural suck like a draining sink. His wife pressed her fingers into the crook of his elbow, and explained how they knew the bride.

The woman cocked her head as she listened, her eyebrows gathering into elaborate shapes of sympathy. 'I didn't even know that could happen,' she said, 'I've never heard of that happening.' Her gaze followed the plate that was lowered before her.

'Oh dear. Well. I'm sorry to hear that. That's very sad.'

Still forcing that pained expression into her brows, she stabbed at a dark lozenge of meat, opening brilliant strata of pink and ruby red. She lifted her fork and paused, the bright morsel quavering at her chin while she waited for Pam to finish speaking.

Pam always finished the same way when she was telling about Sharon, 'So that's it,' and a wet huff of breath. Losing their daughter had mangled many parts of his wife, but it had not shaken her politeness, her consideration. He admired her for that, but he hated the 'so . . .', the way it made people feel like it was okay, the way it let them off the hook. 'So,' they would echo, 'so that's it.' He could hear Pam's breath catch sore in her chest. Her fingers perched tightly on the table edge.

Closing her mouth over the meat, the woman's eyes pulled back to meet his wife's. She chewed for a moment, then pushed the food into her cheek to say, 'Must be hard for you to be here then.'

'Oh. No.' Pam's smile strained thin. 'It was very nice to be invited.' Eoin could feel her shift beside him, crossing and recrossing her ankles under the table. Her shoes were pinching her. She had taken them off in the car after the church, and he had seen the red, hurt squash they had made of her feet.

Turning towards him, Pam plucked the menu from the centre of the table. 'The starter is squab.' Eoin thought of those tin-can phones he made as a boy – the sound was supposed to ride the wire from one can to the other, though it never worked well. That's what Pam's voice sounded like now – vibrations traversing the tiny channel strung between them. 'Seared squab breast,' she said. 'What's squab? Do you know, Eoin?'

The woman in the purple hat answered, relief relaxing her features into friendliness. 'Don't know,' she said, chewing. 'Some kind of game it seems to be. It's a gamey taste. Juniper berries with it.'

'Juniper berries?' said Pam. 'Is that what they are? Pretty aren't they?'

'Yes.'

'A lovely rich colour aren't they? Yes.'

Eoin found his voice then. Grateful, he said, 'It's dove. A squab is a young dove, I think.'

There were five courses. After the squab it was three pillows of nettle ravioli fried to a brown fringe in sage butter.

'Very nice,' said Pam. 'Very fragrant.'

A cold liquid trickled into Eoin's lap, sending a bolt of rage up his throat.

'Oh my God, I am so sorry.' The man to his left was holding a glass at arm's length, struggling with a writhing toddler. He jiggled more wine over the tablecloth as he placed his glass down and scrambled for a napkin.

'Oh, God no,' said Eoin, dabbing at his trousers, 'no, don't worry. I'll get that. You have your hands full.'

A medallion of veal arrived with a squat tower of potato gratin. A kidney dish of garlic asparagus was passed around the table. Eoin offered to hold the child while his neighbour ate, but it clung fast to its father's neck. It was a very blond little thing, with big raw cheeks, gluey stream of snot bubbling softly from one nostril. 'He's a bit under the weather,' said the father, poking at the shut lips with a wad of potato. The child shook its head; 'Want Mama feed me,' and the father sighed and rolled his eyes. 'It's Mama everything these days,' he told Eoin, then to the child he said, 'What about Dada? Please can Dada feed you, Reuben? Mama is being a pretty bridesmaid for now.'

'Come here to me,' said Eoin, 'and we'll see if we can make something with this napkin. What do you think we should make? A fish maybe? Or a swan? What would you like to make, Reuben?'

Reuben moved warily onto Eoin's knee. Eoin folded the napkin while the father spoke between hurried mouthfuls.

'He just won't stay in his bed, you know? He is hung out of his mother day and night and Julie wants another baby now and I'm just thinking, how? She hasn't slept a full night in years...'

'I know,' said Pam, smiling and smiling at the child. 'I remember it well. Gosh, I know.'

The child wanted a plane, and was delighted with the floppy effort that Eoin created with the thick serviette. He flew the creation against his father's shoulders, smashing open the soft folds, 'Baff pchoooo...' and disappeared under the table with the wreckage.

'And our friends all have these babies who apparently slept all night through from birth and I'm like, really? Because no matter what we do, Reuben will not sleep in his own bed...'

'Well they're all different, aren't they?' said Pam.

'So, your own kids must be grown up?' asked the man, and Eoin felt his wife's reassuring fingers on his knee.

They had been young parents, he and Pam, and it was a disconcerting effort for Eoin to align his place in life with the father of the bride, and not the frazzled young dad. When Steve Mahon had grabbed him earlier, Eoin stopped himself from calling him 'Mr Mahon'. He should have thanked him for the invitation, told him his daughter looked happy, but he didn't know how to say it without sounding like a well-brought-up child. Eoin was Steve's junior by ten years maybe, but it wasn't a question of catching up. He could never have afforded something like this for Sharon: all this champagne, all the flowers, the five courses with matching wine.

He watched Pam while she spoke, the tremble and flinch

around her eyes, the climbing breath, the creases threading busily through her cheeks. The lines had played there for decades. Like spider webs, they only showed in certain light, but now there were heavier furrows too, delving her face into pouches and valleys. Had he done that to her?

'So . . . that's that,' said Pam, picking up the menu again.

The child had crawled back up onto his father's lap, a swathe of drying snot smeared across one cheek. The father pecked his head with unsolicited kisses, arms crossed tightly over the little body, shielding him from Eoin and Pam as though their loss might be catching.

'That must have been very hard,' he said. 'I can't imagine . . . I'm sure, I mean. No one can imagine.'

Eoin leaned towards Pam and looked at the menu; a long thing printed on stiff card, gold detail and bottle-green lettering. Up the left margin ran a detail from *The Kiss*, the couple's faces squashed together, the delicate curl of the woman's fingers, the gold swirls of her clothing drizzling down the side of the page.

'Jesus,' muttered Eoin to his wife. 'That's crass, isn't it?'

Pam sighed. 'Don't be nasty, Eoin.'

'Yeah, but really. Would they not think about it like? Did they not look at the painting before printing it on the menu? Would no one tell them, ha?'

Thirteen years ago, they had seen the painting for real.

They hadn't travelled much – not compared to the likes of Steve Mahon – but after Sharon's junior cert they took her to Vienna to see the galleries. Sharon wanted to be an artist. Her bedroom was covered with eerie pictures of sad bodies – pregnant women, fat women, skinny men with messy hair and big, dark eyes. She cut them out of calendars and art books, and arranged them in clip frames amongst her own little sketches and pictures and keepsakes – dried leaves, cinema stubs, photographs of her as a child, doodles of eyes and boxes and teardrops. She had done a project on Egon Schiele for her junior cert and that was what started her obsession with these strange artists – Schiele and Klimt. Their paintings were in Vienna, and Eoin thought, why not? So they had gone around all the museums with Sharon, and Eoin had seen *The Kiss* for real.

All over the city there were gift shops selling *The Kiss*-themed souvenirs; there were lighters and 3D pencil-toppers, and tins of chocolates with the scene printed on the lid and he had assumed it to be a romantic sort of a thing. But when he saw the real painting – tall and personal and alive with intent – he stood stunned and his mouth dried. Eoin didn't know much about art – he'd be the first to admit that – but the painting did something strange to his blood. He closed his eyes and couldn't swallow. It was the stiff resignation in the woman's mouth as she was gathered up into the man's

271

dark shadows, his face turning to devour her, and her hand
– pinkie curled in revulsion and surrender, thumb not quite
touching the fingers, a private dissociation from the scene.
It made him want to flee the room, find his daughter in
front of whatever painting she was lingering at in the high-
ceilinged building, wrap her in his arms and keep her from
the world of men and women.

'It's a bloody rape scene, Pam,' he whispered. 'Who puts a
rape scene on their wedding menu? I thought Clara did art at
college. She knows better, surely?'

Two blotches were beginning high on Pam's cheeks. She
looked at the napkin on her lap, smoothed it out. 'It's not
a rape scene, Eoin. Please stop.'

'I'm just saying, what is that about?'

Pam winced. His noises pained her. 'We are guests, Eoin.
Have some grace.'

Out of habit Pam had chosen a blue dress to complement
the bright eyes she once had and set off her red hair. But the
dress was a luminous, artificial shade, and she had coloured
her greys to shrill orange streaks for the occasion. The
vibrant tones muted her, as though the things she adorned
herself with were drinking all her colour for themselves.

He could remember the weeks after Sharon's birth, Pam
sitting up in bed, feeding, and the way it seemed that all the
heat and blood was draining out of her into the hot bundle

at her breast. Had he looked after her? He had read up about nursing mothers – the need for tea and toast, and a glass of Guinness every day, and he had usually remembered to bring a tray in during the early morning feed.

'I'm going to the bathroom,' Pam said, pushing the heavy chair away from the table and manoeuvring it back weakly. She hobbled a little as she went, uncertain of herself in those shoes. She'd be alright. By the time she got back, she'd be alright. Tensions were high, that was all. And her poor sore feet.

It was good that they had come, good for Pam to get out, get to the hairdresser's and make herself presentable. The invitation had caused them to argue, though. Pam was uncomfortable with the gift Eoin had put together – a perfect gift for Sharon's best friend, but Pam didn't see it that way. Even to the last minute she wanted him not to give it. She had said something very hurtful about it. She said Eoin wanted to drench everyone's joy with his grief.

She wanted to get them the hoover off the list. In the end, they agreed to give both – the hoover and the painting, which Eoin had fitted with an antique gold frame. It was overly ornate, but that was Sharon's style. Her friend would appreciate that. The hoover was just a case of paying online (the price of it!), but he left his own gift – a gift from Sharon, in a way – on the table in a special room near the lobby. 'Mahon-Brown Wedding Gifts' was marked on the door.

'Brown' was a lanky thing who kept touching his bride's spine and lowering his face into her veil. The bride was Clara Mahon, who perhaps – it was something Eoin wondered about sometimes – perhaps Sharon had loved? He had tried to explain it to Pam once, but she didn't know what he was talking about. One Sunday morning he had tapped and entered – it was Pam who had sent him up with tea for the girls – and there they were, Sharon and Clara there in the bed. He had felt all wrong coming in on them like that, but there was a soft joy in the room too – all that fresh morning skin and their cheeks creased from sleep, arms and fingers woven together and the way they froze when he opened the door. His daughter had turned and smiled at him. He recognized the gentle secrecy in her smile, and some light on her face made him squirm. He had frowned when he closed the door, and then he had laughed. He couldn't describe it to Pam, what he had seen: two girls cuddling together, Clara blushing and Sharon smiling, the morning sun on the lovely contours of her face as she turned to look at him. My darling daughter, he thought.

Clara Mahon didn't look very well on her special day, truth be told. She looked tired and ill, walking up the aisle dressed like a little girl in a neat lace robe, shoulder blades skimmed in skin. Eoin couldn't bring himself to tell her father that she looked beautiful. He was afraid the lie would show in his face, and that was worse than saying nothing.

What was so changed about Clara? What age was she? Twenty-seven? Twenty-eight? But she had already lost her looks. Perhaps that was natural. Young people are always beautiful, thought Eoin, and twenty-eight is close to thirty and thirty isn't as young as people think. By the time he was thirty he had a ten-year-old daughter, and felt too old to change career. He hated accountancy, but it was different then. Pam wasn't mad about her job either, but work was work. Work paid for things, and the things were the goal – the roof over his child's head, the food in her mouth, the new bike at Christmas. The holiday that time. There was nothing wrong with providing.

No, thirty was not young. His wife too had started to lose her looks around that time. It was just before her thirtieth birthday when she first asked him, 'Am I still pretty, Eoin?' and he had looked at her and wondered the same. He remembered thinking it must have been the birthday that had her talking like that, but in the years after she had asked him the same question many times, her tone shifting gradually from a question, to a demand, to an accusation – 'You used to think I was pretty, Eoin.'

Time could tangle things. Outside the church there had been women wandering in and out of focus, calling him by his surname, hugging him and patting his arm like mothers, and perhaps it was just the day that was in it, the intimacy they now assumed, or the fact that they were all dressed up and painted, but it took him a while to recognize them as the teenagers who had once filled Sharon's bedroom with the smell of aerosols and antiseptic ointments and all those oily new hormones. Under the dull faces were the girls he had collected from the junior nightclub on dark winter nights. He remembered them huddled together, shivering when he arrived, eyes sooty and lips pale; cold, round cheeks; child bellies and women's shoes. They would lean into each other, linking arms as they approached the car, chewing fruity gum to conceal the toxins he might otherwise have caught on their breath, giggling and whispering in the back while he drove each of them to her door, and then took his daughter home. They had lost their sexiness. He could think that now, not being a father any more. Even if he didn't recognize it at the time, with his daughter in amongst them, they had been full of excitement once, full of sexual energy and wonder, beautiful and each of them destined.

'Is this finished?'

The waiter was hovering at Pam's plate. Eoin nodded. 'Yes, thanks. I think you can take it. Thank you. Thanks.'

As the waiter lifted the dish onto his tray, Eoin spotted Pam approaching. She had brushed her hair to a block of static and clipped it up at one side.

'I let them take your plate,' said Eoin.

'I've been thinking about that gift, Eoin. I think you should take it back and put it in the car. We can give it to her another time.'

'I let them take your plate, Pam.'

She leaned in, put her face in front of his. 'Eoin, did you hear me? I think we shouldn't give that gift just today.'

She had touched up her make-up – red paste already drying to scales on her lips, and a layer like nylon over the hatch of lines that scrunched her mouth.

'I thought we talked about this.'

His wife shut her eyes for a moment, took a breath to speak, and opened them.

'Okay, but Eoin—'

'Just leave it now. Just leave it and enjoy the wedding.'

Pam put an elbow on the table and lowered her forehead into the cradle of her palm. Her nails were like porcelain, and thicker than nails should be. She had been to a salon for them. She wrapped the other hand around the back of her neck, and rubbed back and forth, back and forth. All bulking veins and leathery creases, Pam's flesh was testament to the sleepless nights, the dull work and a mother-joy that had wrung her dry.

'—I just think it might be best to give it to her another time.'

It was hard for Eoin to look at his wife sometimes, at the thick middle of her, and those silver scars that rucked like claw marks across her belly. Making love was hard after, and it was a long time before it stopped feeling like a wrong thing and a sad thing. Pam's breasts had suckled their child and her thighs were the strong things that had fed her into the world. His wife's body had become a site of grief with no natural way to heal, and she had turned on it, turned away from it. She did not often shave her legs now, or have her hair done, or buy pretty things and like herself in them. He did not at all like the way the salon had made her nails.

Eoin lowered his voice. 'I don't understand you, Pam. I think Clara will be delighted . . .'

But the room hushed to the tink of silver against glass.

'When Brona and I decided to raise a family . . .' began Steve Mahon.

Steve Mahon was an eejit. 'Raise a family' – was that even an expression? It sounded like raising pigs, harvesting corn. It sounded like an investment. Steve was mole-eyed with the drink. His comb-over had loosened to cottony tufts. He was proud, so proud of his daughter here today, he said, opening a palm to the room and swinging it around to present Clara, who smiled and touched the sheet of tulle that hung either side of her face.

'I hope you're all enjoying the splendid meal . . .' Steve said. 'The wines are from three of the vineyards near our summer house in Italy . . .'

Eoin felt an ugly grin start on his lips, and he lowered his head. Pam didn't like it when he sneered. Recently, she told him it was the thing she least liked about him, and a thing that wasn't there when she married him – he had become sneery, she said, he 'sneered at others' and it didn't suit him. She had a merciless way of putting things sometimes.

To stop from sneering he kept his eyes off Steve Mahon, flitting his gaze instead over the other guests. There were many strange headpieces – pillbox hats and feathers and gauze. One girl wore a miniature top hat set in a bed of spiky netting. The bright Easter-time dresses seemed foolish now under the dim chandeliers, like flowers opening to the night.

Some flowers folded up at nightfall and opened in the morning – you could catch them doing it if you chose the right time. Poppies were like that, and crocuses. Others stayed blooming until they were ready to die. Daffodils stood soldier-straight on their straws, beaming moronically into the darkness. It made them whackable, easy to stomp or hack, easy to cut and take indoors. Eoin preferred crocuses.

He liked the neat oval beginning of them, the way they cracked clean out of their waxy buds, unfussy in their prettiness. They used to grow at the back of the garden around the roots of the plum tree; pale purple and white and egg-yolk yellow, and a few buttermilk ones shot through with dark flecks like poisoned veins. When had they stopped coming up?

Someone was looking at him. It was the jowly man he had seen perusing the table plan earlier. He was sitting two tables away, a hulking presence, looking at Eoin with that bulldog expression. As Eoin turned away, he caught a mirthless jeer in the man's hooded eyes. Eoin had seen him before somewhere. He had known him, perhaps, but he was changed.

There had been no mention of Sharon at the ceremony – 'Why would there be, Eoin?' Pam shrugged. He thought that perhaps Clara would remember her in the speeches, but the bride didn't speak. Only her father, then the best man, and last the groom.

While his new son-in-law spoke, Steve Mahon sat small in his chair; his flat-topped head low like an owl's in his ruffled neck, the small eyes dark and slow in his pink face. How did Steve feel? What was it like to watch his daughter sit silently like that, skinny and pale and quiet, about to start out on a married life?

It wasn't stoicism that Sharon's death had brought, but a toughness of sorts. Even though Eoin could be brittle now – given to rages and bouts of mute panic, sudden shyness and, Pam said, a tendency to sneer – these were only an outward reflex. A still grief wrapped steely around his core. Nothing quite cut beneath the skin now. But people with children had so much to fear.

A few days after Sharon was born, Eoin had changed her nappy for the first time. He had never thought to wonder what the baby's genitals would be like – not while he waited for her birth. Not when she came out slimy and writhing and was handed to him in a towel. He hadn't thought to prepare himself for anything more shocking than odour and mess, but the baby vagina terrified him – a tense swell and no hint of hair and that strange runnel like a well-healed scar. He thought how a man's penis would measure the torso of his tiny daughter; destroy the complex and tiny intricacies that she was made from. It was a relief, somehow, when he read some years later that baby girls are all sealed up; that no man could manage it, even if he wanted to, though why that fact could offer any kind of comfort was unclear to him.

In the first week of Sharon's life he came home from work to find Pam chopping onions in the kitchen. Slicing so easily like that through crisp layers of bulb, the knife had made him keenly aware of the thin blub and skin that covered his daughter's little chest – the blisters of unsprouted nipples, the tilt of her ribs, and inside her a mystery of movement and blood that chance had set going. He ran immediately to their bedroom, bent into the Moses basket and put his face to the sleeping child until he was sure that the neat parcel of her was all intact, all the organs in their place, the breath moving in and out of her the way it should. Pam had followed him to the door, the knife still in her hand, and it had taken all his strength to keep the images at bay. He had only a blind fear of the harm that could come to their child – the ease with which she could be destroyed, if some madness should send the knife into the tiny chambers, the dark mechanics of her heart.

He had trouble believing in her at first – a pinprick trill on the ultrasound, a belly-swell, a bloody squelch, a cry, and here a whole person looking back at him. He had been shocked and awed by her birth; too shocked, perhaps, too humbled to feel anything as intimate as love for the child. That had come a few days afterwards; her little body resting lengthways on his forearm, her head in his palm. He held her while Pam took a shower. He knew something then that would underpin every concern or joy that came with being her father; the palpable density of her skull in his hand; the secret vibrations of all her cells, and the detail – the specifics of each ear curve and chin fold and the way that one finger lifted senselessly away from her little fists, pivoting blindly.

Eoin had learned to drive later than other men. He was already twenty, which had seemed, at the time, like a shameful thing. His daughter was three months old when he got his licence. Once, on a Saturday morning, he had taken a driving lesson with her in the back, to soothe her to sleep while Pam slept off a difficult night. He had been robbed of a thrill, he thought, for he could never enjoy the speed, the latent danger of it. He was never at ease when he drove. It was the image of Sharon that plagued him – not of Sharon, but of her absence; a vague blot of shadow concealing his daughter's face. Nothing more detailed than that. Whether she was in the car with him or not: when he took a corner a little too hurriedly, when he cut into the fast lane, late for a meeting, his daughter's face was there at his shoulder, obscured by some wound that his recklessness might make.

It was only months after her death that he realized that the fear had gone – the thing had happened, the threat that had anchored his daily life. In the end it had nothing to do with his driving.

It was a violence inside her – a mutiny of her own body – that killed Sharon. She fell in school one afternoon from a heart attack. The hospital said it was probably anorexia, but that did not seem plausible to Eoin. People don't have heart attacks at seventeen, just because they have lost some weight. Pam had said something about Sharon not eating properly – maybe once or twice she had said it, but Sharon had looked fine to him – bright-eyed, energetic, and she was doing well at school. They decided to let things lie until after the Leaving Cert; they decided that together. When that stress was gone, perhaps Sharon would get her appetite back. That is probably what would have happened, if the heart attack had waited.

They sent the GP to the house to persuade Eoin of their diagnosis, but by then he knew it was simpler than that anyway – the mysterious pulsing that had started in his wife had stopped. The organs were no longer in their places, doing the things they should, the lungs no longer filled.

She hadn't been accepted into art college. That had really upset her; it was the one thing she wanted from life – to be an artist. It was Eoin who had gone to collect her portfolio and – he couldn't help it – he had told them what he thought of them. Her art teacher, too, had failed to see Sharon's real talent. It was something Pam didn't quite understand either, because Sharon wasn't good at art the way some more diligent children were – it was more like a special eye she had, a way of feeling things. Once, when Sharon was only ten, Eoin had bought a painting from one of the students who came door-to-door. It was a painting of a grey cat that Pam called mawkish. It cost quite a lot and Pam was angry, because only that morning Eoin had chastised her with the credit-card bill in his hand, yellow highlighter through all the unnecessary purchases she had made that month. 'But she is an artist, Pam,' he had said, and he didn't know himself what he meant by that, except that there was something about his daughter that could be moved by things, and in the cat's eyes, the slant of its head, he thought he saw something that might move her.

When they had gone to those museums in Vienna, Eoin and Pam were, for the most part, bored. The first one they went to had a tiny picture of a witchlike woman holding a womb with a dark foetus curled in it. He and Pam had looked at each other and shrugged, while Sharon stood in awe. In the next room, there was a huge painting of two men, naked, sitting side by side on their bottoms with their legs bent. Beside it was a matching portrait of two women – or two portraits of the same woman – with suspicious shadows beneath their naked bottoms. Sharon stood and wept. Standing beside her, Eoin began to see what was moving her – in the gaze of the women, and the gaze of the men, there was a childlike openness, a baffled understanding opening a chink to the terrible absurdity of matter.

A few months after Sharon's death, Eoin did something very selfish. He 'went AWOL' – that's what Pam called it. He had been back at work a week. One day, instead of going in, he drove to the airport. As soon as he arrived in Vienna, the practical nonsense of the whole thing became real; the cold of the city, the fact that he had no luggage and nowhere to stay. He lay awake fully clothed in a hostel that night and came back the next day. It was he who had wept then, standing in front of those paintings, not because they moved him, but because he could not find the thing his daughter had once seen there.

'Clara, my darling,' said the groom, taking his wife's hand, coaxing her to her feet. 'You have made me the happiest man in the world. Thank you for agreeing to be my wife!'

Clara stood small beside her husband now, peering shyly from the frame of her veil. There was a rumpus of clapping and whooping as the couple kissed. Beyond Pam's profile, the big-faced woman was crying into a napkin. Her purple hat had finally shifted on her head, showing a nest of fine metal pins beneath.

Eoin turned to Pam. 'I was just thinking – what happened to the crocuses?'

'To the crocuses?'

'Remember we used to have loads of crocuses at the back of the garden, all around the plum tree?'

'The little yellow and blue flowers?'

'Purply blue sort of. And white.'

'They're still there, Eoin. We still have them.'

'Pam, I'm thinking I'll go and get the painting. I'll put it in the car. We can ask Clara over for tea maybe, after her honeymoon, give her the painting then. Or we could give it to her on Sharon's anniversary, maybe.'

After the dessert came coffee and a plate of cigars for each table.

The waiter lowered the tray tenderly, as though there was something sensitive and alive in the leathery cocoons. Eoin picked one up and sniffed it. He twirled it between his fingers, and glanced at the large man two tables up, satisfied to see the low-slung eyes dance back at him with mockery. Eoin smiled, and the man nodded doggedly as though responding to a joke he already knew.

Steve Mahon spoke over a microphone. 'The good staff of the Lough Cairn hotel have agreed to serve the cigars,' he said. 'But we have to smoke them outside. There are heaters out on the patio . . .'

A violet bridesmaid – Reuben's mother – folded onto her husband's knee.

'Are they only for the men?' she asked.

'You can have mine,' said Eoin. 'I've no interest in cigars.'

'You two go on outside. We'll keep an eye on Reuben,' Pam said.

*

Eoin closed the door behind him. Relieved by the cool quietude, he pressed his back to the embossed wallpaper and slid to the floor. The room smelled of new carpet.

His had been one of the first gifts on the table, but now there was a pile of boxes wrapped professionally in ivory and silver and steely sheens of blue. He would recognize his gift – it was just a small rectangle. He had used some wrapping paper left over from his nephew's marriage. There were wedding bells on it, or maybe wedding rings, outlined in meagre streaks of glitter. Drink-logged and aching, Eoin laid his head on his knees. He could sleep now. He could stay here and sleep. It was only the thought of Pam, left all alone with the infant and the purple-hatted woman, that hauled him up on his feet to begin his search.

The couple had received many sets of glasses. Through the flimsy cardboard, Eoin could feel the swing of fragile hollows as he moved them box by box to the floor. Sealed envelopes slid about between the gifts. He made a stack of them at one corner of the table. He lifted a shallow, broad box – a cutlery set, thought Eoin, and from the dense weight he guessed silver. He thought of the bright knives lying muffled in rows of cherry-black velvet, fork tines and spoon bellies curving into each other's backs, each held in its private slot. He and Pam had received silver cutlery for their wedding too.

His gift was under what might have been a vase. The heavy cube had been plonked right down on top of the little picture. He pushed it off with deliberate carelessness, toppling it on its side and causing a champagne bottle to thud to the floor. The tag was missing from his gift, and as he lifted it he felt the crunch of smashed glass beneath the bubble wrap.

When he heard someone enter the room his mouth fell open, but no explanation came. It was little Clara. She smiled when she saw him – a big smile that made sinews of her cheeks – sliding her meagre figure in through the gap she had opened. She had her veil in her hand. 'Hi,' she said, shoving the door closed with her back. Without the veil her head looked too large for her neck. He saw that her ears still stuck out. He had forgotten about that. She looked at the gift in his hand. 'What's that?'

'It's for you,' he said. 'But it's . . . it broke, so I'll fix it. I'll give it to you another time.'

She put her hand on his arm. There were patches of sandy make-up on her face, brown-blue pits beneath her eyes.

'Congratulations, Clara,' he said.

Then her bony arms were around his middle. She clung to him, a cool shoulder pushed up against his cheek. He put one hand on her back. With the other, he held the picture.

He could feel the knobbly discs of her spine. Her breath fluttered in her throat. Was she crying?

She pulled away and looked at him.

'So that's that,' she said. 'A married woman now.'

Eoin nodded. He held the gift in two hands and gazed at the paper.

'It's broken,' he said again. 'So I'll fix it and give it to you next time you visit . . .'

'Can I see?' she said. 'Is it a picture?'

He pried open the corner of the paper, and let it fall to the floor. He couldn't see much beyond the blur of the bubble wrap. The frame looked different – newer than he remembered, and shinier. The glass had smashed completely – he could hear it scrape against itself. He knew it would be unwise to unleash all those shards on the fresh carpet, but he couldn't help it. He wanted to see Sharon's painting again – the bowl that disappeared off the side of the page, the blurred tulip that she had placed beside it, its petals streaked watery pink and yellow. What he liked about this painting was the way one petal had come away from the flower and found its way inside the bowl where it lay like a small disc of blood. There was something very interesting about that, which the art college had failed to consider. He could remember Sharon crying about it – her teacher chastised her for not 'plotting' her composition. Eoin needed the reassurance of

Sharon's painting – the marks she had made, the proof of her. Perhaps Sharon had touched the canvas to pad down a peak or make a dot in the distance; perhaps there was a strand of her hair preserved in an oily slice of tablecloth. He had read once that the Mona Lisa's pearls were made with pinkie fingerprints.

He opened only the top of the bubble wrap, hoping that the glass would be caught in the pocket beneath, and tried to slide the frame upwards, but it wouldn't budge. He tugged at the mouth of the bubble wrap and wiggled the picture up out of it, spilling little cubes of glass over the new carpet.

'Sorry,' he said. 'Sorry, someone put something heavy on top of it—'

It was a photograph. Three girls in their school uniforms. Eoin recognized them all. The tall blonde one was Sharon. Sharon with her tongue sticking out to be cool, wearing her school tie as a headband. Clara was in the middle, her cheeks fuller than they were now, thick, low eyebrows, nut-brown hair. The girls had their arms slung over one another. They each made a peace sign with two fingers, but the way they did it looked more like they were saying 'fuck you' to the camera. The other girl was Maud. The stout girl who used to traipse around after Sharon. He had a soft spot for her because she was always so stuttering and polite. The other girls used to fix her make-up for her in the back of the car and tell her she looked fab and he remembered she used to wear black tights with the tiny dresses, instead of going bare-legged like the others. She had died too. My God, could he really have forgotten? A few weeks before Sharon. My God. Yes. She had leukaemia, but it was the hospital bug that killed her.

'Oh,' said Eoin, looking around for his own gift. 'It's the wrong one.'

The tree-planting ceremony. That was where he had seen that big man before – the tree-planting ceremony at the school. One tree for Sharon, and one for the other girl. They stood there – he and Pam, beside the fat man and his short wife, and the headmistress clutching her hands before her like a bouncer. The students were assembled on the lawn. The girls from Sharon's class held each other and wept, crumbling tissues into their faces.

'It's from someone else. It's a photo; from someone else.'

He placed the smashed picture in Clara's hand, and stooped to pick up his own gift. There it was – under the table with the gift tag and the golden ribbon still on.

'I'll give this to you another time, Clara,' he said. 'Congratulations. A married woman now.'

He gave her a dry kiss and moved past her towards the door.

*

The dining room was darker when he came in, and colder, because the big doors had been thrown open onto the patio. There was a string quartet playing a fast waltz, but their sound was feeble, leaching into the dark space outside.

At the far end of the room, some couples shuffled palm to palm to the beat of the waltz, the men in crumpling linen the colour of aged paper, the women in all their murky frills like spring flowers open to the moon.

Pam was still at their table – Table 4, *The Kiss* – sitting amongst empty chairs, the red-cheeked child asleep on her lap. Her eyes were closed and she swayed to and fro like a lapping shore, jaw pressed to the child's clammy hair. Her oval face was tilted like a Madonna's, Victorian pale in the dim light. Eoin stood before her, holding the picture in his hand. They were glittery hearts on the giftwrap – not rings – and doves.

'Pam,' he said, but she didn't open her eyes.

Acknowledgements

Some of these stories have taken many years to write. I have been baffled by the generosity and astuteness of their first readers and critics, as well as the patience and trust of their various publishers. The Arts Council of Ireland played an important practical role in facilitating my work on this collection.

My partner, Seán, dedicated thankless hours to reading and rereading these pieces in their rawest states. His insight often helped me to grasp the slippery heart of the stories they were to become. Without his contribution, certain paths may never have been taken, and without his care and more-than-co-parenting of our three children over the last months, this collection would have been even longer coming.

Thank you, Lisa Coen and Sarah Davis-Goff of Tramp Press, for friendship, time and invaluable feedback over the last years; Daniel Caffrey for championing the work, and providing both the pastoral and editorial care to see it through; John Hobbs for the constant encouragement and sound advice; Joseph Roche for giving me a first-hand account of his Mars One experience; Tom Morris for his quiet support, Colm Farren for his careful readings, Michela Esposito for her discerning and creative eye; Laura-Blaise McDowell for providing a refreshing dose of flippancy, Mary O'Donoghue for her persistent backing, and Eleanor Rees for her sensitive, diligent edits and much needed reassurance.

I am grateful to Marianne Gunn O'Connor for placing this collection, and to my agent, Lucy Luck for her unfailing enthusiasm and support.

Thank you, Antony Farrell of Lilliput Press, for publishing me in the first place, for true collaboration and open mindedness through this process, and for the dishwasher – a gift that has bought me hours of writing time.

Thank you, Neil Belton, for encouragement at a critical moment many years ago, and for your unwavering confidence in my writing. I feel honoured to have you as an editor and truly satisfied that this collection has found a home with Head of Zeus.